What Reviewers Say About Bold Strokes Authors

KIM BALDW

"'A riveting novel of suspense' seems to [be...]
However, it is extremely apt when discus[sing *Hunter's
Pursuit*]. An exciting page turner [featu[ring a...]
bounty hunter...with a million dollar pric~~e on her head. Look for this~~
excellent novel of suspense..." – **R. Lynne Watson**, *MegaScene*

RONICA BLACK

"Black juggles the assorted elements of her first book, [*In Too Deep*],
with assured pacing and estimable panache...[including]...the relative
depth—for genre fiction—of the central characters: Erin, the married-
but-separated detective who comes to her lesbian senses; loner Patricia,
the policewoman-mentor who finds herself falling for Erin; and sultry
club owner Elizabeth, the sexually predatory suspect who discards
women like Kleenex...until she meets Erin."– **Richard Labonte**, *Book
Marks, Q Syndicate, 2005*

ROSE BEECHAM

"...her characters seem fully capable of walking away from the
particulars of whodunit and engaging the reader in other aspects of their
lives." – *Lambda Book Report*

GUN BROOKE

"*Course of Action* is a romance...populated with a host of captivating
and amiable characters. The glimpses into the lifestyles of the rich and
beautiful people are rather like guilty pleasures....[A] most satisfying
and entertaining reading experience." – **Arlene Germain**, reviewer for
the *Lambda Book Report* and the *Midwest Book Review*

JANE FLETCHER

"*The Walls of Westernfort* is not only a highly engaging and fast-paced
adventure novel, it provides the reader with an interesting framework
for examining the same questions of loyalty, faith, family and love that
[the characters] must face." – **M. J. Lowe**, *Midwest Book Review*

RADCLY*f*FE

"...well-honed storytelling skills...solid prose and sure-handedness of
the narrative..." – **Elizabeth Flynn**, *Lambda Book Report*

"...well-plotted...lovely romance...I couldn't turn the pages fast
enough!" – **Ann Bannon**, author of *The Beebo Brinker Chronicles*

Visit us at www.boldstrokesbooks.com

UNEXPECTED
SPARKS

by

Gina L. Dartt

2006

UNEXPECTED SPARKS

ISBN 1-933110-46-5
THIS TRADE PAPERBACK IS PUBLISHED BY
BOLD STROKES BOOKS, INC.,
NEW YORK, USA

FIRST EDITION: JUSTICE HOUSE PUBLISHING 2002
SECOND EDITION: BOLD STROKES BOOKS, INC., JUNE 2006

CREDITS
EDITOR: SHELLEY THRASHER
PRODUCTION DESIGN: J. BARRE GREYSTONE
COVER GRAPHIC: SHERI (graphicartist2020@hotmail.com)

Acknowledgments

I would like to acknowledge Jay for her feedback and conversations. To Helen, Peg, Marcos and Nancy, who have been there practically from the beginning, my deepest thanks. To Shelley, my editor, who is doing her best to teach me how to write properly, no matter how aggravating it is at times, even through a hurricane or two—I tip my hat. And to my mom, family and friends here in the Maritimes, who seem just as thrilled about this as I am, even when they appear in my books—hang in there, there are sure to be more laughs along the way.

DEDICATION

To the late Susan Mullarky and Dru E. Carlson,
both of whom did more than just believe, and
whom I miss tremendously every single day

CHAPTER ONE

Kate was disappointed when Sam Madison entered her bookstore. She liked the guy all right, but today she had wanted the tinny-sounding bell hanging over the door to announce someone else.

"Hey, Kate." Tall and handsome, with dark hair just beginning to turn silver, Sam had kept in good shape over the years, and his expensively tailored suit covered by a long coat emphasized his broad shoulders.

"Sam." Kate watched him stroll over to the magazine rack and wasn't surprised when he grabbed the latest *Penthouse*. She knew he was checking out the photos. He certainly didn't buy it for the articles.

"Lousy weather, eh?" Sam returned to the counter and tossed the magazine onto the polished surface.

Kate idly rang in the purchase. "It could be worse. Remember Juan? When I lost the sign out front?"

Sam nodded. "You know, the way things are going, it's just a matter of time before we're hit with another hurricane. Hey, are you ever going to replace that sign?"

"Are you ever going to pay me the insurance you owe for it?" It was an old argument, and not one that held any heat by this time.

"Act of God, Kate. I would if I could, but I couldn't."

"Remember that the next time you're struck by lightning." Kate knew that a great many women found Sam attractive and charismatic, but something about him had always left her cold. It had nothing to do with the disputed insurance claim either, since that had been only a few hundred dollars. Sam had lost far more in premiums when Kate switched all her coverage to another company. She also recognized that it hadn't been entirely his decision, since his father-in-law ran a head office in the city.

Kate had attended university with his cold, aloof wife, Margaret, in Wolfville decades ago. She had never respected Margaret's opinion, and that extended to any man she married, especially one from Westville. Kate wondered how Margaret had fallen for the hard-edged Sam, and then decided that she must have thought she had discovered a diamond in the rough. Sam had painstakingly developed several layers of charm and wit over the years, and the average person would have no idea which side of the tracks he had started on.

"You know, Kate, you really know how to hold a grudge," he said as he handed her the money.

She smiled without humor. "Not at all, Sam. I just believe in doing unto others. Isn't that your motto as well?"

"Maybe I've learned there are better ways to live life." He grinned as if her comment had struck home in some amusing way.

Kate didn't snort in disbelief, but she wanted to. Instead, she handed Sam the bag emblazoned with the store's name and thanked him for his purchase before he exited her store. Then she promptly dismissed him from her mind as she drifted over to the large display window behind the counter. Peering out at the snowy streets, she searched for signs of a familiar figure coming down the sidewalk, a mix of trepidation and anticipation causing jitters in the pit of her stomach.

Would this Wednesday be the one when she'd finally take the chance she had been thinking about for far too long?

CHAPTER TWO

Trudging through the spongy snow covering the sidewalk, huddled in the coat that was a little too large for her, Nikki Harris wished, not for the first time, that Nova Scotia didn't have to be so blasted damp in the winter. At the corner of Outram and Prince, she carefully mounted the salt-encrusted concrete steps leading to the entrance of Novel Companions, the icy conditions making her move like one of the elderly to prevent any inadvertent slips. Most Maritimers perfected this delicate dance between slush and pavement at a very young age.

Looming over Nikki like a stern, if kindly, kindergarten teacher, the building rose four stories, making it one of the larger structures in Truro. A tarnished gold plaque set in the brick at the side of the heavy wooden double doors read 1865, indicating that it had been built during the town's early existence.

As Nikki entered the warm interior of the bookstore, her wire-frame glasses steamed up from the change in temperature. Pausing just inside, she took them off to clean them with a tissue, glancing around through blurred vision. No other customers were there on this quiet Wednesday afternoon, which gratified her even though she felt ripples of apprehension.

Behind the counter, Kate Shannon glanced up from the book she was reading, her lips curving in a welcome that warmed Nikki far more than the décor. "Cold enough for you?" Kate made the area's traditional winter greeting sound like a personal concern for her well being.

Nikki dropped her head shyly, feeling awkward and remembering the gentle ease that once characterized their friendship. Had it only been a month ago? "It's not so bad," she lied.

Though Kate and Nikki had become friends over the past year, sharing many discussions about their lives and books and international current events, Nikki had recently decided to start distancing herself from Mrs. Shannon. Not because of Kate's demeanor, which continued to be as warm and welcoming as the store, but because Nikki was becoming too attracted to her. A hopeless and unrequited love was the last thing Nikki needed at this stage in her life, especially when she felt as if she'd just finished recovering from the mess with Anne.

Tearing her eyes away from Kate as she drifted over to the mystery section, Nikki tried not to be too obvious in her withdrawal. But her attempt at self-discipline didn't prevent her from feeling what she did or from peering over the top shelf of the counter to surreptitiously study Kate where she perched on a high stool behind the counter.

Standing about five-foot six with a trim, compact form, Kate always appeared fashionable and elegant, even in a simple turquoise sweater and jeans. Reddish brown hair fell neatly about classic features that boasted high cheekbones beneath what Nikki considered to be the most marvelous blue-gray eyes. Kate looked particularly appealing at the moment, a pair of horn-rimmed glasses set precariously on her nose as she flipped through a hardcover. Probably some scholarly tome, Nikki thought wistfully, the understanding of which undoubtedly lay far beyond that required for the mystery novels she preferred.

She supposed that other people wondered why Kate remained unattached after her divorce seven years earlier, just as she did. In all likelihood, she was just holding out for something and someone a whole lot better than she could discover in Truro. Since Nikki had no idea how or why her own feelings toward Kate had changed so drastically in recent weeks, she expected Kate would probably be vastly uncomfortable if she knew. Of course, it also occurred to Nikki that she could stop shopping at the bookstore entirely and return her patronage to the chain store at the mall, but the thought of not seeing Kate at all was too painful to contemplate.

Confused and hurting, Nikki glanced down at the selection on the shelves. Despite Truro's small-town status, Kate stocked her store with a remarkably liberal touch. The alternative lifestyles section easily overshadowed the one belonging to the large chain store, and more than a few gay and lesbian books, which were usually unavailable outside Halifax, were scattered throughout the other sections. Nikki assumed it was merely good business on Kate's part. She was aware that smaller, privately owned stores needed to compete in areas that the larger chains didn't exploit, and she knew she was far from being the only gay person in town or the surrounding area. It just felt that way sometimes.

Nikki looked longingly over the selection of new arrivals, knowing that she would have to limit her indulgences. Her paycheck from her job at Keebler's Building Supplies went only so far, and alternative mysteries cost significantly more than the average mainstream titles. Sighing silently, she left the part of the store where the new books were displayed and strode into the rear where the extensive used section was located. Unfortunately, books with lesbian protagonists rarely made their way onto these shelves. Nikki didn't know why, just that they didn't seem to recycle as other books did, probably because far fewer were in circulation.

As she checked out the mysteries, neatly organized in alphabetical order, Nikki took a moment to appreciate the atmosphere of the store, delighting in the scent of paper and books surrounding her and the gentle fragrance of the incense that Kate favored lingering in the air. The intricate woodwork visible around the ceiling and walls, as well as the polished plank floor, was original, well over a hundred years old, granting the interior a sense of solidness and timeless grandeur. This had become Nikki's favorite place over the past year, not only because of her love of reading and her attraction to Kate, but because it was simply such a comfortable place to be, an inviting place to linger and browse. It was what the chain stores aspired to emulate with their new layouts, which included sofas and coffee bars, but never quite managed to accomplish.

Nikki felt a sharp sense of delight when she discovered a recent book on the shelf by one of the mainstream authors she collected. Pleased at the find, which was half price, she briefly debated with herself whether she could justify the expense before she picked it up and then looked quickly through the rest of the shelves before returning to the front of the store.

"Found something, did you?" Kate glanced at the cover and smiled warmly as she took the book from Nikki to ring it up. "This is one of her best. I read it when it was first released. She really does a good job with her characters."

Nikki felt the heat rise in her cheeks, aware they had to be a glowing pink, and wished that her fair skin would not make it so obvious when she was uncomfortable. The comment was a clear invitation to chat, so similar to the one that Kate had first extended a little more than a year ago. At first, Nikki had welcomed the chance to be friends with Kate, finding their conversations absorbing and challenging. But now, just the slightest bit of attention from Kate made every nerve in her body sing with energy, and the feelings were becoming so intense that she couldn't even look the shopkeeper directly in the eye. "I was planning to buy it new," she managed, studying the bookmark display on the counter with intensity. "I'm surprised it showed up in the used section so quickly."

"She's a very popular author, so a lot of her books are in circulation." Kate accepted Nikki's money. "Did you see the newest Rita Mae Brown?"

Their fingers brushed in the exchange, and Nikki felt the tingle move all the way up her arm. *I need to get out of here.* She tried desperately not to react visibly. "I did, but I'm not really into her new series."

"Is it because she doesn't include any gay characters?" Kate's expression was quizzical.

"That's part of it. She doesn't have to always write about gays, but since the gay in the first book is a villain, and no others appear even in a supporting role through the rest of the series, it's like she's denying us. It's too bad, since we were the ones who bought her first books, after all—not the Midwestern housewives she's apparently trying to appeal to now."

Nikki stopped, not particularly liking the sharp edge that had appeared in her tone; gay issues were not something she really wanted to discuss, particularly not with Kate at the moment. Sometimes it seemed that Kate tried too hard to steer their conversations onto that subject, as if she was somehow trying to prove that Nikki's sexual orientation didn't matter to her. But it mattered to Nikki. "I have to get going. I've…uh, I have things to do at home."

Kate lifted her eyes, the thoughtful and compassionate gaze mesmerizing Nikki. "Is something wrong? You've seemed a little uncomfortable with me lately. Have I offended you in some way?"

"Not at all." Nikki was horrified that Kate would think that, though a tiny part of her was quite pleased that she cared enough to notice. "I'm fine. I just…I need to go." She couldn't remain in the presence of that intense gaze, humiliated at being unable to deal with these feelings of desire and longing. She expected better of herself. "Thanks," she mumbled as she picked up the bag and hastily made her escape, conscious of Kate's soft eyes following her from the store.

Out on the sidewalk, the damp chill hit Nikki like a shock, and she stuffed the book into the large pocket in the front of her jacket. Still stinging from the conversation, feeling unbearably lonely, she bent her head and forged into the stiff breeze that had come up, bringing with it the scent of more snow.

A few minutes later, she unlocked the door to her small apartment with a sense of relief. Deliberately forcing Kate from her mind, she dropped her purchase on the portable washer in the corner before shrugging out of her jacket and hanging it in the closet. Leaving her wet boots on the mat, she pulled on her slippers as she moved into the tiny kitchen just off the entrance.

Nikki heard a soft thud from the bedroom as Powder leapt from the bed where he liked to curl up, and before long, he was winding around her ankles, purring audibly. "You realize that if things get any tighter, I may have to skin and eat you," she told the pure white cat sternly as she pulled a can opener from the drawer and opened a tin of cat food. He appeared suitably unimpressed by this threat and shoved his face into his dish as soon as she placed it on the floor.

After making a tuna and Swiss cheese sandwich, putting some rice chips into a bowl, and pouring a glass of milk, Nikki retrieved her book and moved into the living room where she curled up on the threadbare sofa she had inherited from her parents after her mother had gone on one of her redecorating binges. She had always meant to replace it with a new one, but that was another expense for better times.

She relaxed as she munched and opened her new acquisition, feeling the same sort of comfort and expectation in starting a new book that she always did. Suddenly, dropping from the inside pages, a small card fell onto her lap. It wasn't the first time Nikki had found something from the previous owner of a used book, a makeshift bookmark, something utilized to mark the page and forgotten, now offering the opportunity to peer through a small window into the life of the person who had read it before her.

Curious, she opened it and read the script sprawled over the interior: "Dear Kate, just a small token of our weekend at the Keltic Lodge. It was wonderful, and I can't wait to see you again. Soon, we'll be together for the rest of our lives. All my love, Sam."

Kate was a fairly common name in Truro, and it was unlikely this had anything to do with the owner of the bookstore or with Sam Madison, the odious man who owned the insurance office down the street from Novel Companions. But Nikki still felt a little dagger pierce her heart. It was ridiculous, of course, but that didn't lessen how it felt or the thread of loneliness that rippled through her.

Suddenly depressed again, she dropped the card into the nearby wastebasket. She placed the book, no longer something she wanted to read, on the end table and desolately took a small bite from her sandwich, although she wasn't really very hungry any more.

Powder leaped up beside her and rubbed his cheek along her arm, almost as if he knew she was upset and wanted to comfort her, though she suspected he probably hoped for a morsel from her supper. "At least you love me," Nikki muttered as she obligingly fed him a small piece of cheese. "Even if I am just a food source for you." He meowed appreciatively and bumped her hand gently with his head.

Reaching for the remote, she began yet another solitary evening of television and an early bedtime, wondering when she would ever start living her life rather than merely existing within it.

CHAPTER THREE

Turning the lock on the door to her shop, Kate peered out the window at Prince Street before lowering the shade. She had remained open a little late, losing track of time as she read her book behind the counter, and hadn't looked up until 5:25. Outside, darkness had descended and snow was falling heavily, swirling in the wind that rattled the large pane glass of her display windows. It had been a hard winter. Several storms had hit the area since the middle of November, in distinct contrast to the predominantly mild and rainy winters of the past five or six years, much like the ones in England.

This was a harsh reminder to the inhabitants that they were still in Canada and why it proudly claimed the title of Great White North. The buildup of snow, along with the effort and aggravation required for its removal, had fueled a steady stream of conversation in the nearby diner, though if anything was more futile than complaining about the weather, Kate had yet to encounter it.

Feeling vaguely depressed, she glanced up and down the empty street where the rest of the businesses had already closed, their interior lights dimmed, their display windows already dusted by the storm. Truro tended to roll up its sidewalks early through the week and on Saturdays. Only on Thursday and Friday nights did the downtown stay open later.

Kate lifted her head, watching as the snowflakes danced in the yellow streetlights, feeling a little of her dark mood evaporate. It was pretty, particularly if one didn't have to walk anywhere or navigate a vehicle on the streets rapidly being covered with a thick layer of slush. A car drove past, slowed, and stopped in front of Madison Insurance, a block down the street from Novel Companions. Kate watched as a figure got out of the Lexus and entered the building. The bulky winter clothing and obscuring snow made identification impossible, but she was left with the distinct impression that it was female.

Undoubtedly Sam's latest flame, Kate thought with wry amusement. The man saw more action than the lottery machines at the taverns, but his wife either didn't mind or didn't know about it. Such obliviousness was a trait that Kate never would have ascribed to Margaret, but ultimately it was none of her business, and she lowered the blind before checking the locks a final time.

Walking back through the store, Kate transferred the money from the register to the safe and then took a moment to straighten the cardboard display for a new release. She was reluctant to leave the store, to go upstairs to her apartment, though she was unsure why. A small part of her wondered if her unusual lethargy wasn't due to the earlier encounter with Nikki Harris.

Idly, Kate traced her fingers over the raised embossing on the bestseller, trailing over the blond head of a generic female character, though the fantasy figure lacked the exact shade of Nikki's hair or the amazing depth of her eyes. She wondered why Nikki had been so distant lately. Over the past few weeks Kate had wanted to reach out to her beyond their spirited discussions, to ask her out for coffee after work, or perhaps even to dinner.

How many times had she gathered up her courage between each visit, only to promptly lose it when she actually looked into that brilliant blue gaze? Had that secret desire somehow showed in her words or actions? Had such attraction scared or disturbed Nikki? Nikki's visits had steadily decreased the past month until she was only coming by once a week, and then she stayed only a few minutes, resisting any invitation to talk.

It was an entirely new experience for Kate to want someone this strongly. Even during her marriage, her emotions had been based on accepting what was expected of her rather than anything she truly desired. She had known at the time that she wasn't really physically attracted to her husband, but the marriage had seemed the correct thing to do, not only for herself and David, but for her family and friends as well.

Once she had extricated herself from the union, she had enough self-respect to vow not to make the same mistake twice. Celibacy held its own form of peace, and it wasn't as if Kate found women all that attractive, either, so it hadn't been necessary for her to seriously consider that she might be gay. She merely contented herself with the theory that she was asexual by nature, lacking any sort of physical desire. She had wanted to believe that she did not require anyone to share her life with, even during her more lonely moments over the years. Until Nikki Harris had walked into her store.

It was like being struck by a bolt of lightning, and Kate cherished the memory of that first meeting as she would a beloved family heirloom. Her heart had pounded so oddly as she waited on the young woman who placed the lesbian mystery novel defiantly on the counter, probably the first customer who had openly dared to buy one since the store started carrying them.

Kate inhaled slowly, hearing the wind batter the windows with small pellets of snow. She wondered occasionally if Nikki ever felt the same...if she *could* ever feel the same, particularly for an older woman. *God only knew how much older.* Kate winced. She wasn't sure she had the right to even think about it, considering Nikki's youth and how little they had in common beyond a mutual love of books.

Shaking her head in an effort to clear her thoughts, Kate walked to the rear of the store where a stairwell led to the upper floors. On the second-floor landing, she entered her apartment and crossed the dining room to the kitchen where she immediately switched on the coffee machine. Through the window over the sink, which was angled toward the east part of Prince Street, she could see a light shining from the second floor of the insurance office where Sam Madison maintained an apartment. It had to be for his own use, because as far as Kate knew, no one had ever rented it. Remembering the late arrival to Sam's office, she shook her head. How could she condemn others for being unduly inquisitive when she managed to keep tabs on nearly everything that happened in the downtown area without even trying?

Kate made herself a small salad, losing herself in the rhythm of slicing vegetables and mushrooms, and then filled a mug with coffee before carrying her meal out to the dining table. The heavy wooden table was really too large for the room, but remained a possession that she had not wanted to give up after the unexpected and devastating deaths of her parents. She consumed her solitary supper to the soft sounds of the radio tuned to the classical station, keenly conscious of how alone she felt.

The treble of the phone after she dumped her dishes in the sink came as a welcome relief, and she picked it up, pleased to discover that it was Susan Carlson. She and her oldest friend in the world weren't as constantly close as they had been before Susan moved to Halifax when her husband had been transferred, but they did keep in contact regularly.

"So what are you doing next Saturday night?" Susan asked after they had made it through the initial greetings, her breezy tone apparent over the phone line.

"Why?"

"I want you to come down to the city. You can spend the evening, we'll go out for dinner..."

Immediately wary, Kate hesitated. After her divorce, she had managed to divert the majority of honest, if misplaced, attempts by her friends to hook her up with someone new, first by insisting that it was too soon, then later with a host of other excuses, until finally most had simply given up with the conviction that she was hopeless. Only Susan persisted in coming up with possible suitors on a regular basis.

"Just you, me, and Ted?" she asked suspiciously.

"Well, Ted's invited along a friend from work—"

"I'll probably be busy." Kate closed her eyes and shook her head.

There was a wounded silence on the other end of the line. "Katie, don't be like that," Susan scolded finally. "You can't live your life alone."

"I'm doing fine so far."

"What about love, Katie?"

"If I require love that badly, I can buy a dog."

"Then the hell with love. What about sex?"

Despite herself, Kate chuckled. "Believe it or not, I don't miss that either."

A somewhat exasperated sigh sounded in her ear. "I swear, Katie, I'm about ready to give up on you."

"I do live in constant hope of that occurring." Kate smiled wryly.

"So you're not coming down?"

Stringing out the long cord, Kate carried the phone over to her plush sofa and settled onto it. "Seriously, Susan, while I'd love to see you, Ted, and the girls, I really have no interest in any kind of setup. I'm content with my life the way it is." A lie, of course, but not one she was about to elaborate on with an admission that the only relationship she might be interested in had to do with a young woman.

"Maybe I should come up and visit you," Susan said. "Heaven knows, I could use a bit of a break from hubby and the kids. It's been awhile since we've had some quality time together."

"Are you serious? That would be wonderful."

"Let me see what's going on for the next few weekends, and I'll get back to you. I've missed you, Katie."

"I've missed you, too."

They exchanged a few more pleasantries, with Susan once more urging her to get out and experience life more before she finally said farewell. Kate hung up and returned the phone to the kitchen counter, determined not to think about things like relationships or the possibilities inherent in them, despite Susan's encouragement.

Instead, she sat at the desk in the living room and dug into the stack of paperwork that had been languishing there since the end of the year. She wanted to have the taxes for the business done and out of the way early, instead of waiting until the last minute as she always did. It was her New Year's resolution, and a few hours later she felt a real sense of accomplishment and triumph as she finished.

Then she realized how truly empty her life had become when she considered that sort of thing cause for this degree of celebration.

Sighing, she headed into the bedroom where she prepared for bed, finally slipping between the sheets. Picking up a book from the nightstand, she read for another hour before weariness made her pillow more attractive than the adventures of the main character, who was apparently incapable of figuring out what Kate had known not long after the first chapter. Turning out the light, she settled back against the pillows and wondered when she would ever have the chance to experience some of the things that she had only read about, such as desire and passion and possibly even the type of love that could provide her with the happiness she had yet to experience, but still believed in.

She wasn't sure what woke her up hours later. It had been something unusual, she knew, blinking in the dim illumination of refracted streetlights through the window blind. Disconcerted, she finally realized exactly where she was as her eyes managed to pick out the familiar shapes and shadows of her bedroom. A glance at the clock radio on the nightstand showed it was early morning, the glowing green LED digits reading 1:13.

Has someone broken in? Kate listened intently. Moments passed as she tried to determine what had interrupted her sleep. Finally, she decided that it had been nothing more than a sound that, while unfamiliar enough to disturb her, hadn't really meant anything. Perhaps merely the storm, her subconscious reacting to a particularly sharp gust of wind from the Nor'easter rattling her windowpane.

Kate eased back onto the mattress, relaxing into the cozy comfort of her bed, trying to go back to sleep. From the street, she heard the soft sounds of a muffled car engine starting, idling for a moment before driving off, eventually fading away to leave nothing but the soft patter of snowflakes against her window and the wind whistling about the eaves. Soothed by the quiet, she started to drift off, only peripherally aware when another faint sound insinuated itself into her consciousness, something crackling beneath the thin howl of the storm. She didn't immediately recognize it, and while she floated in that sea of twilight between wakefulness and sleep, it danced along her senses until her mind finally pinpointed what it could be.

Jolted, she felt her eyes fly open, and she stared at the reddish glow scattering odd shadows along her bedroom wall. The next moment, she was flipping back the covers and rolling out of bed, scrambling over to the window. The glow was brighter, and over the roof of the building across the street, she could see smoke rising thick and dark in the driving snowstorm.

Pulling on her robe hastily, she left the bedroom and ran out to the kitchen. The flickering illumination was more intense and apparent, and lifting the blinds on the window over the sink, she peered through the swirling snow toward the buildings down the block.

The smoke was billowing from the windows above the insurance office, accompanied by flames licking up the front, whipped by the wind. Her mouth went dry as she realized the apartment on the upper floor was already engulfed, and she lunged for her phone. Fingers shaking, she quickly punched in 911, breathless as she stared at the inferno, and informed the dispatcher of the emergency. Trying to keep her voice calm, Kate couldn't help but notice the snow filling in the ruts on the street, leaving only minor depressions at this point. There *had* been a car, she decided, undoubtedly the one she noticed parking there earlier in the evening. The tracks began right in front of the insurance office and proceeded east, down the street where the trail disappeared beneath a blanket of white.

Had the driver been aware that the building had been on fire before he or she left? If so, why hadn't they called for help?

CHAPTER FOUR

The high wail of sirens woke Nikki. Sitting up abruptly in confusion, she looked around with blurred vision. After fumbling for her glasses on the nightstand, she jammed them on, frowning as she saw Powder up on the bedroom windowsill, the tip of his tail flicking spastically as he stared intently through the frosted glass.

She could discern more sirens as she jumped out of bed. Truro had its share of sirens in the night, but never this many. Heart pounding, Nikki stumbled across to join Powder at the window, peering through the white fog created by the blizzard outside. She finally saw the reflection of lights in the distance and the darker shadow of smoke over the rooftops. It didn't take her long to realize that the fire was only a few blocks away in the general vicinity of Prince Street. Possibly even at the intersection of Outram where Kate's bookstore was located.

Horrified, she scrambled for her clothes, not really understanding the reasoning behind her actions, only knowing that if something had happened to the store...had happened to Kate's business...she needed to be there.

Nikki flew down the stairs of her apartment building and was immediately brought up short by the heavy drift filling the sidewalk. Floundering in the snow, she decided to go back inside where she dressed properly for the weather. While she cursed a constant streak, she pulled on some waterproof pants over her sweats, a pair of heavy boots, a thick wool hat, some mittens, and her oversized jacket before forging a trail into the storm.

She wasn't the only one drawn outside by the commotion, Nikki noticed, as she plowed determinedly through the storm. Other people in the neighborhood, seeming curious and excited at the unexpected drama, also headed in the direction of the flames and smoke. She was still a block away when she realized it wasn't Novel Companions going up in smoke, but one of the buildings farther down on the opposite side of the street, the relief sharp and strong in her chest.

Heart easing its pounding, she surveyed the garish scene of flashing lights and roaring flames. From the number of trucks, Nikki realized that other departments had been called in from the surrounding areas, indicating that the situation was serious. Still concerned about the bookstore, she cut across the side streets to approach the scene from Outram. The fire department also had this street blocked, but only where it opened onto Prince, so she was able to find a spot alongside the building housing the bookstore. Other people had also chosen this as the best place to view the proceedings, and a crowd milled behind the barricades as if they were anticipating some sort of parade or celebration put on for their entertainment.

Nikki looked up worriedly, trying to determine if the flames might spread up the block. Fortunately, the wind was howling in the other direction, but because of it, the firefighters had their hands full trying to prevent the fire from jumping to a nearby restaurant, separated from the fire by only a small parking lot. Luckily there weren't any apartments in the buildings directly nearby, but many of the area residents had left their homes just the same, perhaps afraid it might spread toward them. They stood huddled in coats and jackets pulled hastily over pajamas, some holding young children, the eerie splash of emergency lights washing over their drawn faces.

It was difficult to hear above the roaring of the flames, the shouts of the firefighters, and the confused conversation of the onlookers as the firefighters worked frantically to bring things under control. The water was freezing as it rose into the air from the hoses, and ice was forming everywhere, in addition to the blizzard dumping more snow with every passing minute. Nikki thought the precipitation would help dampen the flames, but the high winds apparently offset any potential benefit.

"Nikki."

The call originated from above her, faint, almost carried away by the wind. Startled, she looked up, astounded when she saw Kate Shannon's head poking through the second-story window directly above her.

"Go to the door at the back," Kate instructed, gesturing toward the rear of the building.

Nikki frowned and then glanced around at the crowd, none of whom seemed to have noticed her being summoned by the woman in the window. After all, why would anyone care that the most gorgeous woman in town wanted to invite the local lesbian upstairs? Shrugging off her worries of being scrutinized, she obediently moved back to the sidewalk and along the side of the building. At the rear, she discovered a door, a mailbox with the street number, and a small brass plaque just below the doorbell with the name "K. Shannon" inscribed across it. A sizable, nondescript vehicle covered with snow was parked next to a large dumpster.

Nikki realized Kate didn't just run her business from this building; she also lived in the upstairs, and Nikki wondered why she hadn't known that. Tentatively, she reached out to push the bell. The door opened before she could touch it, revealing a somewhat mussed bookstore owner motioning Nikki inside. She was dressed as informally as Nikki had ever seen her, in an oversized white T-shirt and loose drawstring pants, with bright blue fuzzy slippers adorning her feet. Nikki found the ensemble unbearably adorable.

"Come on in," Kate told her. "It's a lot warmer upstairs."

Dazedly, Nikki followed her up the stairs that led to a second floor landing where Kate opened the door to her apartment. Nikki paused inside, astounded by the lavish rooms she had been unaware existed right over her head all the times she had visited the bookstore. "I didn't know you lived here," she said, somewhat inanely, as she shrugged out of her jacket and removed her hat and scarf. "I thought there was only storage or empty offices up here."

"I renovated when I bought the building." Kate smiled as she took the garments from Nikki. Hanging them in the closet, Kate moved Nikki's boots over to the mat where the melting snow could drain. "After Mom and Dad died, I sold their house and redid this floor above the store. It didn't make sense to maintain a separate residence when I could work and live in the same building."

"That does make sense." Feeling nervous and extremely conscious of being in unfamiliar territory, Nikki recognized that the décor in the apartment was far more tasteful and cultured than she was used to, looking more like something from a magazine layout than a place where someone she knew actually lived. At the same time she was elated to be invited into an inner sanctum that not many had the privilege of discovering.

"May I get you something?" Kate asked as she moved toward the kitchen, past the dining table. "I think it's going to be a long night."

"Uh, thank you," Nikki said as she followed.

"Coffee?"

"No, I don't drink it."

Kate looked at her as if she had just said she didn't breathe on a regular basis. "Oh." There was a pause. "Tea?"

"Um, water would be fine." It wasn't the first time Nikki had run into this sort of awkward situation. Not drinking tea or coffee seemed to be something of an oddity to most people over twenty, particularly in a town that boasted eight chain restaurants specializing in coffee and donuts, in addition to the privately owned shops. She had simply never developed a taste for it, finding it bitter and unpleasant, and couldn't comprehend why other people enjoyed it.

"How about some hot chocolate?" Kate suggested in a gentler tone. "You must be cold."

Nikki seized on this offer with relief. "That would be great." She glanced around the kitchen, which appeared sunny and bright even in the dead of night. It had to be some trick of the wallpaper, she decided. "I'm surprised you still have electricity."

Kate stopped in midmotion while pulling some mugs from the cupboard. "You're right," she said, eyeing Nikki. "I hadn't thought of that. Maybe I should find some candles, just in case."

"This side of the street is probably on a different line than the other," Nikki said, aware she was just filling the moment with something…anything…to say, because the thought of suddenly being in the dark with Kate made it difficult to swallow. "Otherwise, I think you would have lost it by now. Uh, I wonder who noticed the fire."

"I called the fire department," Kate said, busying herself with preparing Nikki's hot chocolate, filling the mug with water and placing it in the microwave before retrieving a tin from another cupboard. "But I'm not sure if I was the first. They arrived here quickly enough, and it didn't take long before they were calling in others. I think both the county and Bible Hill departments are here."

"The sirens woke me up," Nikki said, suddenly feeling self-conscious about rushing down to the scene of a disaster in the making.

Unexpected Sparks

"When I saw the smoke from my window, I was afraid it was the bookstore. It's not like I go out of my way to gawk at accidents or anything."

Kate flashed her a brief grin. "I'm flattered you were worried about me."

Nikki decided not to pursue that one. Instead she asked, "Did you see it start?"

Kate's features darkened, and Nikki wondered why.

"The top floor was fully ablaze when I called it in. Something woke me...maybe the sound of the flames."

The sudden ding from the microwave interrupted anything else she might have said. Kate removed the mug and placed it on the counter before handing Nikki the tin of hot chocolate, along with a spoon. "Help yourself," she said. "I'm not sure how thick you want it."

Nikki obligingly scooped the dark powder into the mug, aware of Kate pouring herself a cup of coffee from the pot on the coffeemaker. Shyly, she stood next to the other woman at the large window over the sink, wondering why she, out of all the people on the street below, had been invited in. Lifting her mug carefully, she sipped her drink, not wanting to spill it either on herself or on the tile floor that was cool beneath her sock feet. Sneaking a peek at Kate's profile as she observed the action outside, Nikki hesitantly cleared her throat. "You said something woke you?"

Kate drew down her brows and lifted her chin, though she didn't turn her head. "Yes. It was...a noise...similar to a backfire from a car." She shook her head. "It was probably just the glass breaking as the fire broke the windows."

"Perhaps it was an explosion of some sort," Nikki mused. "Or it could have been a gunshot."

Now Kate did look at her, and Nikki was astonished to see that her eyes altered color to reflect her mood, shading from a light blue to dark gray. She wondered why she had never noticed that before.

"Why would you say that?" Astonishment edged Kate's tone.

Nikki shrugged, embarrassed. "I don't know. Too many mysteries, probably." The woman continued to stare at her, and Nikki felt very uncomfortable, sorry that she had ever opened her mouth.

"You do like to read a lot," Kate said after a few seconds, which seemed like hours. "I know you like the outdoors. What else do you like to do, Nikki? In your spare time, I mean."

"Uh, not much," Nikki said, wondering why Kate was asking, and why now. "I like sports, I guess. I'm into computers quite a bit, and I like going to movies. I'm really into camping and hiking. I play tennis in the summer." She darted a glance from the corner of her eye. "Why?"

Kate looked away, color touching her high cheekbones. "I was just curious. I don't feel I know you very well, even after all the times we've spoken in the bookstore."

"Why would you want to?" Nikki blurted, amazed at the disclosure.

"Why wouldn't I?" There seemed to be a touch of defensiveness in Kate's tone. "I find you an extremely interesting and intelligent person, Nikki."

Nikki couldn't think of an immediate response. "When did you call the fire department?" she asked finally, thinking that was a much safer topic.

Kate lifted her brow but didn't challenge the change of topic. "I woke up around quarter after one."

Nikki considered that information. "The taverns let out at one. If anything was going on earlier than that, you'd think someone would have noticed. How late is the Dairy Queen open?"

"It closes at ten." Kate pursed her lips thoughtfully. "Besides, I only saw tracks from the car parked in front of the insurance office. The storm seems to have kept everyone else at home."

"What car?"

Kate took a breath and explained about the unidentified person she saw going into the office earlier, as well as the fact that she heard a car drive away shortly after she woke.

Nikki frowned. "That's weird."

"Probably a coincidence."

"Yeah? A car drives away, and only a few minutes later, the building it was parked in front of suddenly bursts into flames? I don't know much about how fires work, but I don't think they take off that quickly unless they were 'helped' a little bit."

Kate regarded her, obviously disturbed at the thought, and Nikki felt embarrassed again. "I'm sorry. I'm just thinking out loud. I'm probably way off base."

"Maybe." Kate's expression appeared troubled. "But at the same time, something odd did wake me up." She seemed about to say more when her doorbell rang. She looked vaguely annoyed at the interruption but nodded at Nikki. "I'll be right back."

She disappeared out the door, leaving it ajar and, curious, Nikki drifted over to it, eavesdropping as she wondered who else would be knocking on Kate's back door at this time of night, particularly when all the entertainment was out front.

CHAPTER FIVE

K ate was startled to see Rick Johnson on her doorstep. Large and ruggedly handsome with broad shoulders and the beginning of a potbelly, the constable had been a dear friend to her since high school. A laidback individual who kept tense situations under control with a joke or a calming comment rather than by trying to intimidate anyone, he was well liked and an excellent law enforcement officer who commanded respect rather than fear.

"Rick? What can I do for you?"

"Sorry to bother you, Kate." Snow heavily dusted the shoulders of his bulky uniform jacket. "Even though I doubt you'd be asleep with all that's going on out front."

"No, I wasn't asleep. Come on in."

She hesitated as she realized she didn't want to take him upstairs where Nikki was, though why she was averse to that, she really didn't want to examine. Instead, she reached behind her and opened the door to the store. Leading him through the used section to the front where they could watch the firefighters still battling the blaze through the large display windows, she turned to him expectantly. Rick had his notepad out, his pen at the ready, letting her know this wasn't a social call. "You called in the alarm?"

"I called 911," she said, crossing her arms over her chest. "About two-fifteen."

"You didn't see anyone else around?"

She thought it a somewhat odd question. "You mean, when I looked outside?"

"Exactly." He was being very formal with her, undoubtedly attempting to maintain a professional distance as he investigated.

"No." She hesitated, wondering if she should tell him about the car.

"What?" He was watching her intently, and she realized her expression had given her away. He had always been very good at reading between the lines with her.

"I don't know what woke me up," she said. "There was a kind of noise. For some reason, I keep thinking it was a car backfire."

"Did you notice what time this was?"

"When I glanced at the clock, it read 1:13. While I lay there, I heard a car start up and drive away. That was about...oh, twenty to two, I guess. I was just going back to sleep when I heard a crackling sound and saw the glow from the fire on my bedroom wall. That's when I got up and called the fire department." She shrugged. "That's all I know."

"Did you see the car?"

She shook her head. "Just the marks from where it drove away from its parking place in front of the insurance office. The tracks turned left at Walker Street." She tilted her head, studying his face. "What's this about, Rick?"

He looked very serious, his jaw set. "It's possible the fire was started with gasoline, Kate. We won't know for sure until an investigation team checks it out, but from what the firefighters are saying, they're pretty sure it's arson. If that's the case, I decided I wasn't going to wait around to start asking questions. It's not as if I'm waking anyone up."

Which was why Rick was considered an outstanding constable, Kate reminded herself. She was disturbed someone might have set the fire deliberately, particularly after what she and Nikki had been talking about upstairs.

"You didn't get a look at the car, Kate?"

"I don't know if it was the same one," she said slowly, "but a car did park there just as I was closing down around five thirty. It was a dark sedan, a Lexus, I think. I didn't really notice much more. I definitely didn't get a license plate or anything like that."

"What about the driver?"

"It was already snowing heavily." She felt as if she was somehow at fault for not noticing more. "I'm not even sure if it was a man or a woman, but—"

"But?"

She exhaled audibly. "I was left with the impression it was a woman." She put her hand on Rick's forearm. "That's just a guess, Rick," she added. "It's not anything I would swear to."

"I know, Kate. You're a good witness. You would never say anything beyond what you saw."

She felt even more disturbed. "I'm a witness?"

"If it's arson, I'm afraid you are." He made another note in his book. "Are you and Sam Madison friends, Kate?"

Kate lifted her chin, not sure she liked how Rick had asked the question. Perhaps it had been the emphasis on the word "friends." She had become pretty good at reading between the lines with him over the years, as well.

"What do you mean?"

He had the grace to look vaguely embarrassed. "It's no secret that Sam...plays around." He lowered his eyes, his cheeks darkening slightly. "You're a very attractive woman, Kate, and you're right down the street..."

"So I would be convenient?"

"I'm sorry, Kate. I have to ask. We haven't found Sam yet, and frankly, if anyone knows insurance—"

"It would be him. Do you think that's what this is about?"

"Again, we don't even know for sure if it's arson. I just can't figure out why we can't find Sam Madison at three in the morning while his business is burning to the ground. He's not at home, and his wife hasn't seen him since yesterday morning at breakfast." He lifted his head. "That in itself is sort of disturbing. Even when he's 'working late,' Margaret says he always manages to make it home on the weeknights."

"Rick, if he wasn't in that car that drove away, is it possible—"

"That he's still in the building?" Rick looked very serious again. "We've considered it, Kate. The first truck on the scene sent some guys in, but they didn't find anything. Until it cools down a bit, they don't want to risk anyone else. If he *was* in there—"

"Oh, dear."

"Try not to think about it." He hesitated. "I don't suppose you know who his latest flame is?" He winced. "No pun intended."

She smiled despite the circumstances. "No. I don't think I'm being rude in saying that it altered a lot over the years. Who kept track?"

"Not his wife, that's for sure," he said, and flushed. "Sorry, that was—"

"Accurate." She studied him in the rosy reflection of the flames. "Rick, if it's arson, and he was in there—"

"Then it's murder," he said flatly.

There was a creak above their heads, and Rick looked up. He frowned. "Is there someone else here, Kate?"

She felt the heat rise in her cheeks, even though she managed to keep her voice perfectly even. "I noticed one of my friends in the crowd and invited her up to the apartment to...well, watch the fire in comfort."

He grinned. "Oh yeah? Who?"

"Nikki Harris." She could have said nothing, since it was none of his business, or dissembled about the identity of her visitor, but she didn't want him or anyone else to think she had something to hide or was somehow ashamed of having Nikki in her apartment. For her own self-respect, and out of respect for Nikki, she refused to let herself fall into that trap. She did notice that Rick's face altered perceptibly.

"Lorne and Adele Harris's daughter," he said, an odd tone in his voice. "She just moved back to town last year."

She hesitated, wondering how he knew. "That's my understanding."

His gaze on her was speculative, as if he had somehow come to a conclusion about her that had been troubling him for some time.

She felt a spark of annoyance. "Is there anything else?"

He started slightly, as if her question caught him off guard or her sudden coldness affected him. "No. I'll get back to you if I have any further questions."

"Of course." She let him out the front door, rather than returning back through the store, and he offered her one more unfathomable glance before walking out onto the street. She locked up behind him and then headed back up the stairs.

Nikki had already pulled on her boots and retrieved her coat from the closet by the time Kate reached the apartment. The acute stab of disappointment that shot through her when she realized Nikki was preparing to leave surprised her. "You're not staying?"

Nikki appeared uncomfortable. "I think I'd better go." She hesitated. "I didn't mean to eavesdrop, but I heard you talking to the police."

"Rick had a few questions. I did call it in, after all."

Nikki pulled on her mittens. "It won't do your reputation any good for people to know I visited you this time of night."

Kate lifted a brow. "My reputation?"

"I'm gay," Nikki said, as if this would be news to Kate. "I don't flaunt it, but I don't make any secret of it either. If someone straight is seen with me, that automatically makes them gay in a lot of people's eyes. You probably don't need that hassle."

"I'm not sure I understand what you're saying, Nikki." Kate remained in the doorway, preventing Nikki from moving past her and down the stairs, though Nikki's greater height would have made it easy for her to brush by her if she really wanted to.

Nikki seemed to have difficulty meeting her eyes. "I'm just saying that if you become my friend, other people will think you're...like me. For someone like you, that probably wouldn't be any good."

"Someone like me. What does that mean?"

Nikki frowned, flushing furiously, obviously very uncomfortable with the whole situation. "Someone who's preeminent in the business community. Someone who's active in all the social things that happen around town, someone who's on the town council. It could hurt your business, maybe even a lot."

"Ah." Kate remembered how much stir she had caused in that same town council when she first began carrying gay and lesbian books, primarily from the mayor's wife. Abigail Jenkins claimed she was carrying pornography and threatened to start a protest outside her store. Facing down the woman with the coldly logical explanation that even if these books were predominantly adult-oriented, which she wasn't prepared to liken to pornography in any way, Kate explained that she needed to expand her customer base or the store would go under, as had a great many other businesses in the downtown. She finished by saying that she certainly wasn't going to run her shop according to the outmoded beliefs of a woman who was obviously far more worried about what consenting adults did in the privacy of their homes than she was about keeping the downtown core active and thriving, which was what the meeting had been about in the first place.

Kate's cool, calm presentation had quieted Abigail, though it undoubtedly had made her a lifelong enemy. She apparently impressed the other council members, because not another thing had been said about it. But she also agreed that Nikki had a point. *Was that why she had suddenly started to curtail her visits to the store? Was it an effort to protect her somehow?* A glow abruptly spread through Kate that she might care so much. "I choose my own friends."

Nikki suddenly lifted her gaze. "You do? I mean...it really wouldn't bother you—"

"Nikki, I don't invite just anyone into my home." Kate reached out and put her hand on Nikki's arm, feeling her warmth even through the thick coat. "I appreciate that you're trying to protect me, but it isn't necessary. I do thank you for the gesture, though, despite how misguided it is."

Nikki was looking down again. "I just don't want you to...be embarrassed to be my friend."

Kate's heart ached. *Who had hurt Nikki so badly to put that amount of pain in her voice?* "I can't imagine that ever happening."

Nikki regarded her uncertainly for a moment and then looked away. "I still better go," she said quietly. "It's almost five-thirty."

"God, so it is." Kate gave a brief laugh. "I have to open up in a few hours." Nikki smiled suddenly, and Kate felt her heart give a sudden twinge.

"I guess I'm lucky I don't have to be at Keebler's until ten."

"You're fortunate."

Nikki tried to edge past Kate. "Still, I have to go."

"Of course." Kate stepped aside. "I'll see you later?"

"Yeah, I'll talk to you later."

Then she was gone, and Kate was left with the distinct impression that this night would forever change her life...in more ways than one.

CHAPTER SIX

The Mayflower Diner was abuzz when Nikki walked in the next afternoon. Existing for as long as she could remember, the small restaurant was owned by a couple who provided excellent food at reasonable prices. Furthermore, the garishly colored vinyl booths along the walls and scarred wooden tables in front of the large windows looking out onto Inglish Place offered a place to socialize and chat for those who lived and worked in the downtown. The fire had been the most exciting thing to happen in years, and it was obviously good for business. The place was crowded even though it was well after lunch and a little too early for supper. Fortunately, Nikki's timing was unnaturally perfect for just as she walked in, a couple rose from the table near the window. Nikki wasted little time in grabbing it, removing her coat, and draping it over the chair.

"Nikki, did you hear?"

Nikki looked up as Kim McKinnon promptly plopped down in the chair opposite her. "The fire, you mean? I saw it."

"No, I'm talking about the body they pulled out of the rubble early this afternoon." Kim shrugged out of her jacket, which sported a logo for the Sportsplex where she was an aerobics instructor. A wiry strawberry blonde, she had always been into sports, and her basketball records at Truro High would probably stand for years. Kim and her partner, Lynn, an accountant with her own business, had been the first gay people Nikki had ever met when she hesitantly walked into their potluck gathering not long after she had graduated high school. They had helped make the acknowledgment of who she truly was a much easier transition. Nikki was aware that she could easily have fallen in with another type of crowd during such a delicate stage in her life, one which didn't consist primarily of couples in long-term relationships...

one where she could have developed a somewhat damaging perception of what being gay was all about.

Nikki felt dizzy. "Body?"

"A lot of people think it's Sam Madison. But there's been no official identification yet." Kim leaned closer, lowering her voice. "I also heard there was a hole in the corpse's head...maybe even a bullet hole."

"Jesus," Nikki blurted. She took a breath and composed herself. "Are you sure?"

Kim shrugged. "It's not as if I was there when they hauled it out. I'm just repeating what I heard from people who were."

"A murder." Nikki leaned back in her seat and found it somewhat difficult to breathe. She wasn't sure why the news was impacting her this hard, unless it was the fact she had watched the fire last night from Kate's apartment and didn't for one moment think of someone being inside, burning in the flames, their flesh shriveling... She swallowed hard and cursed her overactive imagination. She couldn't imagine a worse way to die. "That's just...incredible."

"Did you see anything last night, Nikki?" Kim and Lynn lived across the Salmon River Bridge in Bible Hill, and it was unlikely they had even seen the smoke from their house.

"Just a lot of firemen and spectators." Nikki hesitated, not sure if she should add this last part but decided to go ahead. "Mrs. Shannon invited me in to watch the fire from her apartment."

Now it was Kim's turn to lean back in her chair as she stared at Nikki. "Kate Shannon? The owner of the bookstore?"

Nikki nodded.

"Why would she invite you in?"

Nikki started to respond, hesitated, and then shook her head. "I don't know."

Nikki seemed about to add more when Addy, the diner's primary waitress and part owner, finally made it over to their table to take their order. Kim ordered a hamburger platter, totally at odds to the image of health and fitness she was supposed to represent. Nikki ordered only a glass of milk.

Once the waitress had slipped away, Nikki asked, "What have you heard about Kate?"

"'Kate,' is it?" Kim eyed her narrowly. "What happened to 'Mrs. Shannon'?"

Nikki's face grew warm. She felt like she was about to be forced into admitting something she wasn't ready to face, and finally Kim relented when she didn't say anything further.

"I haven't heard much, Nikki. She's active in everything in town, yet at the same time, she's pretty private. Since her divorce, she's stayed out of circulation, at least as far as sleeping around is concerned, unless she and her partner, or partners, are far more discreet than this town is known for." She shrugged. "The basic conclusion is that 'Kate don't date.' You don't think she's hanging in the closet?"

"No." Nikki felt a tug of regret at her certainty. "She's just...really nice." She glanced down and felt awkward. "I like her."

"God, let's not go there again," Kim said, and Nikki raised her eyes sharply.

"I'm not, so forget it."

Startled, Kim looked at her and nodded. "Sorry. It's just...there's no future in straight chicks, Nik. You should know that, especially after Anne. Even if they do give it a try, it's only because they're curious, and it's only on their terms. Once the fun has worn off, they're back to what they're most comfortable with, and they don't even want to know you exist anymore."

That was what had hurt most about the whole situation, Nikki remembered. Not so much that it hadn't worked out, but that when it was over, Anne no longer wanted to talk to her, not even in passing, apparently wanting to forget the relationship had ever happened. As if it had been embarrassing...as if being with Nikki had been shameful. With an effort, she swallowed back the misery that rose in her chest whenever she thought of the woman she had fallen so hard for, had actually moved into the city to be near, leaving behind her friends and family. It had been hard to give up her heart so completely, only to have it handed back dismissively as nothing anyone would want.

"I'm just saying Kate's friendly. What's wrong with being friends?"

"Well, you could do worse than to make friends with Kate Shannon," Kim said, glancing sideways as her meal arrived. "She knows just about everyone in town, and if there are any better jobs floating around, she can probably put you on an inside track for them. Have you come across any?"

"Not yet." Nikki sipped her drink. She had been attempting to find a better-paying, more stable position than her clerical job at Keebler's, but such positions were scarce in Truro. "Besides, that's not why I want to be friends with her."

"Nikki."

"What?"

"Don't do this again."

"I'm not."

"Good." Kim bit vigorously into her hamburger. "I really don't want you to get hurt or move away again." She nudged over her plate. "Have some fries, will you? They always pile on way too many."

Which was exactly why she had ordered the platter, Nikki knew, but she didn't demur, readily helping herself to the crispy home-cut potatoes and dipping them in the barbeque sauce that Kim had poured onto the side of her plate.

"Listen, why don't you come over Saturday night? We'll get some of the girls together, have a few drinks, and commiserate over your new state of affairs."

"I could use some cheering up." Nikki felt a flash of genuine enthusiasm. As far as the town's small, tightly knit community of lesbians and gays went, Kim and Lynn were, without question, the leaders. They coordinated all of the social events, with some smaller gatherings occurring right in their home. Though Nikki sometimes felt very much like a fifth wheel because everyone else in the group was paired off, it still promised her a good time, something she desperately needed.

"It'll work out." Kim took another bite of her hamburger before dragging the subject back to the hot topic of the moment. "If it *was* Sam they dragged out of the ashes, I wonder who did him in."

"Kate said..." Nikki began, and then stopped.

Kim's eyes assessed her alertly. "What?"

Nikki sighed and repeated what Kate had told her the night before. "Don't spread it around."

"I won't." Kim looked thoughtful. "If a woman was visiting Sam last night, it's pretty quiet as to who it could have been, which is unusual for him. He couldn't keep anything secret."

"Did he really get around that much?"

"If it had breasts and breathed, he had a go at it. Christ, he even made a pass at me one night while I was working the front desk. He was really nice about it, though."

"You're kidding."

Kim shrugged. "I'm not saying I was interested. I'm just saying that he had a way of doing it that was charming in an odd sort of way."

Nikki wondered if Kate Shannon had ever succumbed to his apparent charms, conscious of the card, which she had retrieved from her trash basket and now had tucked into her jacket pocket. "How do you know about...the others?"

"Hey, you pick up a lot where I work. The Sportsplex is the only place in town, with the exception of the liquor store, where everyone shows up at least once."

Nikki granted that was true. Built only a few years earlier as part of the effort to revitalize the downtown core, the large structure sprawled over the area where a gigantic old warehouse had once been located, not far from where the insurance office had burned down. It included a heated pool, a gym, and a virtual golfing range, providing a lot of jobs and a central recreational facility for Truro. It had also significantly increased business in the surrounding area. Its use wasn't limited to the sporting community either, also providing space, at a very minimal charge, for various organizations, from the War Veterans to the local Quilting Society, to hold their meetings.

Nikki had attended classes there for her computer courses and had visited the gym often for her morning workouts. The local Gay & Lesbian Support Group held their committee meetings there once a month. Sooner or later, everyone who participated in any activity in Truro visited the complex.

"Listen, was Sam a regular?"

Kim nodded. "Religiously. He worked out every day, even on Sundays and holidays. To my knowledge, the only time he missed was a weekend in January when he was out of town."

"Where'd he go?" Nikki asked, remembering the message on the card.

"How would I know?" Kim tilted her head slightly. "Why are you so interested? Trying to solve the mystery all on your own?"

Nikki laughed and shook her head. "I'm just thinking out loud. Do you think one of the women he was involved with killed him?"

Kim frowned. "You know, I'd be quicker to think it was a husband or boyfriend rather than any of the women." She popped a fry into her mouth. "Or maybe it had nothing to do with sex."

"You could be right. Most crime does seem to come down to one thing, and it usually isn't passion."

"Money," they both said in the same breath, and then laughed. They quickly stopped as they remembered what they were laughing about.

"God, he's really dead, isn't he?"

"Someone is." Nikki shook her head. "A hell of a thing to happen in a town this small."

"Don't kid yourself. There are a lot of secrets in small towns. In this case, one of them was terrible enough to kill for."

Nikki lifted her brows. "Or die for."

CHAPTER SEVEN

As Kate went over the invoice for the next week's order, noting which of her books needed to be shipped back due to slow sales, Sheila Fisher waited on the Thursday-evening customers. The high school student worked two evenings, as well as on Saturdays, freeing Kate from spending her entire time in the store. Though Kate often worked anyway, the latitude Sheila's help afforded her made every penny of the teenager's wages worth it.

When the bell above the door jangled, Kate glanced up from her invoice and was astounded at the way her stomach clenched as Nikki walked in. She immediately rose and motioned for her to come over, almost overwhelmed by Nikki's smile. The open expression made Nikki's previous withdrawal even more striking, and Kate's reaching out to her the previous night had obviously played a part in the change. Once more, Nikki was the warm, sweet person she had come to know, and Kate experienced a small moment of disorientation, wondering just where their friendship would lead. Then Nikki was standing in front of her, and she forgot everything but the devastating blue of her eyes.

"Hi," Nikki said, seeming breathless.

"Hi." Kate decided she had pretty much used up her inanity quotient for the day. She swallowed and smiled. "Two visits in one week. I'm amazed."

When Nikki flushed and drew back, Kate mentally kicked herself. Becoming more intimate with the young woman would apparently be similar to befriending a wild animal. It would take both time and patience, not to mention a great deal of care. What surprised her was how much she needed and wanted to do it, regardless of how much work it took or what the end result would be.

"I wanted your opinion on something." Nikki peered at her from beneath lowered lashes. "If you're not too busy."

"Of course." Kate motioned toward the back of the store. "Come on up to the apartment, and you can tell me over some hot chocolate." She glanced over at the counter. "Sheila, I'll be upstairs for awhile."

The teen raised her hand absently, seeming to be completely focused on the customer she was helping, and Kate led Nikki through the used section to the rear staircase. Upstairs, Kate took her jacket and hung it in the closet. "Have a seat." She gestured at the chairs lining the breakfast bar as she walked into the kitchen.

While Nikki perched on the high, wooden stool, Kate prepared the drinks, remembering how many spoonfuls of hot chocolate Nikki had used the night before and pouring a coffee for herself. Kate placed the mug in front of Nikki as she sat down beside her. "What's up?"

Nikki dug into her pocket and placed a card on the counter. "I found it in the book I bought yesterday. Maybe Madison is the 'Sam' who signed it."

Kate picked up the card and read the inscription inside, then frowned as she looked at Nikki. "Possibly, but I would have no way of knowing."

Nikki looked extremely uncomfortable. "I thought...Does the card belong to you?"

"Did you honestly think it did?" She wondered if she should be insulted. First, Rick and now Nikki...did everyone think she was that desperate? "I've never been out with Sam."

Nikki nodded, her features relaxing. "Okay...I'm glad."

"Why?" Kate eyed her keenly. "Why are you glad?"

Nikki flushed. "I didn't..." She floundered. "It's..." She swallowed so hard that the muscles in her throat moved visibly. "You could do a lot better than being Sam Madison's mistress. I'm just glad that you know that, too."

Kate was suddenly amused. "Ah." She regarded Nikki evenly, then added with a touch of wickedness, "What constitutes 'better'?" Nikki's eyes rose to meet hers intently, warm and frightened at the same time, but she didn't respond, and Kate's common sense urged her not to pursue the subject...not yet. Instead she asked, "Why do you think this might be a 'clue'?"

"It might not be, but the book is a new release from last November, and I know it wasn't in the used section last week, so it was probably brought in recently by a customer."

"You think that means this other 'Kate' is Sam's current paramour?"

Nikki shrugged. "No one seems to know who that person is. Which in itself is pretty unusual. Most of the time, it's no secret who he's seeing...unless she's married. Which also might be a clue."

"Just because the book is a new release, the card might not be," Kate said. "In fact, since it was used for a bookmark, chances are it's not. Assuming that the card is even from Sam Madison in the first place."

Nikki nodded. "I know." But she looked deflated at Kate's lack of enthusiasm. "You're right, of course. I'm probably making something out of nothing." She studied the counter. "Too much time on my hands, I guess."

Dismayed at how quickly the light went out of Nikki's face, Kate reached over and covered the slender hand with her own, steadfastly ignoring the tingle that shot up her arm. "Still, it could be important. I don't know that it's enough to take to the police, but it might be something to investigate if that's what you really want to do."

"You're just humoring me now."

Startled, Kate opened her mouth to protest and then reconsidered. "Yes, I suppose I was though that wasn't really my intention." She tilted her head slightly. "Why are you so interested, Nikki? Is it just because the murder hit so close to home or, in this case, the bookstore?"

Nikki blinked, almost as if she hadn't thought about it. "Maybe. Maybe it just makes me feel like I'm doing something more important with my life than working at Keebler's."

"Perhaps you have a leaning toward this sort of work. Have you ever thought about going into law enforcement?"

"You mean, like a police officer?" Nikki shook her head. "Not really."

"Maybe you should. You could get a student loan..."

Nikki winced. "I already have a student loan. I took some computer courses from Compu-Learn when I came back from Halifax."

Kate remembered the fly-by-night school which had popped into town at the height of the high-tech boom, took the money, and promptly run before the courses were finished, leaving the students without diplomas yet still carrying the bank loans they had arranged for the tuition. "I'm sorry."

Nikki shrugged. "I did learn a lot about computers before the school closed, so it wasn't a total loss. I know word processing and spreadsheet programs. They also taught me how to type. I don't know if it was worth what I paid them, and I never received a diploma, but it did get me a job in Keebler's accounting office. It's better than a cashier's job."

"You want more." Kate was pleased at the knowledge. "Those skills should be able to get you another job fairly quickly."

"Maybe somewhere other than Truro. It's pretty slow right now. The main problem is that I don't own a car, which limits my options. I may have to take the bus down to the city, find a better-paying job and an apartment there."

"You're thinking of moving away?" The thought made Kate's chest hurt in an unfamiliar and totally unpleasant manner.

"I don't want to. I know there are more opportunities in the city, but I didn't like living there. It was crowded, and you had to watch where you walked all the time. I like living in Truro. It's near where I grew up, and I went to the high school downtown. It's where all my family and friends are. I want to stay here if I can."

"There's nothing wrong with that." Kate understood perfectly. She liked the town as well, appreciated its peacefulness and cleanliness, even if it sometimes felt a little too small. She took a sip from her coffee, peering at Nikki over the rim. "Uh, do you mind if I ask how old you are?"

"Twenty-six." Nikki flushed and looked away, as if the question embarrassed her. "I guess I should know by now what I want to do with my life, but I don't. If I did, I would get another loan and go to college for the proper training."

"Not necessarily," Kate said, feeling a sudden gulf in years between them. "I was thirty-three before I finally figured out what I wanted...or rather, didn't want...from life, and I was damned lucky to have the store to fall back on. I discovered that I had gone through four years of university and ten years of marriage without developing any useful job skills at all."

"What did you take in college?"

"Literature, but unless I'm going to teach or work in a library, which never really interested me, there are simply no jobs requiring it around here."

Nikki tilted her head slightly. "Then why did you take it?"

"It fascinated me. Still does. In those days when we applied to university we didn't always think in terms of what we were supposed to do afterward. Now, it seems like people only pursue secondary education in order to find a job that will provide them with the most money. I can't remember the last time I talked with someone who went to university simply to learn rather than...what did you call it? Train for a career." She chose her next words with care. "You know, if you want to stay in town, you should. I'll start sending out feelers to see what's out there. Hopefully, my contacts can provide some leads for you."

Nikki was blushing again. "That's not why I came to see you."

"I know. If I can help you, though, I'm going to. That's what friends are for. But you're right in saying things are a little depressed at the moment. I don't know how much longer it will be financially feasible to keep the store open. The overhead is steadily rising, while the profit margin is growing slimmer, and it's the same for everyone here in the downtown. Still, computer skills are always useful, and I'm sure we can find you a position somewhere."

Nikki took a breath. "There's also the other thing."

"What other thing?"

"The lesbian thing. Most people know."

Kate waved it off. "Anyone who wouldn't hire you because of that is no one you'd want to work for anyway, regardless of what kind of job it was."

She was pleased to see this was exactly the right thing to say. Nikki's eyes lit up at her casual assurance and encouragement. It was obvious that whoever had done a number on her self-esteem had been quite thorough.

Kate was caught off-guard by the anger that realization stirred within her and positively shocked at the sudden desire to meet this person, preferably with a baseball bat in hand. She wondered if Nikki was aware she was capable of inspiring the most intense and primitive emotions within her. If it weren't so damned disconcerting, it would almost be funny.

"In the meantime, let's follow the lead with the card you found in the book." Kate picked it up. "What was the name of the book again?"

"*Mummy's Legacy.*"

"The archaeologist mysteries." Kate recognized it now. The fact that it was a new release returning so quickly had stuck in her mind and made it easy to pinpoint the day she had put it on the shelf in the back room. "The auction."

"What?"

"It was in a box of books I picked up at the auction in the hotel last Tuesday night." Kate rose from her chair and walked over to her desk, rummaging through her receipts. "Here it is."

"Does it say whose estate it was?"

"No. If it was mentioned, I wasn't paying attention." Kate shrugged.

"Could we find out?"

Kate glanced over at her. "Do you really want to?"

"For my own curiosity, if nothing else." Nikki's eyes were steady.

Kate gazed at her a moment longer, acknowledging to herself that she would do just about anything in order to spend more time with the woman sitting at the breakfast bar. "All right," she said. "Let me make a few calls."

She returned to the kitchen where the phone was and put a hand on the receiver but didn't lift it from the cradle as she flipped through her address book, picking her most likely contact before she dialed. Aware of Nikki watching her, an impressed expression on her face, Kate resisted the urge to feel self-important. After all, she knew everyone in town only because she had no personal life, just a professional one. She was just now starting to notice how empty it was.

"Bill, how are you?" she said, when the phone was picked up. "This is Kate Shannon down at Novel Companions. Listen, I was wondering about the auction in your hotel last week. You don't happen to remember whose estate was on the block, do you?"

CHAPTER EIGHT

K atherine Rushton was the name that Kate had finally tracked down from her friends at the hotel, which possibly identified the name on the card. Once they discovered the previous owner of the book, Nikki no longer had an excuse to remain at the apartment, though she certainly wanted to. A small part of her sensed that Kate also wanted her to stay a little longer, but she wasn't completely sure, so she didn't take the chance on imposing.

By late Friday afternoon, Nikki had yet to find any use for the information, but she hoped that she could uncover something just by using her ears for a while. As she strode down Prince Street after work, the wind had picked up, heralding more snow for the evening, and she was forced to bow her head as she headed toward the diner, finding the footing uncertain on the sidewalk still covered with a layer of slush from the previous storm. Turning the corner, she noticed the blackened and gutted shell of the insurance office, which stood like an evil sentinel at the end of the street, barricaded by orange barrier fencing and making her shiver. The glowing warmth of the diner was a welcome change.

Because she was a little early for the supper crowd, it wasn't difficult to find a free booth. She knew it wasn't financially prudent to eat out a lot on her budget, but she couldn't discover anything by remaining in her apartment all the time. Scanning the menu, she finally decided on homemade soup, a selection that would fill her up and not cost too much. Plus, it had been sitting in the pot since early morning and actually tasted the best by this time of the afternoon. Nikki was discovering that by being out on her own and forced to watch her pennies, she was developing new spending habits, and not all of them necessarily served as a form of deprivation. When she lived with her parents and in the city with a well-paying job, she had not considered herself an extravagant person, but now she understood how much she had indulged herself when it came to groceries, computer accessories, music CDs, and books.

Being totally independent with a much smaller income, she was learning how to spend her money more efficiently. She had the same amount to read, thanks to the public library, and, by being more creative when she went to the supermarket, she was actually eating better. Instead of the quick and convenient processed dinners, which were easy to make, but expensive, she was buying raw ingredients and making herself a stir fry or a chili which would last for a week. Instead of junk food, she bought popcorn, a bag of which cost half that of potato chips, but provided plenty of snacks and was lower in fat to boot.

She wondered how Kate kept her trim figure or if she was just naturally compact. Recognizing where her thoughts had immediately trailed without even trying, and unable to fool herself by pretending her feelings for the other woman were only friendly, Nikki still hoped that if she maintained her discipline she would get past her adolescent crush. She didn't think she would be able to remain a part of Kate's life otherwise. Certainly, no straight woman would want a lovesick lesbian mooning around her, any more than a lesbian would want some lovesick straight guy drooling over her.

Addy brought over her soup as Nikki straightened in her seat. The waitress didn't seem to mind the young people who occasionally used the diner as a social center, respecting their need to hang out during slow times, particularly when it was cold outside. In turn, they quickly vacated the place when she quietly suggested the table was needed. As a result, there were no clashes or awkward scenes, and the diner kept them as loyal customers as they grew older, just as their parents had been.

"Quiet around town," Addy said, taking a moment to linger. "Especially for a Friday."

"Yeah," Nikki agreed before trying her soup, a thick beef barley, and finding it absolutely delicious. She alternated with mouthfuls of warm buttered roll. "Maybe there's been too much excitement already this week."

"You can say that again." Addy sighed and sank onto the seat opposite Nikki, who eyed her curiously. "So, what's new with you?"

Nikki shrugged. "Not much. I'm still looking for a new job. What's going on around here? Any word on the fire?"

The morning newspaper had broken the story that the body was indeed that of Sam Madison, but while officials declared the fire had been arson, they weren't yet calling his death a murder, nor was there any mention of the mysterious figure who had visited him that night. She wondered if the police were holding that tidbit back for their own reasons.

"Nothing more than what's already been in the paper," Addy said. "The funeral is on Tuesday."

"You going?" Nikki wondered if Kate would be attending and, if she was, whether she dared find an excuse to tag along. Despite her courageous words and stance on her choice of friends, Nikki didn't want to put her new acquaintance in an awkward position. She decided she would have to be content with a secondhand account if Kate attended the memorial service.

"Sam was a little out of our social circle," Addy remarked. "Even in a town this small, the lines are drawn. Just because we knew him, and he knew us, doesn't mean that we *knew* him, you know."

"I know." Nikki tilted her head. "Addy, have you ever heard of Katherine Rushton?"

"The stockbroker?"

"Is that what she does?"

"Yes." Addy lowered her voice to a confidential tone and leaned forward, her massive breasts resting on the tabletop. "She's from the city and still commutes to her office there, as far as I know. She bought Edwards House out in Old Barns a couple of years ago and spent a fortune restoring it, but something must have gone wrong. She had to put the house on the market for a really low price…a lot less than she probably paid for it. She's living in a condo over on Highland Drive now. I've seen her in here on occasion with Terry Bishop. I think he's her lawyer."

Nikki considered the information. That explained the auction and how the book might have fallen into her hands. But was the "Sam" on the card actually Sam Madison, and if so, was the affair recent?

"Do you know whom she was seeing romantically?"

Addy laughed. "I don't think she's playing on your team, if that's what you mean. She's a really good-looking woman, though."

Nikki blushed. "I was just wondering." She supposed that if people thought that was why she was asking, perhaps she wouldn't alarm anyone. Then she wondered why she was worried about alarming anyone, and what the repercussions of that could be. Savoring her soup, she considered what Addy had told her.

"So why are you looking for a new job?" Addy asked, obviously curious.

"Money. Keebler's pays the bills, but I want more than that."

"Don't we all." As a few more customers came into the diner, Addy glanced up and eased her bulk out of the booth. "Duty calls."

Nikki finished her soup slowly, surreptitiously observing the people who were starting to filter into the diner, listening to the various conversations. The fire and death of Sam Madison was still the hot topic of the town, and everyone seemed to have an opinion. But no one seemed to know why Sam had been in his office that time of night or who, if anyone, might have wanted to kill him. Nikki ordered dessert, an extra expense, but it allowed her to legitimately remain in her booth a little longer.

As she savored every bite of her chocolate cream pie…another side effect of being poor, she appreciated every indulgence so much more…she centered her eavesdropping on the men in the booth behind her who, unlike everyone else there, were discussing Sam's financial status rather than his demise.

"I'm telling you, he was in a lot of trouble," one voice said. Nikki didn't dare turn around to identify the pair. That would be too obvious. Instead, she just sat tight and listened intently. "Between the money he had invested in the company, and the five hundred thousand he never accounted for with me, Maggie could find herself in a lot of trouble when the tax people come calling."

"I don't think we need to discuss this here," another voice, smoother and more cultured, admonished quietly. "We'll take it back to the office."

Nikki recognized the silken tones of the town's biggest lawyer, Terry Bishop, without needing to look. The sudden bulk of Addy appearing next to her diverted her attention, and she glanced up at the waitress, knowing she had lingered as long as she could, especially with the supper crowd starting to appear.

Addy laid her bill on the table. "How was the pie?"

"Wonderful. Does Eddie ever bake a bad one?"

"Never." Addy grinned. "At least, not any that we'd serve to the customers."

Nikki laughed and rose, picking up her bill. As she pulled on her jacket, she snuck a peek at the men in the booth next to her. Seated across from Bishop was Jack Dennis, a chartered accountant with Dennis, Moore, and Trip. Apparently, he was also Sam's accountant. She wanted to stay longer and find out if they said anything else about the dead man, but once Addy had dropped the bill, she didn't allow much leeway.

Paying at the counter, Nikki threw a wave at Addy's husband, Eddie, working feverishly in the back. The big bald man grinned when he spotted her and raised his spatula briefly. Nikki hoped the restaurant was doing well, mindful of what Kate had said about the area being depressed. She couldn't imagine the downtown core without the Mayflower Diner.

Snowflakes were starting to fall as she came out of the diner. She looked up, appreciating the sensation of them feathering softly over her face, and it actually took her a few seconds to realize her feet had turned toward the bookstore, rather than her apartment building.

Ruefully, she discovered that if she didn't see Kate at least once before she went home, her day simply wasn't complete. What that meant for the future, she didn't know, but for now, it filled her with a warm bubble that seemed to expand as she waited for Kate to answer the door.

CHAPTER NINE

As Kate neatly placed the newest arrivals on the shelf, she was aware of Sheila lingering near the end of the aisle. Curious, Kate looked up, wondering what she wanted. Sheila wasn't tall and carried more weight than she should for her age, but having a job had done wonders for her personality. Achingly withdrawn when she first applied for the position at her teacher's urging, she had blossomed because of working with the public, and Kate had even managed to slip some hints to her about her appearance, which had brought out some unexpected qualities.

To Kate, hiring a different high school student every year wasn't just a matter of having some extra help around the store. She considered it an opportunity to teach each one some necessary social skills, which is why she tended to choose the more awkward and insular applicants. She had made that arrangement with her friend Lydia Fennell, who taught Grade 12 History at the school, and it had resulted in some very positive experiences for all concerned, not just the students.

"Mrs. Shannon?"

"Yes, Sheila?"

"I was wondering..." she began, hesitated, then finished in a rush. "Could I possibly get next Friday night off? Billy Wallace asked me to the Valentine's Day dance and, well..."

Kate stifled a sigh. That was the other side to providing the young girls with some confidence and style. Suddenly, boys discovered them, just as they discovered boys, and the next thing Kate knew, she was losing her part-time help.

She took her time to consider the question carefully, aware of Sheila's hopeful gaze. On one hand, Kate didn't want to discourage what was obviously a very exciting event for the girl, but on the other, should she allow Sheila to abdicate her responsibility simply by requesting it?

Kate shrugged mentally. At that age, priorities were a trifle different, and Sheila would find herself caught up in the burden of life soon enough. Certainly, being dedicated to business hadn't helped Kate's social life. Why make it any more difficult for the girl? Besides, if she phrased her permission properly, Sheila would realize that Kate was not just granting the request because she had asked for it, but because she had earned it.

"You've managed to make it to the store every day since I hired you last September, even during the snow storms, Sheila. And you've done extremely good work. I think that deserves a night off, particularly for such an important event."

Sheila beamed. "Thank you, Mrs. Shannon. I'll work any extra hours you want to make up for it."

"I might take you up on that. Some in-service or snow day, when I want the afternoon off."

"Anytime. I'll be here."

Sheila returned to the counter, almost wiggling in her pleasure, and Kate turned back to her task, wondering if she had ever been that young, when things were new and fresh, and every emotion didn't just happen, it exploded within you. But she couldn't remember feeling that way for another person—at least not until she had met Nikki. Though if that wasn't enough to give her pause, she thought uncomfortably, she wasn't sure what was.

She certainly hadn't felt that way about David. David had been… well, comfortable…a good friend and a kind boyfriend who had subsequently became a kind, if perplexed, husband. She wondered if they'd still be bumbling along with each other if the issue of children hadn't diverted them. David had wanted desperately to be a father, while Kate had never felt any desire to be a mother. It had been one thing to get married under what she now realized were false pretenses, but she refused to allow innocent children to be dragged into the mix.

As a result, they had shed a few tears, exchanged a few heated words, but ultimately parted as amicably as possible under the circumstances, neither of them contesting the divorce. She suspected that David was far happier in his new life, which now included two little boys who were the center of his existence. Whenever she ran into him, he absolutely beamed with pride and didn't hesitate to show her his newest batch of pictures.

Kate finished shelving and rose, dusting off her knees. Glancing around, she detected three customers in the store, about average for a Friday afternoon. Later, after dinner, the downtown would become a little busier, and she would garner some sales, particularly since one of the more popular authors she carried had just released a mass-market paperback of his latest. Checking the time and realizing it was past five, she decided to go upstairs for dinner before tackling some paperwork for a charity, one of her volunteer tasks.

Halfway up the staircase, she heard the chime of the back door, and she grumbled a bit under her breath as she turned to go back down. When she saw Nikki on the back steps, her irritation vanished instantly, and her heart executed an excited little flip. Her cheeks grew distinctly warm, and she hoped her unfamiliar and unusual feelings weren't as apparent on the outside as they were on the inside.

"Hi," Nikki said, gazing at her with those lovely blue eyes. "I'm really sorry if I'm bothering you. I know you don't normally work Friday nights, so I took a chance you'd be home. I know I should have called first."

Kate lifted a brow, noting that Nikki kept track of her schedule. Was that a recent thing, or had she just noticed in passing? "You're not bothering me at all. I'm on my way upstairs for supper. Would you care to join me?"

Nikki looked embarrassed. "I'm sorry. I've already had dinner. I'll pop by tomorrow. It's not important."

"Please." Kate reached out, took Nikki's arm, and drew her inside the warmth of the landing before she realized what she was doing. "I'd love the company…unless you'd be bored watching me eat?"

Nikki smiled. "I can't imagine anything you do ever boring me."

Kate withdrew her hand. That hadn't quite been the response she anticipated, and she wondered what exactly she had been expecting as she led the way up the stairs. Was it possible that Nikki was actually attracted to her?

Nikki hung her own jacket in the closet, which made Kate feel warm inside, as if Nikki felt she somehow belonged in these rooms, no longer a mere visitor. Something was seriously going on for her to react so strongly to every little thing Nikki did.

Was this attraction? This physical, lustful, emotional yearning, this needing-to-be-with-Nikki-beyond-reason feeling that filled her every waking moment? Kate was totally at sea. She had never experienced anything like this before, so she had nothing to compare it with. All she knew was that the more contact she had with Nikki, the more she wanted. How far did she intend to pursue this situation?

"What are you having?"

Kate jumped slightly. "What?"

Nikki looked at her with a bit of a frown, and Kate knew she was behaving oddly enough for Nikki to have noticed. Taking a deep breath, she drew on her formidable composure. "I think I'll have some soup and a sandwich."

Nikki's eyes brightened. "That's what I had," she said with a lilt in her voice, as if the coincidence was significant in some way. "Down at the diner."

Her visitor perched on the stool she had sat on the day before as Kate began to prepare her meal. "Are you sure I can't get you anything?"

Nikki shook her head. "No, I had pie for dessert. I'm stuffed."

"What kind?"

"Chocolate cream."

"Obviously, you're one of the fortunate ones who doesn't have to be concerned with weight," Kate said lightly. "You have an absolutely spectacular figure." She wanted to snatch the words back as soon as they left her mouth. It was an incredibly personal and presumptuous thing to say and completely inappropriate.

The pink rose in Nikki's cheeks. "Thank you."

"You're welcome," Kate said, concentrating hard on her hands as she placed some cheese, ham, and lettuce on a steak sandwich bun, hoping that the moment would just disappear. The microwave chirped cheerfully, indicating the soup was finished, and she snatched at it with relief.

"Uh, actually, I had an ulterior motive for eating out this afternoon," Nikki said after a few moments while Kate carried her meal out to the dining room. She sat in the chair midway down the large table, separating herself from Kate with another chair. "I was hoping to pick up some more information on the fire."

"Did you?" Kate asked, glad for the change in topic.

"Maybe." Nikki told her all that she had learned at the diner.

Kate listened intently as she ate her soup and sandwich, not really tasting them. "So this might actually be financial rather than a crime of passion."

"If what I heard about Sam was correct, he was in a lot of trouble money-wise. Furthermore, so was Katherine Rushton, if her having to sell her home at a big loss is any indication. It sounds as if some deal they made went bad, and they were both going under."

"Assuming they were in it together." Kate held up a cautioning finger. "We're placing a lot of emphasis on a card that may or may not link them."

Nikki nodded, looking serious. "You're right, but if it really does connect them, we're the only ones who know. From what I heard, no one has a clue who might have had it in for him or might have visited him that night. The coincidences are starting to add up." She stopped as if struck by a sudden thought. "'We?'"

Kate inhaled slowly. "You bought the book from me. We watched the fire together. We've been sharing information. I think that makes it 'our' case."

"I like the sound of that."

Kate wondered if it was the word "case" she liked or the use of "our." She wasn't sure she dared find out at the moment.

"So where do we go from here?"

"I'm not sure," Kate said. "A lot of the information we would require is confidential, and we have no authority to be digging around in it."

Nikki waved that technicality aside. "Probably, but you'd be amazed at how much you can pick up just from gossip. The whole town knew the Ames boy was the one behind the break-ins at the lake cottages long before he was ever arrested."

Kate winced. She knew the boy's parents, and they had been devastated to discover he had been feeding a drug habit by burglarizing the vacation homes in the area. But it was true that the story had gotten around quickly and, in fact, it was possibly the reason he was finally apprehended. If he had been a little smarter, he would have taken note of the various rumors and backed off, because until Rick Johnson caught him in the beam of his flashlight during a routine patrol, the police didn't have enough evidence to charge him. He ended up being tried as an adult and wasn't due for parole for another two years. "You may have a point," she said. "It's a small town. But it's one thing to follow leads like this for a theft. It's quite another when we're talking about arson and murder."

"They haven't declared it a murder, yet," Nikki pointed out. "It might have been suicide."

"No, I didn't date Sam, but I've known him for a long time. He just wasn't the type."

"That's been said a lot," Nikki said in an oddly flat tone. "Particularly after someone's killed himself."

Kate inhaled slowly. Nikki sounded as if she was speaking from personal experience and, disturbed, she eyed her covertly. Nikki shook her head slightly, as if pushing away some unpleasant memory. For a moment, Kate wondered if she should pursue the subject, but then decided not to. Whatever it was, she suspected Nikki would tell her in her own time. Meanwhile, she drew herself back to the topic at hand. "Suicide doesn't explain the car that drove away. It was parked in front of the insurance office. Somebody was with him that night and only left when the fire had started."

"You're just playing devil's advocate, aren't you, Kate? Everything I say, you come up with a countering argument."

Kate tilted her head. "I guess I am, but doesn't every Sherlock need her Dr. Watson?"

Nikki abruptly offered that breathtaking expression again, and Kate found it difficult to swallow. She looked down at her meal, surprised to see she had finished, unable to remember having consumed any of it. "Well, if we're being serious about this, we should start soon, before the trail grows cold," she said as she placed the plates gently into the sink. "What if we use this weekend to track down all the leads we can?"

Kate turned around and started abruptly as she discovered Nikki immediately behind her. She had her head inclined slightly, gazing down into Kate's eyes, and for a moment, the floor seemed very uncertain beneath her feet.

"That sounds wonderful," Nikki said, her voice incredibly soft.

Kate could feel the heat of Nikki's body brush against her, and a trickle of perspiration slipped down the back of her neck. Swallowing hard, she felt almost lost in that blue gaze, mesmerized. "Fine," she squeaked, and had to pause to clear her throat. "Fine," she said again, in a stronger tone. "Sheila can cover the store. I'll take the day off. You and I can do some research."

Nikki tilted her head, studying her closely. "Why are you doing this?" She sounded baffled.

Kate managed a smile. "Let's just say that I've been feeling a little bored lately. A little adventure may be exactly what I need to figure out what I'm missing in my life." However, she wasn't sure if she was talking about playing detective or exploring how far the feelings stirring inside would take her.

CHAPTER TEN

Nikki opened her eyes and saw the sun casting a narrow beam across the bed from the slit between the blinds and the sill. A small bubble of joy expanded within her chest, and a glance at the clock revealed that she still had an hour before she had to meet Kate behind the store. Part of her wanted to leap from the bed immediately and dress, but another part decided to lounge in the blankets just a little longer in order to appreciate this new sexual tension she had discovered between her and Kate.

It had been so thick the night before it was almost visible. She knew that Kate had felt it too, had seen it in her eyes, though Kate had done her best to hide her responses to Nikki's physical closeness. Yet, despite what must have been a disturbing sensation to her, Kate didn't draw away. Instead, she was reaching out even further, planning a whole day that they could spend together, possibly to explore what was rapidly growing between them.

What *was* growing between them?

The cynical aspect of Nikki's personality, born of past pain and previous disappointments, refused to allow her to simply enjoy her feelings. After all, she and Anne had experienced plenty of sexual tension between them, but once they had indulged themselves, Anne had soon started looking elsewhere for her next adventure. The fact that Nikki was deeply and completely in love with Anne hadn't seemed to matter at all. In retrospect, Nikki had recognized that Anne wanted only the novelty, to explore something new and different, and, once sated, she was no longer interested.

She didn't blame Anne entirely. Nikki had vaulted into her first love affair without reservation, picking up and following Anne into the city where she found a job and took an apartment in the same building just so she could be near her, caught up helplessly in feelings and sensations she had never before experienced. But Anne never once said that she loved her. In fact, she had made it clear on more than one occasion that she didn't, but Nikki hadn't wanted to listen, until it was finally clear even to her that Anne felt nothing special for her. Even then, Nikki continued to ache long after the breakup, feeling as if Anne had ripped a part of her soul away, leaving a wound that would never fully heal.

That's when she found out who her friends truly were, and, somehow, they got her through the rejection even when Nikki wanted to die because it hurt so badly. She didn't ever want to experience that type of relationship again, and for a while, it seemed she wouldn't need to worry. She had met a few other women, become attracted to them, even dated them, but no one had come close to stirring those wild, wonderful, and completely irresistible sensations that falling in love evoked. She had started to think that maybe she would never fall in love again, that Anne would be the only one who made her feel that way. Then she started visiting Kate's bookstore.

"Oh, God," she murmured as Powder abruptly landed on the bed, stepping lightly over the blankets to settle on her chest, purring audibly as he tucked his paws under his snowy chest. "What the hell am I getting myself into, Powder? Am I making the same mistake all over again?"

Powder blinked, his large green eyes regarding her intently as he declined to answer.

"Kate was married, for crying out loud," Nikki muttered, reaching up to scratch his head, inciting a deeper purr. "Even if she *is* attracted to me, it's probably just what Kim says—a walk on the wild side because she's bored. Even Kate said as much last night. She's only pursuing the investigation with me for the adventure. Maybe that's all the 'friendship' is, too."

She caught her breath in a sob, feeling tears sting her eyes, the elation she had felt upon waking dissipating immediately under the sharp reality of past experience. "It just feels so good when I'm with her."

Powder meowed, seeming sympathetic, and rasped his tongue over her chin.

"Damn," she said, and pushed the cat off her so that she could roll out of bed. She took a quick shower before dressing in the ski pants she had received for Christmas and a new sweater she had never worn. After drawing back her hair in a ponytail, she put in her contacts, which she rarely wore except when going out on a date. When she started eyeing her pitiful supply of makeup, she groaned, realizing how desperate her situation had truly become.

She fed Powder and left enough food to keep him for the day, then made an omelet for her own breakfast because she didn't know how long it would be before she would have a chance to eat on this little excursion. After consuming it with little appetite, she finished in the bathroom and took a last despairing glance in the mirror before heading for the closet containing her outerwear. The day outside was beautiful, crisp but not brutally cold, the fresh dusting of powder a brilliant white and sparkling beneath a sky so blue it almost hurt to look at it.

Tramping through the snow that squeaked slightly beneath her boots, she took deep gulps of the clear air, giddy as she quickly made her way down the sidewalk. Behind the store, Kate was busy clearing the snow from her car that, minus the snow, proved to be a black sports utility vehicle highlighted in silver trim. She wore jeans, boots, and a blue jacket that looked more stylish than warm, but it was the SUV that really caught Nikki's attention.

"A dyke-mobile," she crowed with delight.

Kate looked at her, a startled expression on her face. "A what?"

"Uh, it's just that a lot of lesbians tend to drive this type of vehicle. It's almost…well, a stereotype." She hesitated, then added daringly, "You're not trying to tell me something, are you?"

Kate stared at her, the pink rising in her cheeks before she smiled, continued to brush the snow from the hood, and said lightly, "You never know."

Nikki blinked in astonishment.

The interior of the SUV was gray and very plush, as well as extraordinarily clean. It looked as if it had just come off the showroom floor, and Nikki could faintly smell that unmistakable "new car" fragrance of upholstery and plastic. "Did you just buy this?" Nikki drew the seatbelt across her chest. She cringed as the snow fell from her boots. Fortunately, ridged rubber floor mats caught the moisture.

Kate appeared slightly embarrassed. "I bought it a year and a half ago, but I think I allowed the salesman to influence me too much. Frankly, it's too large for me and hard on fuel compared to a car. At least I don't need to drive it too often." She grinned as she put it in gear. "And it's great in snow."

"In this part of the world, that's a good thing." Nikki glanced at her. "So, you don't use it for camping?"

"No," Kate said in a way that indicated that she hadn't even considered it, and Nikki thought how much she would love to introduce Kate to camping. They turned left onto the street from the parking lot before stopping on Prince, waiting for a break in the traffic.

Nikki peered at the shell of the insurance office. "How long before they tear that down?"

"Not long. It's an eyesore and isn't doing the downtown core any good. As soon as the insurance company..." Kate glanced at Nikki with an odd expression on her face.

Nikki laughed. "Right. What happens when the insurance company's been burned to the ground? I can't see that Sam would insure it with anyone but his own company."

"It may take longer to straighten out the legal wrangle than the town council thinks."

Nikki leaned back against the comfortable seat and looked around as Kate made another turn on Walker and then motored back up the Esplanade. Prince was a one-way street, connected at several places to other one-way streets and as such required the town's inhabitants to occasionally do some extra maneuvering to reach their destination. It was rare that she had the opportunity to ride in a vehicle this high off the ground, and it gave her a sense of power that amused her. She wondered if this feeling had contributed to Kate's decision to buy the vehicle.

"Do you drive?" Kate asked suddenly. "I mean," she added, looking sideways at her, "do you have your license?"

"Yes. But not a standard."

"This is an automatic. Want to try?"

Nikki glanced at her and started to laugh, unable to help herself. "What?"

"I'm sorry." Nikki tried to get a handle on her mirth. She really was too giddy for her own good. "It's just that I have a friend who's really into cars. Audrey would sleep with someone before she'd actually let her drive her car. She says that sex is one thing, but letting them behind the wheel of her baby is just too damned intimate. We knew she was really in love when she lent Deb her car to take down to the city."

"Oh," Kate said, looking a bit flustered. "It wasn't a... proposition."

Nikki didn't dare look at her, suddenly very somber. "I know," she murmured. "It just made me think of Audrey."

After a moment's silence Kate asked, "Is there some kind of code? To being gay, I mean. Like letting someone drive your car to show you're...interested?"

"No. I think we claim a few cherished behavioral patterns that differ from those of straights, but everyone's pretty much the same regardless of who they love, Kate. Sure, stereotypes exist, because there's been enough evidence over time to create them, but gays don't have a set way to act, just as straights don't."

"But there are certain ways of acting within any society."

"Cultural restrictions, dynamics between various levels of class society." Nikki stared through the tinted front window, probably a costly option. The salesman really had gotten to Kate, she thought idly. "For example, even in the twenty-first century in this country, it's still possible to 'marry beneath one's self.'"

"Or become involved with a romantic relationship that damages one's standing within the community."

"Yeah, you might say we gays wrote the book on that type of relationship."

Kate seemed about to say something and then hesitated as if reconsidering. When she spoke as they stopped at another light, her comment was somewhat off the line that Nikki thought she had been headed. "It's been said that Margaret Madison married beneath her. She came from a certain stratum in the community, and her father put up the seed money for Sam to start his business."

"Is that where we're going? To visit Mrs. Madison?"

"God, no," Kate said, glancing at her in horror. "That would be completely inappropriate, even if we did have some kind of authority to be investigating this. She's just lost her husband."

Nikki grinned at what was a perfect example of cultural behavioral patterns, though she didn't point that out. "Where are we going, then?"

"Paulo Realties. They're the ones who have the Edwards House on the market. I'm stopping by to pick up the key."

"They'll just give it to you?" Nikki said, vastly impressed with Kate's contacts, yet slightly appalled that a real estate office would hand out keys indiscriminately.

Kate shrugged minutely. "I know all the real estate agents. My ex-husband has his own office, and they all cooperate."

Nikki looked out the window at the casual words, feeling the tremor inside again, that defensive wash of pain to remind her how she had felt before and how foolish it would be to go there again. Whatever else this woman might be, she had a distinctly heterosexual past woven directly into the fabric of the town. It wasn't something Nikki should be involving herself in, regardless of how strongly she felt about Kate or what she wished could be between them.

"It only took a couple of calls to track down the key." Kate didn't miss a beat, obviously unaware of how her words had affected Nikki.

Nikki wondered if Kate's ex-husband had been one of those calls. "Do you think we'll find anything in the house?"

"Probably not, but it might give us a sense of who this Katherine Rushton is. James said that not all the furniture was auctioned off and won't be removed unless the new owners indicate they don't want the pieces. Rushton might have left something behind, forgot it in the confusion of all the packing or in the aggravation of finding her finances taking a downturn." She turned into the parking lot of the real estate office. "Do you have a better idea?"

Nikki shook her head. "No."

Kate parked and patted Nikki absently on the thigh. "Wait here. I won't be a minute."

Frozen by the sensation that flashed from her leg to impact with the top of her head, Nikki couldn't manage a coherent response. She just made a strangled sound of assent as Kate, seemingly oblivious to the havoc she had just caused with her casual gesture, slipped out of the truck and walked into the real estate office.

Nikki had managed to bring her heart rate and respiration under control by the time Kate returned, tossed the key into the console between the seats, and shifted into reverse. When they were back on the street and heading for the countryside where Edwards House was located, Nikki had found her voice again, though it was a trifle unsteady. "Won't there be a problem with us roaming around up there?"

"There won't be any other potential buyers around. This is a bad time of year to sell houses, and this house is a particularly poor prospect no matter what the season. It's too far out of town to turn into apartments, too large for most people to maintain properly, too unattractive property-wise to the business community, and has no real historic significance. Truthfully, they were remarkably lucky to sell it the first time to Rushton. I doubt they'll be able to find another buyer, regardless of how far she agrees to lower the price."

"If you say so."

Kate flashed her a smile. "I do."

Kate turned her eyes forward on the road, and Nikki caught her breath at the sight of the classic profile. *That's what makes me a lesbian. Not that I want to sleep with every woman I see, but because just looking at a woman like her makes me want to cry, the sound of her voice makes my heart sing...being able to love her and have her love me back would be the greatest joy I could ever imagine.* She guessed that was how straight people probably felt about the opposite gender, that a lot of women felt that way about men.

She was falling fast for Kate Shannon, and she was falling hard. And the inevitable impact, when it came, might not be one she could survive.

CHAPTER ELEVEN

O h my God."
Kate swallowed as she stared at the long driveway leading up to Edwards House. Perched on a hill, the mansion sat at the end of a lane that was nothing more than a snaking depression between high banks deposited from previous plowing. Obviously no blade had touched it for the past week, and at least a foot of snow had built up in the driveway itself, higher where the wind had drifted it.

Nikki appeared unsettled. "You mentioned that the property couldn't be sold this time of year. Is that because no one can get to it?"

"No." Kate sighed. "If a client indicated interest, the realtor would arrange for the lane to be plowed before they showed the house."

"But not for a couple of inquisitive chicks who just want to nose around."

"Exactly," Kate said. *Chicks? Has that already made a comeback?* She took a breath. "So what do you want to do? Try it on foot?"

"Well, is this really an off-road vehicle," Nikki asked, a hint of challenge in her tone, "or just one of those wannabe trucks that doesn't have what it takes to really live up to its butch reputation?"

Kate hesitated, though she smiled at the words. "I don't know. I never tried anything like this. If we get stuck..."

Nikki grinned. "I notice you have a shovel and sand in the back. Do you have a cell phone? We can always call for help in an absolute emergency."

"I suppose we could. It was my suggestion to come up here, after all."

Nikki shrugged lightly. "We don't have to, if you really don't want to. It's your truck. I was just teasing."

If she backed down now, what would that say about her, Kate wondered. That she had bought a truck designed for forging into the unknown simply because of a sales pitch? That she had spent a fortune on a status symbol, only to have it sit behind her store most of the time? That she would support her friend in her pursuit, but only so long as it didn't really inconvenience her?

That she would go only so far when it came to doing something risky?

Kate shifted the vehicle into a lower gear and firmed her jaw. "Hang on." She clutched the steering wheel, hoping no ditches lurked beneath the obscuring white, and tried to figure out just where to aim so she wouldn't crash into the banks that were so high she couldn't see over them. It was like driving through a tunnel, seeing open sky above and occasional glimpses of the house during the harrowing journey. Sliding, skidding, engine growling in protest at the first real test she had ever given it, the SUV clawed its way around two hairpin curves to reach the courtyard in front of the mansion. Kate parked there with a sigh of relief, finally prying her gloved fingers from the wheel, straightening them with difficulty.

"Wow." Nikki had been silent for the whole hair-raising journey, except for an occasional whimper at each shift of the vehicle. "I guess this is a real four-by-four after all."

"Sure is," Kate said, proud that her voice didn't shake, and tried not to think about the return trip down the hill. Opening her door, she climbed out of the truck, taking a small leap from the running board to clear the top of a drift. But she discovered that the courtyard was sloped, and what she thought was level ground was actually even deeper snow. Off balance because the ground wasn't exactly where she expected it to be, Kate plunged into the soft, frozen moisture, falling sideways up to her waist, her hips and legs trapped as she struggled helplessly.

She must have made a slight sound because Nikki, who had left the vehicle without incident on the other side, immediately worked her way around the front of the truck, sinking knee-deep in a lot of places. "Kate? Are you all right?"

Kate tried to wiggle free and couldn't manage any leverage. "I'm stuck."

"What?" Nikki, bracing herself with one hand on the hood, stared at her. "What do you mean you're stuck?"

Kate exhaled slowly in exasperation. "I'm sorry. Which part of 'I'm stuck' are you not understanding?"

Nikki opened her mouth, shut it, and then turned away, leaning weakly on the truck as she laughed until she could barely stand up.

Immobilized, Kate was initially outraged before the humor of the situation began to work on her, and she started to laugh as well.

"And you were worried about your car?" Nikki gasped between her giggles. "Should we call for a tow truck now?"

Kate immediately gathered up a snowball and pegged Nikki on the shoulder. Wide-eyed, Nikki promptly gathered her own snow, pausing only when Kate held up her hand imperiously. "No. I can't move."

"Fair enough," she said, letting the snowball fall back to the ground. "I owe you one."

"Understood. Now get me the hell out of here."

Nikki laughed again, but she plunged through the drift toward Kate, and with both of them digging the snow, they were able to loosen it enough to free Kate, pulling her back onto flatter ground.

Her jeans soaked, still a little embarrassed by her fall, Kate promptly began to forge her way to the front door through a narrow path just to prove she could, as Nikki followed close behind. More than once, they had to help each other and support themselves on the snow banks running alongside as they struggled through the drifts.

They leaned against the wall and caught their breath on the doorstep. Nikki coughed. "Next time we do something like this, let's bring snowshoes."

"Good idea." Kate plunged her hand into her coat pocket. "Let's hope I didn't lose the key when I fell down."

"Bite your tongue."

Both women exhaled frosty clouds of relief when Kate pulled out the key and fit it into the lock. The door was a bit reluctant, but with both pushing, they managed to force it open and almost fell into the cold interior.

"Holy cow." Nikki looked around, her mouth falling open.

"It is rather ostentatious."

Regardless of how much money Katherine Rushton had at the moment, it was clear that at one time she must have been rolling in it. The interior of the home looked more like a resort than a place where someone had once lived. Kate's tastes tended to the luxurious, but this was far too much. It was almost like a shrine to the almighty dollar, a place where worshipers could come and pay homage to the gods of currency. In an area where bed-and-breakfasts were the typical tourist retreat, this was as out of place as if someone had built a mall on a dirt road.

"I'm afraid to move. I may break something." Nikki's voice sounded tiny in the large space. "I'd be in debt for the rest of my life."

"What a waste. Look at the natural woodwork. The gilding on the ceiling has overwhelmed it."

"I think it's all overwhelming."

Kate glanced at her. "Let's look around."

"What about our boots?" Nikki had barely moved inside the door, and already a small puddle of water was forming around her feet. Obviously, though it felt cold inside, the owner maintained enough heat to melt snow and keep the pipes from freezing.

Kate frowned, then opened a nearby closet door. Sure enough, several boxes of inexpensive slippers stood inside, put there by the real estate office for just this sort of thing. "What size are you?"

"Nine," Nikki said, with only the faintest hesitation.

"I'm an eight." Kate drew out the appropriate boxes and handed Nikki one box of slippers before pulling on her own, amused to find the company's logo embroidered on the top. She had actually suggested providing slippers back when her husband had worked with Paulo Realties, prior to starting his own office. "Souvenir. They're freebies for the clients and work as advertising as well."

Nikki removed hers from the box and put them on, wiggling her toes a bit as she looked down. "Not bad."

"They only last about two months before the soles start to wear out, but for tramping all over a house when deciding whether to buy it, they're fine. Let's start upstairs and work our way down."

Each room contained only a few random pieces of furniture, and Kate could tell that the most expensive and highest-quality items had been at the auction. These pieces, primarily individual chairs, bedsteads, and bureaus with depressingly bare drawers, hadn't been worth the crating and shipping charges. Occasional tables, along with several odd little curios, filled spare corners and made the long halls seem emptier than if there had been no furniture at all. Kate noticed a significant number of bedrooms with attached bathrooms. Unquestionably, Rushton had been planning to turn the house into a hotel of some kind.

Only when they returned to the ground floor and the library did they find anything worth the drive out. A large, heavy desk dominated the area in front of French doors that led out into what might have been a garden, but was presently a snow-covered square bordered by a three-foot cast-iron fence. Examining the furniture, they discovered that the two drawers on the right side were locked.

"Odd. Why lock the drawers?" Kate murmured when Nikki drew her attention to them. "If the furniture comes with the house, then it doesn't make sense to make it inaccessible to a buyer who might want to look at it."

"It's a nice desk. Why leave it here at all?"

Kate reexamined it. "You're right. The rest of the pieces were mediocre, at best. This is a real antique, worth more than all the rest combined."

"You know a lot about antiques?"

"You should see what I have in the top two floors of my building. I keep some of the smaller pieces in my apartment but store most of the furniture my parents left me upstairs. I keep meaning to sell it, but a part of me wants to keep it in case I ever buy another house. I suppose if the bookstore goes under, I can always open an antique shop."

Kate attempted to open the single remaining drawer that ran along the underside of the desk, but had difficulty. It wasn't locked, but it slid open only about an inch. "It's jammed. There must be too much moisture in the house, and it swelled the runners." She hated to see nice things neglected.

Nikki ducked underneath, looking at the desk from below. "That's not why it isn't opening," she said, a touch of excitement in her voice. "There's an envelope taped here." She glanced back over her shoulder at Kate, her features entreating. "Dare we open it?"

Intrigued, Kate knelt beside her, looking at the small, letter-size envelope taped to the side of the desk near the back, its corner obstructing the runner. "What made you think of looking here?"

"Too many mysteries." Nikki's eyes were bright. "Shall we?"

Kate inhaled quickly. She realized a part of her had never really expected to find anything in the house. She had only suggested the excursion as an excuse to spend more time with Nikki. But now she would have to decide just how far she was prepared to go with this adventure. "This is private property. Obviously whoever put that there didn't want just anyone to handle it."

"Don't you want to know what's inside?" Nikki urged.

Kate hesitated and then nodded. "Of course," she said, amazed at her strong desire to take this situation to the absolute limit. "But that still doesn't give us the right to poke around."

"We're talking arson and murder. It might not have anything to do with this crime, but what if it does? What if this is the vital clue which brings a killer to justice?"

"Now you're just being melodramatic."

Nikki grinned. "I watch mysteries on television, too. All kidding aside, I can get it off and put it back without anyone ever knowing. We came all the way out here for this. Where's the harm?"

"Fine," Kate said, wondering if she would regret her decision later. "Let's do it."

CHAPTER TWELVE

Nikki carefully pried the tape along one side of the envelope, using the jackknife that she always carried in her pocket. Kate had eyed the blade briefly when Nikki brought it out but didn't comment as she set to work. With a little more effort, she peeled back the tape, and the heavy envelope fell down and dangled from the tape along the other side.

"If it's sealed, we're not opening it," Kate said. "There are laws about this sort of thing."

"I know." Nikki wasn't as fanatic as her companion apparently was about this sort of thing, but she did respect other people's property. If it hadn't involved a possible murder, she wouldn't even be attempting this. "It isn't sealed. The flap is just tucked into the envelope." She slid her fingers into the opening and discovered a hard lump. Capturing it between her fingertips, she drew it out. "It's a key!" She glanced back at Kate, who was peering over her shoulder. "I bet it opens those drawers."

Kate looked disturbed. "Do we have the right to go digging around in there?"

"Probably not. But since we've come this far, why stop now?"

Kate frowned but didn't say anything else, moving back as Nikki crawled from beneath the desk.

Nikki was almost dizzy with excitement as she eased the key into the lock on the top drawer and sighed with relief and anticipation as it slipped in easily. She turned it, heard the click, then wrapped her fingers around the handle and pulled it open, her heart pounding with suspense. She could feel Kate's body brush against her back as she leaned over her from behind.

Lying on the bottom were two paper clips and a dust bunny the size of a golf ball.

"Shit," Nikki said before she could stop herself.

Kate snorted laughter and, responding to her amusement, Nikki started to laugh as well, relaxing with the release of tension and at the absurdity of their discovery.

"That was rather anticlimactic."

"No kidding," Nikki said, feeling quite the opposite about Kate's nearness. Shaking her head, she slid the drawer shut and locked it again. Almost as an afterthought, she tried the key on the other drawer that was much smaller than the top one. "Nothing in here either."

"Well, it was fun while it lasted."

Disappointed, Nikki started to slide it shut when Kate put a hand on her arm. "Wait," she said, staring intently at the drawer.

Nikki was confused. "What?"

"The interior isn't big enough."

Nikki looked back, wondering what she was talking about, and then abruptly understood. "That's right," she said, her excitement rising a little. "It's too shallow."

"It might have a false bottom."

Nikki pulled out her jackknife again and slipped the tip against the small depression in the joint where the bottom met the front of the drawer. It came up easily, and she held her breath as she extracted the panel. Beneath lay a file folder and a handgun. Nikki supposed if she were a real detective, or one of those characters in the mysteries she enjoyed, she would have been able to identify the make and model of the weapon. As an abortive graduate from a fly-by-night computer college, all she could note was the way the light glinted on the blue metal, ugly in its implication.

"Oh my God," Kate said.

Nikki clenched her jaw. "I heard that Sam had a bullet hole right between the eyes."

"That doesn't mean it came from this gun. You saw for yourself that no one's been up to the house for a while. Certainly not since Wednesday night."

"Are you sure? That was a hell of a blizzard that night, and it's snowed twice since then. It could have covered up any tracks."

"You could be right."

Nikki picked up the file folders and put them on the desk. Opening the first one, she glanced down at the papers inside, unsure what she was looking at. "What is this?"

Kate, obviously reluctant to go further but not quite willing to stop just yet, scanned the first sheet, then a few more, her eyes dark as she read them. "Contracts," she identified. "Papers for a company called Mosaic Estates, invoices, itemized lists of supplies for this house..." She suddenly pointed at the bottom of one page. Her face tightened, the lines around her mouth and eyes growing deeper. "Here's your connection in black-and-white."

She tapped her finger on the lines at the bottom of the page, and Nikki bent slightly as she tried to decipher the signatures. "Katherine Rushton and Sam Madison both signed this. According to this date, they've known each other for awhile."

"No mere flavor of the month, our Miss Rushton." Kate flipped through a few more pages, her frown growing deeper with each one. "They weren't necessarily lovers, Nikki. They were business partners. And according to what I'm seeing here, the business wasn't exactly on the up-and-up."

Nikki raised her eyes to meet Kate's. "Money, not passion." She felt dizzy. Suddenly, this was no longer a game, no fun excursion to occupy her time and grant her the opportunity to become closer to Kate. They could be looking at a motive for a murder here, as well as discovering the identity of the killer. "What should we do?"

Kate straightened the papers and closed the folder. "We put this back. We replace the key, go back to town, and then I call Rick Johnson and tell him that I heard that Rushton and Madison were in business together and that he might want to look into it. If it's necessary, I'll tell him what I found here."

"What *we* found."

Kate started to respond, then her face gentled. "There's no need for you to even be involved, Nikki. I'm the one who borrowed the key from Paulo Realties—"

"I'm not a child. Don't presume to make decisions for me. Or are you just embarrassed at the thought of him knowing you were alone up here with a lesbian?"

Kate's eyes shaded to gray before her mouth turned down. "That's not it at all." Her tone was unnaturally even.

Anger dissipating as soon as it appeared, and keenly regretting what she had said, Nikki exhaled slowly. "I'm sorry." She glanced at Kate.

"I'm a little scared suddenly, and it's making me say stupid things."

Kate studied her. "All right," she said, her voice devoid of inflection.

As Nikki carefully placed the folder in the drawer and picked up the panel, fitting it back into its spot, she felt miserable, knowing that she had overreacted to Kate's honest attempt to shield her. She wanted Kate to admire her, to think highly of her, not regard her as some stupid kid messing around with things that didn't really concern her. "Why do you suppose Rushton leaves this stuff here?" she asked, needing to break the silence that had fallen between them.

"She probably believes that no one would be here who isn't supposed to be. If a client's interested in the property, then James would call her to let her know he's showing the house on such and such a date. In that event, she'd have plenty of time to get up here and remove anything she wanted."

"So as a result, all the evidence linking her to Sam is tucked away here instead of in her condo in the event that it was searched. Clever."

"Rick wouldn't necessarily be able to get these papers from her," Kate said. "Not unless he had proof a crime had been committed."

"But he wouldn't know about the gun."

Kate bent down, slipping the key back in the envelope and replacing it beneath the desk, pressing against it in order to make the tape stick. "No, he wouldn't know about the gun," she said as she straightened. "Which is why I may have to tell him that I…we…were up here."

"If that's what we have to do, then we'll do it. He'll probably lecture me about 'playing detective.'"

"You say that like he's done it before."

"He has." Nikki shut up as they left the library and headed for the foyer, aware of Kate's curious look but not about to satisfy it. It had been an embarrassing incident, and she rather hoped he had forgotten all about it. She had only been sixteen, after all. "Should we check the rest of the house?"

"I think we have all our answers. Besides, I'm starting to get cold."

Startled, Nikki looked at her, abruptly aware of Kate's discomfort and ashamed she hadn't noticed it earlier. "Your jeans got wet when you fell in the drift." The jeans had dried somewhat, but they still looked damp. "You should have said something."

"I'll warm up once I'm back in the truck." Kate removed her slippers and pulled on her boots.

Nikki tucked the slippers in her coat pocket as they made their way back to the SUV, finding it a great deal easier on the return journey than they had in breaking the path to the front door. Inside, she looked at Kate as she started the vehicle, surprising herself when she reached over and covered the hand on the steering wheel. "I'm really sorry about what I said in there," she said. "It was stupid and childish. I just... I react badly when other people decide things that are supposedly for my own good whether I have a say in them or not."

Kate didn't turn her head, just looked straight ahead through the windshield. "Someone must have hurt you a lot at one time, didn't they?"

Startled, Nikki immediately took her hand away and moved back to her side of the vehicle, crossing her arms over her chest. Her withdrawal was so abrupt that even she was aware of how blatant it was, and she flushed hotly. "I guess you could say that."

"I'm sorry."

Nikki glanced out the window, taking measured breaths. "So am I."

Kate started the truck.

Taking hold of the brace on the door, Nikki gripped it tightly as Kate eased the truck around, making even more tracks in the whiteness. Anyone could certainly tell they had been there, she noted as she glanced back at the churned-up snow.

Kate seemed more confident in the drive down the lane. Perhaps a little too confident. As they neared the bottom turn, the SUV was moving faster than it should have been. Nikki felt it lurch beneath her and watched Kate twist the wheel to no avail as the vehicle slid gracefully into the bank on the corner as if in slow motion, the wheels spinning in place while she attempted to drive out of it. "Damn," Kate muttered. Even the curse sounded elegant in that husky voice. "I think we're stuck."

"Seems to be a recurring theme with you today."

Kate shot Nikki an arch look. "Cute. We'll try digging ourselves out before I call for a tow."

"You should stay in the truck where it's warm." Nikki opened her door. "Your jeans are almost dry, and it won't do to get them wet again. My ski pants are much better in this stuff."

"I guess I should have dressed better," Kate said, but she remained where she was as Nikki walked toward the rear of the vehicle.

Pleased that Kate had listened to her, Nikki retrieved a shovel from the rear and evaluated the situation, trying to figure out the best place to start digging. She discovered that she wanted to take care of Kate, and the fact that Kate would allow it, even this much, warmed her heart. She tackled the snow at the front of the truck with enthusiasm, lifting with her legs, throwing it in front of her, just as her dad had taught her on the farm. She cleared a path back onto the lane and then stood off to the side as she motioned Kate to try it.

It took a little rocking, but once the SUV had forward momentum, Kate was able to extricate it, and Nikki waved her onward rather than let it stop and possibly become stuck again. As she jogged down the lane in its wake, she spotted a car pull into the end of the driveway, blocking Kate's exit onto the road. Seeing the woman get out and glare at Kate, she somehow knew this was the mysterious Katherine Rushton.

CHAPTER THIRTEEN

K ate barely managed to stop in time to avoid colliding with the car pulling to a stop at the end of the lane. She shifted into park and watched curiously as a statuesque woman got out of a dark sedan and slammed the door behind her. Kate narrowed her eyes as she realized the vehicle seemed somewhat familiar to her...and where she might have seen it before.

"What are you doing here?" the woman demanded in a shrill tone as she stomped toward the truck, though it was difficult to stomp effectively when one was in grave danger of going ass over teakettle at any given second.

Kate rolled down her window even though the antagonistic tone immediately put her on guard, as did the memory of that deadly little weapon tucked away in the desk drawer. Kate felt her indomitable composure take control. "Who are *you*?"

"I own this place. I'm Katherine Rushton. And you're trespassing."

Kate placed her hands on her hips. "Miss Rushton, I'm Kate Shannon, the owner of Novel Companions on Prince. I was interested in looking over your property. I'm sure James Stanton told you I'd be by to check it out."

Clearly taken aback by Kate's assumption of having every right to be there, Rushton paused, her outrage seemingly blunted.

Kate assessed her dispassionately, noting the expensive cut of her clothing, the polished finish to her makeup and light brown hair, the faint artificialness of her cheeks, nose, and jaw that suggested plastic surgery. The telltale signs around the eyes indicated that she was a little older than she appeared to casual inspection, and she was obviously very used to money and what it could buy. For all that, however, she seemed to possess very little natural mien...or was far more agitated about something than she should be displaying, particularly if she wanted to hide it.

"No, he didn't," Rushton said, her tone lowering, becoming more controlled as she seemed to finally take a good look at Kate. She kept shooting glances at the house, as if to make sure it was still there. "Why didn't you wait until the lane was cleared?"

Kate shrugged. "My vehicle is capable of going most places," she said in a carefully calculated tone of boredom. "I had the time free to look at it today, which wouldn't be the case Monday. James couldn't arrange for the plow this quickly."

"Didn't Stanton come out here with you?"

"I don't require assistance," Kate responded with a touch of patronizing aplomb. "After all, I was married to the owner of Shannon Realties for ten years, so there's very little that I can't figure out for myself when assessing a property."

"Can you afford this property?"

That was definitely not a question anyone of class would utter, and Kate proceeded to stare at Katherine evenly, as if she were a bug that had just landed on her arm and she was contemplating exactly what she was going to do with it now...brush it away or merely squash it. It was a very effective look, one her mother had cultivated to a level of artistry and painstakingly taught her daughter, who knew exactly how it appeared to others. It had extricated Kate from more situations than she could count and never failed to intimidate the most obnoxious of opponents.

It clearly intimidated Rushton, the woman's fair skin flushing a dull red, though the reaction could easily spring from anger as well. Kate didn't budge, merely maintained the stare until Rushton stepped back from the truck.

"I don't suppose you'd mind moving your vehicle so I can pull onto the road?" Kate asked, in that devastatingly polite tone that only a person with a certain panache could use with absolute authority.

Rushton stared at her a few seconds longer and then backed away from the truck, teetering unsteadily on heels that were really too high to be wearing in snow deeper than an inch.

Kate took the opportunity to glance at the other mirror, discovering that Nikki had been standing quietly by the side of the truck, out of Rushton's sight, though she was obviously listening to the conversation.

It was as if she were hunting, waiting for her prey to make a false move, and Kate wondered why she felt that way about Nikki's demeanor. When Rushton turned away from the truck, Nikki quietly opened the door and slipped inside, as if trying not to draw attention to herself. It was an astonishing performance, particularly when Kate saw Rushton glance back into the interior of the SUV to say something else and actually twitch violently, presumably when she saw Nikki in the passenger's seat. Kate was hard-pressed not to laugh.

Rushton jerkily brushed her hair back over her ear and stalked over to her car, getting in and starting it. She backed up onto the road and Kate easily slipped past her, beeping her horn in acknowledgment as she headed toward town.

Nikki was twisted around in the seat, staring out the rear window. "I think she's going to try to drive up to the house."

Kate, observing in the side mirror, slowed as much as she could without being obvious, watching as the car disappeared up the lane. "I wouldn't think she'd be able make it," she said, pulling off to the side of the road, the engine idling as she also glanced back, trying to spot the vehicle. "Not in that car."

"Do you think we scared her?"

"She was definitely agitated about something," Kate said. "At first, I thought James had called her and that's why she showed up, but now I'm wondering if someone else was keeping an eye on the property for her."

"Who?"

Kate looked around. The area surrounding them was comprised of snow-covered fields, dotted by occasional copses of trees. An isolated farmhouse sat on the rise in the distance, with a clear view of the road and Edwards House. "I'm guessing whoever lives there," she said, nodding her head at the property.

"The Nelsons. She wouldn't even have to pay them. Mildred's such a nosey old biddy."

Surprised, Kate looked over at Nikki. Though she was familiar with most people in Truro, once she moved out to the surrounding rural areas, she was somewhat lost. "You know them?"

"I grew up around here." Nikki gave a crooked grin. "I'm a country girl."

"I see." Kate filed away yet another tidbit of information about her new friend.

"Anyway, do you think she made it up the driveway?"

"If not, then she'll just have to deal with it. She obviously didn't want us around."

Nikki looked agitated. "She'll probably move the evidence. What did you tell this James guy when you asked for the key?"

"I told him I wanted to check out the rest of the antiques in the house after seeing what was available at the auction. If she asks, that's what he'll tell her." She tapped her fingers lightly on the steering wheel. "She may not move the evidence. There's no reason for her to believe we even found it. We put the key back exactly where it was."

"But were we that careful with the file?"

"Maybe not, but I'm not sure it's enough reason to call Rick."

Nikki looked torn and then took a breath. "We'd better. If it really is evidence—"

"You're right." She flipped open the compartment between the seats and drew out her cell phone, punching in the numbers of the Truro police station. "Hello, Sandy? Is Rick around?"

The dispatcher told her to hang on, and Kate waited until he came on the line. "Hi, Kate," he said, his tone robust, even over the cell connection. "Remember something about the fire?"

"Not exactly. But I may have found something else that could be connected. Do you know who Katherine Rushton is?"

There was a pause. "The woman who's selling Edwards House," he said, a hint of wariness in his tone.

She assumed that meant he knew very well who she was, at least in connection to Sam Madison. "Yes. My friend and I were up there, checking out the antiques that were left over from the auction, and we found something by accident."

"Friend? You don't mean Nikki Harris by any chance?"

Kate wondered why he had asked. "Yes."

"Go on."

"We found some papers in a desk. They indicated a business partnership between Sam Madison and Katherine Rushton. We also found a gun."

"A gun?" His tone suddenly became gravely serious. "Any indication that it's been fired recently?"

Kate felt her lips thin. "Rick, I own a bookstore. Forensic science isn't one of my specialties."

"You always were a smart-mouth, Kate. Even when everyone else thought butter wouldn't melt in it. In any event, did you touch it?"

"No, but we did look through the file folder." She paused, glancing over at Nikki. "We found both it and the gun in a false-bottomed drawer."

"Ah, so it wasn't just in passing. Nikki's playing detective again, isn't she? And she's dragged you into it, as well."

Kate raised an eyebrow. Obviously, there were things about Nikki she needed to find out. She trusted it would be a pleasurable investigation. "Regardless of whether we were being inquisitive or not," she said, "the gun and files are there, but they might not be for much longer."

"What does that mean?"

"While we were leaving, we ran into Katherine Rushton, and it appears she went up to check the house. She's there right now, assuming she managed to get her car up the lane."

"Where are you?"

"Sitting in my truck about half a mile down the road from the house."

"You know, that's outside town limits. It rightfully belongs to the Mounties."

"Should I call them?"

There was a silence on the line before Rick finally spoke, his tone rueful. "Sit tight. I'll come take a look. Call me immediately if Miss Rushton leaves."

"Fine. See you in a bit." Kate cut the connection and glanced over at Nikki, who was regarding her expectantly. "Rick wants to know if you're 'playing detective' again. Is there something you would care to tell me about before he gets here?"

Nikki flushed and looked forward through the windshield. "It was stupid."

"Can I decide that?"

"You'll decide it was stupid."

"Try me." After a while, Kate wondered if her friend was going to confide in her or not.

Finally Nikki sighed and began to speak. "When I was sixteen,

I was convinced that one of the teachers at the high school was on America's Most Wanted list. I followed him all over town and finally caught him in a somewhat indelicate situation."

"What kind of indelicate situation?"

"You know the mayor's wife?"

"Abigail Jenkins?"

"Yeah, she and him...well, they have a thing for leather, and while it's sort of disgusting, it's not illegal. Sitting in a tree watching them through the bedroom window is."

"Oh, dear," Kate said, putting her hand over her mouth.

"They didn't press charges, mostly because they didn't want any of it to come out, particularly Mrs. Jenkins, but I had to agree never to tell anyone." She peered at Kate. "You have to swear not to tell. I only told you because...well, I guess I just *trust* you." She looked away, her voice trailing off to a whisper. "More than anyone I've ever met."

"Thank you," Kate said gravely. "I won't betray your trust."

The sudden flashing in her mirrors alerted her to the arrival of the sheriff, and with a smile of encouragement to Nikki, she opened her door and walked back to speak with Rick.

CHAPTER FOURTEEN

K atherine Rushton's car was already in the courtyard when Kate pulled in, closely followed by Rick in the police SUV. Nikki examined the tires on the sedan, noting that they were studded and top-of-the-line. Exchanging a look with Kate, she decided that they were thinking the same thing—the vehicle might have easily made it up here within the last week, even if the snowfall had erased all traces of it.

"She must already be inside," Rick said as they tramped toward the front door. In the foyer, a wet trail of melting snow led in toward the library.

"Must not like the slippers," Nikki muttered as they followed the watery path, none of them wearing the footwear designed to spare the flooring.

Katherine Rushton was bent over the drawers of the desk and looked up with a flare of anger as they entered the library. "Who the hell do you think you are?"

"I think you recognize me, Miss Rushton," Rick responded.

"This is private property," Katherine said, but she backed up, leaving the drawer open and the panel removed to expose the contents of the false bottom.

Rick walked around the desk, lifting his brow as he spotted the weapon. To Nikki's surprise, he reached down and picked it up, apparently unconcerned about fingerprints. "Is this the gun you were talking about, Kate?"

She nodded but Nikki frowned, struck by a thought but unable to pin it down.

"What's this about, Sheriff?" Rushton asked, managing a more civil tone.

"It's actually 'Constable,' and it's about your connection to Sam Madison. Is this your gun?"

The woman regarded him warily. "Yes, it's mine. It's registered and I have a license for it. It's to keep wild animals clear of the property. When it's not in use, it's locked up in the drawer. Is something wrong with that?"

"Was Sam shot, Rick?" Kate asked, her cool tone indicating that she didn't necessarily want to know the gory details but accepted that it was vital information.

"Yes, he was." Rick smelled the barrel and then laid the gun on top of the desk. "But it wasn't with this particular caliber of weapon."

Nikki felt deflated and disappointed. Had she and Kate been completely wrong in their conclusions? She perked up when she saw Rick pull out the file.

As he began to flip through it, he said, "I know you and Sam were in business together. Is this part of that business?"

"Some of it," Katherine said, with a little more assurance than Nikki would have liked. Suddenly, she had a bad feeling about the situation, afraid they were missing something very important.

"Would you mind if I took these in as evidence?" Rick laid the folder next to the weapon.

"I'll want proper receipts."

Nikki really started to wonder. As agitated as the woman had been down at the end of the lane, why was she suddenly the picture of composure now that the police had arrived? Rushton was sneering at Kate and ignoring her.

Rick glanced at Kate himself. "Mrs. Shannon, is the car outside the same as the vehicle you saw parked in front of the insurance office Wednesday night?"

His question seemed to give Rushton a bit of a pause, Nikki noticed with satisfaction, and she grinned slightly.

"It looks...very similar," Kate said. "It's the same color, and they were both four-door sedans made by Lexus. It has the same general outline and shape."

Rick turned to Rushton. "Did you visit Sam Madison Wednesday evening?"

She hesitated, gave Kate an angry look, and finally nodded. "We had some business to go over, but I was only there for awhile. I assure you, he was very much alive when I left."

"What time was that?"

"Around eleven-thirty."

Kate, who had said she didn't hear a vehicle leave until well after midnight, remained silent.

Nikki, glancing back and forth among all the participants, wondered if Rushton realized she had just tripped herself up.

"Why didn't you come forward with this information?" Rick asked, not telling her of the discrepancy either. "Surely, you were aware a crime had been committed, and as one of the last to see him alive, your information could have helped us."

She shrugged. "I guess I'm just not very civic-minded."

"If what those papers indicate is true, that's an understatement," Kate interjected, to Nikki's surprise.

Rushton's face turned a little ugly, but she didn't react directly to the comment. Instead, she turned to Rick. "Neither of these...women... have the money to even stay in this hotel, let alone be interested in buying it. Obviously they're here on false pretenses. Isn't there a law against that?"

Rick's face altered, his First Nation heritage suddenly becoming even more apparent in the hollows of his features and dark eyes as he regarded the woman. He tapped his fingertips on the folder lying on the desk. "Was it just business between you and Mr. Madison?"

"Of course."

Before she could stop herself, Nikki blurted, "Is that why you went to the Keltic Lodge together? Business?"

Rushton stared at her as if she had just grown another head, but Nikki knew she had undoubtedly scored by the way Rushton's face altered.

"I know who you are," Rushton said suddenly, staring at Nikki. "You're one of those...deviants...from the group of dykes that meet at the Sportsplex every month."

"Well, we certainly can't afford to meet at the Keltic Lodge," she said, not allowing herself to be diverted by the deliberate slur. The resort was one of the most expensive in the province. "Did you and Sam go there often?"

Rushton shifted her eyes to the police officer who was regarding them both impassively. "Fine," she admitted slowly. "Sam and I did spend a weekend together, but it was only the one time, and it wasn't serious on either of our parts."

Rick glanced at Nikki, undoubtedly wondering where she had picked up her piece of information, but didn't refer to it as he retrieved the file and tucked it under his arm. "You're very quick with a lie when the truth is required, Miss Rushton. I think you and I should return to the station to discuss these papers further."

"I'll want my attorney there," she said as she picked up her gloves. She glared at Nikki and Kate, especially the latter. "Mrs. Shannon, I wonder if the town council knows about your...extracurricular activities." Her slight sneer at Nikki left no doubt as to what she was alluding.

"Come on," Rick said, taking Katherine by the arm and nudging her toward the door. In the courtyard, he directed her into her car with instructions to follow him back to town before motioning Nikki over to his truck. "Keltic Lodge?" he asked.

Nikki dug out the card she had been carrying with her and handed it to him. "It fell out of a used book I bought Wednesday." She lowered her eyes. "It sort of started the whole thing."

"Well, I'm ending it," he said, tucking the card into his pocket. "This is a murder, Nikki, and I don't want to see you messing around in it just because you have some free time on your hands. You could find yourself in serious trouble." He glanced over at Kate. "Just spend more of your energy looking for a new job and less of it getting in the way of a police investigation."

Chastised, Nikki trudged back to the truck, where Kate was waiting with a displeased expression on her face. Nikki suspected she was embarrassed by the entire situation. The drive back to town was excruciatingly quiet, Nikki miserably convinced that her presence had undermined Kate's credibility in Rick's eyes and was mortified at the condescending way Rushton had treated Kate.

When Kate stopped in the lot that belonged to a nearby business behind her apartment building, Nikki put her hand on the handle and started to open the door.

"Nikki."

She flinched, certain Kate was about to tell her it would be best if she didn't come by the store any more. She couldn't imagine how the day, which had started out so promisingly, had ended so badly. "Yeah?" Despite her best effort, her voice was a little unsteady.

"Your composure with Katherine Rushton was amazing. You really pinned her to the wall with the information from the card and never let her wiggle out, even when she became, well, unpleasantly personal."

"Being called a dyke isn't unpleasant, Kate. It's what I am. As for the rest, it doesn't mean anything. But I'm sorry she made assumptions about you just because you were with me. That's unfair."

Kate shook her head. "It's irrelevant. Katherine Rushton's opinion is of no consequence to me. And anyone else who's suffered her presence for more than ten minutes would probably feel the same way."

Nikki glanced at Kate sideways. "Uh, what about someone else's opinion? Someone who *does* matter to you?"

Kate was silent as Nikki watched the snowflakes once more beginning to fall, sticking wetly to the windshield. The incident at the Edwards House had taken them into late afternoon, and dusk had fallen with an overcast sullenness that contrasted greatly with the sunny dawn earlier in the day. At length Kate said, "It doesn't bother me that people assume you and I might be...together."

Nikki absorbed that statement, feeling a sudden thrill of some kind in the pit of her stomach, unsure of exactly what it was, but wanting to pursue it desperately. After another still, quiet moment, she cleared her throat tentatively. "Uh, are you hungry?"

"Starved. We didn't have lunch."

"Would you...like to come up for a while?" Nikki was finding it hard to formulate the words. She wanted to sound smooth, but was afraid she was blithering like an idiot. "I could make us something to eat. We could listen to some music."

Kate's eyes were gray in the fading light, her expression unreadable, but she said, "I'd like that."

Nikki wondered if her heart was going to resume its beat anytime soon. She was fairly certain that a regular rhythm was required for continued survival, even if the lack didn't seem to be hindering her mobility as she slipped out of the truck.

Kate locked the vehicle after Nikki assured her it was all right to park in the lot and followed Nikki up the side stairs to her apartment on the second floor. Originally a warehouse, the building's top floor now contained three apartments, while the lower floor housed two businesses—a used-clothing store and a flower shop.

Nikki opened the door and motioned Kate in, grateful that her apartment was as spotless as possible, considering that she shared it with Powder. As if aware she was thinking of him, the cat promptly flowed off the bed to greet her and her visitor, eyeing Kate warily from the bedroom doorway.

"Male or female?" Kate asked, eyeing him with equal ambivalence.

"Neutered." Nikki took Kate's coat and hung it in her closet. "His name is Powder."

Leading Kate into the living room, Nikki abruptly realized how small her place was. She had always liked the apartment she had found after moving back from the city, but now it seemed cramped and drab, a far cry from the elegant rooms above Novel Companions.

"It's charming," Kate said, as she took a seat on the couch.

"Thanks." Nikki suspected Kate was being kind. She moved into the small kitchenette and looked into the fridge, relieved to find some leftovers. "Do you like lasagna?"

"I love it."

Nikki cast her eyes upward in silent thanks and set about preparing it. When she began to place dishes on the small table in the area beside the living room, Kate stood up. "May I help?"

"Uh, it's under control," Nikki said, watching her sit back down.

As she saw Kate rub her hands lightly on her thighs, she realized Kate was also nervous, but rather than helping her relax, the knowledge made Nikki feel even tenser. She inhaled deeply and moved over to the small bookshelf stereo, putting on some music before she returned to the table. Hesitating over the candles, she finally placed them in the middle and lit them as she waited for the timer on the microwave to ding.

As she fiddled with these tiny tasks, she was keenly aware of Kate taking inventory of her apartment, checking out the seascape photos on the walls and the tennis trophies on the shelves. She watched her examine the titles of the books in the large wooden case that lined one end of the room, then eye the acoustic guitar leaning in a corner next to it.

"Do you play?" Kate asked, glancing over her shoulder from where she knelt in front of the bookcase, reaching out to put her fingertips on the golden curve of the instrument.

Nikki shrugged. "A little. I'm not very good."

"Would you play for me sometime?"

She hesitated briefly before finally nodding. "If you'd like."

"I would."

Nikki was relieved when the microwave sounded. "Dinner's ready."

Kate rose gracefully from the floor and walked over to the dinette set where she took a seat.

Retrieving the casserole, Nikki slipped a respectable portion onto Kate's plate before she served herself. She suspected her guest would prefer wine with her meal, but since she wasn't in the habit of drinking, she didn't have any to offer. "Juice, soda, or water?"

"Water's fine," Kate said, taking a bite from her slab of lasagna as Nikki went to the fridge and pulled out a jug of spring water, filling two glasses with ice from the freezer. When Nikki returned, Kate said, "This is absolutely delicious."

Nikki smiled, pleased. "Once in a while I get it right. It's Mom's recipe, actually." As she took her seat, she was struck by how incredible Kate looked in the flickers of the tiny flames of the candles.

They ate companionably for a few moments before Kate glanced up. "Do you still see your parents a lot?" Her tone seemed careful, tentative.

"Are you asking if they still speak to me?" She feigned indifference, though her heart gave a little twinge. "It was a bit tense when I first came out, but they...adapted, I guess. They don't march in the Pride parade or anything, but it's all right. I know some lesbians who can't even see their families anymore. Then there are others who moved away from home, and when they go back, they just pretend they're not gay at all."

"How do you feel about that?"

Nikki thought about how it was when she was home. Although she wasn't pretending to be straight, talking about mythical boyfriends or playing a role to cover up who she really was, she was still aware that her parents weren't prepared for her to bring someone home to meet them. The usual feelings of hurt, resentment, and regret surged within her chest, but tonight was not the time to be hashing over old wounds. With an effort, she shoved the feelings deep inside. "I think everyone has to decide what's best for her. It's not my place to judge or demand certain behavior from anyone else."

"I admire you," Kate said. "It takes a lot of courage to be different."

Nikki bent her head, feeling embarrassed. "I'm not courageous. It's just a little easier for my generation. I've spoken to older lesbians, and they have stories that would curl your hair, but I've never really run into anything too outrageous. I know a lot of people are like Katherine Rushton, but since they rarely have the guts to say anything to my face, it's pretty irrelevant."

"Does that include your parents?"

Nikki studied her fork, unsure why Kate was so interested. "Mom and Dad aren't so bad," she insisted, and wondered if Kate believed her. "They don't like to talk about it at all. Sometimes Jeff and Julie are a little tough to be around."

"Your siblings. Ah. You don't get along?"

"I think they're scared being gay is a communicable disease."

Kate smiled faintly. "I see."

They ate quietly for a few moments before Nikki noticed Kate watching her with an oddly vulnerable expression. "Are you…um, seeing anyone in particular at the moment?"

Nikki felt her heart start to pound. "No."

Kate placed her fork on her plate and linked her fingers, peering over them at her. "You're very attractive," she said, and though her voice was suddenly cool, its underlying quaver made Nikki think that the controlled tone in no way reflected how Kate really felt. "It's difficult to believe there hasn't been someone who could appreciate that before now."

Nikki felt her ears grow warm, not quite knowing how to respond. "That's very flattering," she said, suddenly feeling bashful. "The few relationships I've been in…haven't worked out as well as I might have wanted."

"I guessed that to some extent." Kate swallowed visibly, the muscles in her neck moving. "What would you...expect from a relationship?"

"I think honesty is the most important," Nikki said slowly, scrutinizing Kate as she tried to figure out what was going on. "I want someone who isn't afraid to be with me, who can trust me. Someone *I* can trust without hesitation." She forced a smile, attempting to lighten the mood that had become especially intense. "Pretty much the same as everyone else, I guess."

Kate seemed to relax slightly. "I guess people aren't really all that different, no matter what walk of life they're coming from."

"We all just want to love and be loved. Everything else is...just filling time, I guess."

They stared at each other in the candlelight for a few moments, before Kate glanced over toward the living room as a slow song began on the stereo. "I've always loved that song," she said, tilting her head slightly as she listened to the music.

Nikki gathered her courage, then took the plunge. "Would you care to dance?"

Kate looked back at her, slightly startled, her eyes wide and dark in the candlelight. In a small voice, she said, "All right."

Nikki took a deep breath before reaching out to Kate. The small fingers trembled in her grasp like a bird attempting to take flight, and she squeezed them reassuringly. Leading Kate over to the space in front of the couch, Nikki took her into her arms, feeling her compact body press lightly against hers, and she grew dizzy at the sensation. Kate, of course, was an incredible dancer, light on her feet, and Nikki instinctively led, realizing that the other woman would be used to that. She felt Kate's soft body, breathed in the wonderful fragrance of hair and perfume and womanly scent, listened to the soft whisper of breath so close to her, and wondered if she would be able to keep from fainting from the sheer intensity of it all.

After the song was over, Nikki didn't release her, reluctant to surrender the feeling. Kate also didn't pull away. They continued to dance as the next song began, fortunately also with a slow tempo. Midway through, Kate lifted her face, and it seemed the most natural thing in the world for Nikki to close the distance between them and kiss her. She felt no hesitation, no hint of surprise or shock on Kate's part, just the sensation of lips yielding beneath hers, kissing her back, tentative at first, then with more assurance—tender, sweet, infinitely alluring.

An eternity seemed to pass, the connection so perfect, before Nikki could bring herself to end it. Even then it was apparently more her choice than Kate's. She swallowed hard and gazed down into eyes that were the softest blue she could ever imagine. Huskily, she murmured, "I didn't invite you up here to seduce you."

"I know." Kate's expression was achingly open and yearning. "I didn't come up here with that in mind either."

Nikki felt the emotion surge thick and strong within her chest, leaving her weak and afraid. "Kate, you're an incredible person. I'd be lying if I told you my feelings were limited to only friendship." She smiled tremulously, her fingers glancing over Kate's cheek. "But I know from experience that sex changes things, and it's not always for the better. I honestly don't want to pursue this attraction if, in the end, it means you won't be a part of my life anymore."

Kate exhaled audibly, her breath brushing warm over Nikki's throat as she lowered her eyes. "I don't know what lies in the future," she said quietly, her voice shaky. "I only know that I've never felt this way about anyone in my entire life. The more I'm with you, the more I want to be with you, in every way possible." She leaned into Nikki, as if seeking strength from her. "And while that scares me on one level, the alternative of running away from it scares me even more."

Nikki bent her head, brushing her lips lightly over Kate's. "Then don't," she whispered. "Don't run away."

CHAPTER FIFTEEN

Kate wasn't sure how they had eased over to the couch and sat down without ever losing the connection of their kisses... those incredible kisses. She felt as if she had never kissed anyone in her life. Nikki's mouth was so tender, so very gentle, the flavor of sweetness and warmth. And she held her so protectively, her embrace strong yet light, comforting, not at all restrictive.

Thinking she could probably spend the rest of her life in Nikki's arms, Kate was lost in sensations and feelings that she could no longer suppress or deny. She wanted her, actually craved her touch, in a way that she had never experienced before. The feel of Nikki's hands on her body made her shudder, and Nikki wasn't even touching her intimately yet, merely caressing her torso lightly through suddenly constrictive clothing. Kate found it hard to breathe and felt a sweet ache between her legs that shocked and titillated her with its intensity. She knew she was wet, could feel the stickiness between her thighs as Nikki's lips trailed over her neck and throat.

The trill of the phone was an unwelcome and unpleasant surprise, and Nikki reached over and unplugged it.

"It might be important," Kate whispered, drawing back long enough to catch her breath.

"Nothing is as important as this."

Kate searched Nikki's face and saw her own expectation mirrored there. The passion, the desire, the absolute, overwhelming need alternately frightened and elated her. Had she ever felt this way before? She couldn't remember. Perhaps she should be thinking about what all this meant for her future and where the consequences of her actions would lead her. But it was extremely difficult to think about anything but Nikki's lips and arms and body, and how much she wanted more of them with every passing second.

She supposed she should be surprised at how she was reacting to Nikki's touch. Had she considered it beforehand, she would have predicted tentativeness in her response, fear at making a wrong move, and uncertainty at what would be expected of her. Instead, it all felt so wonderfully right, as if everything else she had been doing up until this moment had been completely wrong, as if she had only been playing a role and could finally be her true self only now in this embrace.

Breaking momentarily to catch her own breath, Nikki stroked Kate's cheek lightly. "Are you sure about this?"

"I've never been more sure about anything."

Nikki hesitated, as if something disturbed her, then smiled weakly. "I didn't think I'd be the one trying to slow things down."

Kate was struck by a sudden qualm. "Are we going too fast, Nikki?" She felt shy. "I don't want you to think this is just...physical for me. I'm not here for a one-night stand."

"All right. I'm just worried we're not ready for this."

Kate cupped the young face in her hands. "It may seem like this... all this...has only happened in the past few days," she said, "but to be perfectly honest, I've spent the last year falling in love with you."

Nikki jerked, apparently stunned by the declaration. She stared at Kate for a moment, and then, slowly, a luminous smile spread over her face, filled with such joy that Kate felt tears sting her eyes in immediate response. "Oh. Okay." She inhaled deeply, leaning forward to kiss Kate again, and this time, the connection was deeper, more profound, as if she was no longer holding back.

Kate responded to the more emotional touch by gentling her own, slowing her building passion, channeling it into a more controlled action, settling into Nikki's arms as she concentrated on how it felt to actually kiss her after her many fantasies about it. Her lips were so soft, so gentle on hers, and she tasted so sweet. Yet Nikki was aggressive at the same time, her tongue running over Kate's lips, then slipping between them to invade her mouth. Kate understood finally what she had been missing. This was true need, demanding and powerful. This was what it meant to really want someone, to actually ache for them.

This was *desire*.

She welcomed Nikki's tongue in her mouth with a hunger that shook her, wanted her own in Nikki's, and the duel between them only added to the sensation. She wanted to absorb her, to imprint her flavor so deeply upon herself that she would be able to taste it years from now simply from a passing memory of this night.

Somehow, in all the stroking and kissing, they had shifted on the couch. Kate felt her sweater pulled out of her jeans, and she made a sound, a half moan, as she felt warm hands on her back beneath the material. Parting briefly to breathe once more, Kate lost herself in Nikki's gaze of adoration. She drew her fingers down Nikki's cheek, leaning closer to brush her lips over that wonderfully full mouth—teasing, brief touches that inflamed them both.

Nikki fumbled at the catch on Kate's bra. "May I?"

"God, yes." Kate didn't wait for her. Instead, she drew back slightly and reached down, pulling both sweater and bra off over her head in one motion, tossing them carelessly behind her.

Kate noticed Nikki swallow visibly, felt her blue eyes devour her torso with palpable heat, and for the first time she felt self-conscious, aware of certain areas surrendering to gravity and age, of never having been particularly endowed in those areas to begin with. She had always been wiry rather than voluptuous, slender rather than curvaceous. Freckles were scattered over her fair skin, and she knew the swell of her belly had never achieved the flat ideal so many gadgets and drugs in television commercials demanded the viewing public aspire to. She murmured, "I know...I look better with my clothes on."

Nikki reached up and kissed her, cupping her cheek in a warm palm. "Don't even think that. You're the most beautiful woman I've ever seen."

Flattered, pleased by the compliment so freely offered, Kate inhaled sharply, her head falling back as she felt Nikki's fingertips slip gently over her breasts and carefully circle her nipples, the sensation more powerful than any she could remember experiencing. Perhaps it was the fact that it had been so long since she had been physically intimate with anyone, but Kate suspected it had more to do with who was fondling her so lovingly. Nikki didn't just touch her, she blessed her, adored her, worshiped her with her hands and then with her mouth, leaning down to cover one brownish nub with her lips, kissing lightly at first, then flicking it provocatively with her tongue.

"Oh!" Kate cried with part pleasure, part surprise. She arched as Nikki moved over to the other breast, according it the same treatment, the same loving attention, and almost wept when she drew away. "Nikki?"

"Right here," she assured her quietly. She gazed up at Kate, her features flushed with desire and arousal. "But I do think we'd be more comfortable in the bedroom."

Nikki's words slowly penetrated the hazy heat that filled Kate's head, forcing her to consider moving. "Yes," she said, finally able to voice a coherent thought. "That's a good idea. In fact, that's the most incredibly spectacular idea I've ever heard."

Nikki laughed, and with a bit of maneuvering they managed to untangle from each other, rise from the sofa, and move out of the living room. Nikki picked up Kate's sweater from the floor, switched off the stereo, and blew out the candles on the table. Kate waited impatiently for her to take care of these details, wanting to drag Nikki to the bed instantly and peripherally aware that the ferocity of her desires would have shocked her had she taken the time to analyze them fully.

Finally, Nikki switched on a lamp on the nightstand in the bedroom, revealing Powder curled up in the center of the comforter, eyes slitted at them in outrage. He seemed even more affronted as Nikki promptly and unceremoniously scooped him up, tossed him out in the foyer, and shut the door behind him.

"He'll probably never forgive us for that," Kate said as Nikki turned to her and slipped her arms about her waist. She trembled as she rested her hands lightly on Nikki's shoulders, feeling the warmth of her body through her sweater.

"He'll get over it," Nikki said, smiling faintly. Then she sobered, eyes intent on Kate's eyes as she reached down and deliberately unbuttoned her jeans.

Kate exhaled slowly and surrendered to her lead as Nikki removed her pants and undergarments, laying them neatly next to the sweater on the cedar chest at the end of the bed. She didn't extend the care and consideration she gave Kate's clothing to her own, but stripped her garments from her body without hesitation and flung them into the far corners of the room.

Kate discovered that she had been correct in her previous assessment of Nikki's figure, gulping as it was revealed to her. Pert breasts stood out proudly from her chest, and Kate feasted her eyes over a flat stomach, down to lanky hips framing a thatch of pale hair. Nikki's skin was smooth, creamy, and incredibly hot as it pressed against hers. They sank onto the bed in wordless demand for each other, Nikki's hands and mouth exploring eagerly yet tenderly.

"Nikki." Kate may have been older and certainly more experienced in social and business matters, but when it came to making love for the first time with a woman, she was completely lost.

Nikki lifted her head briefly, looking down at her. "What?" she murmured, brushing her lips teasingly over Kate's mouth.

"I…I've never done this before…I mean, not with a woman." Kate was terribly afraid she'd be a disappointment to her.

"It's okay." Nikki nibbled a line along her jaw. "Anything you do will be wonderful."

Kate made a sound. It wasn't quite a laugh, but it was undeniably nervous. She wondered what had happened to all that confidence she had felt out in the living room. "Are you sure? I don't know if—"

"Shh." Nikki kissed Kate's ear, drawing the tip of her tongue along its edge, and took Kate's hand in her own, guiding her to the heat between her legs. "Just touch me like I touch you, and don't worry about where we're going. The real fun is in how we get there, and believe me, there's no hurry."

Kate caught her breath as she felt the silky wetness on her fingertips. "Oh…Nikki…"

"That's what you do to me, Kate," Nikki whispered, her breath hot and quick. "I want you so much. You're beautiful and wonderful, and just being here with you is all I need." She groaned quietly as Kate hesitantly moved over the firm nodule she had found. "That's it. That's so nice. Take your time."

Kate whimpered when she felt Nikki's fingers find her, stroking her with loving tenderness, and she tried to mimic the pace and pressure her lover provided. Before long, she wasn't worried about anything, caught up completely in how it felt to be touched by Nikki and how incredible it felt just touching her. "Oh, this feels so good." She didn't realize she had said it out loud until she heard Nikki's breathless chuckle.

"It's beyond good." Nikki circled Kate's opening, teasing her lightly. "I want to go inside you. Please—"

"Oh, God, yes." Kate spread her legs wider, quivering as she felt the slender fingers slip in slowly, not invading, but drawn into her heat as if they belonged. Nikki didn't thrust, she merely explored and flexed over the interior as if seeking something. It was like nothing Kate had ever felt before as she felt their pressure against a sensitive spot. The motion of Nikki's thumb rubbing over her ridge at the same time was shattering in its intensity. She clutched at her desperately. "Nikki, I can't—"

Climax swept over her almost before she fully understood what was happening and gripped her so tightly that she was left helpless. Distantly she was aware of her lover shuddering against her at the same time. Somehow, Kate had continued her caresses, maintained the motion of her fingers even as she was tossed mercilessly by her orgasm and knew a sudden, humbling awe at Nikki's climax in simultaneous rhythm with her own.

She gulped for air, feeling Nikki ease away, and she immediately gentled her touch even as Nikki lightened her own. The aftershocks were as powerful as the initial strike, and she wondered dazedly if this was what was considered a multiple orgasm. Certainly it seemed to go on for much longer than anything she had experienced before, even by her own hand.

"Kate." Nikki's kiss was demanding, and Kate returned it as hard as she could, reaching up to wrap her arms around her neck and hold on tight.

"That was...my god, Nikki."

Nikki uttered a low laugh. "It was fantastic. You're fantastic. Now lie back."

Kate didn't have time to ask why, and very shortly, she didn't need to as Nikki traced a searing path down her body with her mouth. She should have felt awkward, she thought dazedly at one point in the hours that followed. She should have been hesitant, afraid of the unknown, reluctant to explore where Nikki led her, but no. Instead she experienced only pleasure and wonderful discovery of a brand-new kind: tempestuous and tender, glorious and gentle. Touches that scorched and soothed, that drove her out of her mind even as they finally brought her to a place so peaceful she never wanted to leave.

Lying in Nikki's arms afterward, bound together in sweat and satisfaction, Kate wept silently, not only for the new existence of love Nikki invited her into, but for her old self who had spent so many years without it. Beneath her cheek, she could hear the rapid beat of her lover's heart, only now beginning to slow, the soft whisper of her respiration as it slipped warm over her forehead where strands of her hair stuck to her brow. Beyond the warm comfort of bedding and the small expanse of mattress, she could hear the wind rattling the pane and the quiet ticking of snowflakes against the glass, just as it had three nights ago when this all began.

"Kate?"

"Yes, my love?" Kate whispered, still lost in her glow, wetting her lips with the tip of her tongue, Nikki's piquant flavor lingering there like a fine wine.

"That was...just so incredible."

Kate lifted her head, studying her face in the low illumination. "It was," she said wonderingly. "It was the most amazing experience I've ever had. Is it like that all the time between women?"

Nikki made an amused sound low in her throat. "Not usually. I mean, some of my experiences haven't been as...great...as others, but they've always been pleasant. But I've *never* experienced anything that *intense* before." She stroked her fingers through Kate's hair. "I guess love does make a difference...not just on my part, but when the person I'm with loves me back."

"I do," Kate said, lowering her head back to Nikki's chest. "Oh, God, I do love you. That's what this is, isn't it? Love."

"Yes," Nikki whispered. "It is."

Outside the door, an affronted meow indicated that as pleased as they were with the results of the past few hours, at least one resident of the dwelling was royally offended.

"Oh, dear," Kate said. "I suppose I'll have to make peace with him, won't I?"

Nikki hugged her. "Only if you want to. I'm not one of those demanding love-me-love-my-cat pet owners."

"I'll make the attempt anyway," Kate promised, snuggling closer. A pleasant languidness drew her down and she yawned. She hadn't thought that she would be so comfortable with Nikki that she would consider spending the entire night, particularly since sleeping with another person had always been difficult for her. Even during her marriage, she and David had ended up buying twin beds simply because of her insomnia, but with Nikki, she felt so secure and content, she could barely keep her eyes open. "May I stay with you tonight?"

"Of course." Nikki pulled her closer. "I certainly don't want you to leave." She nuzzled Kate's ear as a particularly sharp gust rattled the window. "Besides, I'd never send you out into weather like that. What kind of hostess would I be?"

Kate laughed. It felt marvelous to lie here in the darkness with Nikki, as if the rest of the world had disappeared and they were the last two people on Earth, huddled together from the storm. It was an intimacy she was unfamiliar with. "I don't know how acceptable I'll be to sleep with. I may snore."

"I might, too," Nikki said. "Or I might take the covers away from you."

"I'll just have to pull them back."

"Or crawl under them with me."

"That too."

Nikki laughed, and they settled in, as if they had done it a thousand times. Just before Kate fell asleep, she thought she heard Nikki mutter something about 'the same,' and she opened her eyes. She was apparently unconscious, and Kate wondered if she had imagined the sound. Too tired to pursue it at the moment, she exhaled and drifted off, curled around her lover as if afraid to lose contact in the night.

CHAPTER SIXTEEN

Nikki stretched out in blissful repose as she watched an unselfconsciously nude Kate study the CDs scattered over the dresser, enjoying the play of morning sunlight over her back and buttocks.

Kate started to reach for a disc and glanced back over her shoulder at Nikki. "May I?"

"Of course. Why would you even ask?"

"I didn't want to be presumptuous."

Staring at her, Nikki realized that Kate honestly meant it, obviously unaware of what she was saying. "I think after last night, you have every right to be presumptuous."

Kate shook her head and started to laugh. "I wasn't thinking. I'm completely comfortable with you," she said, regarding Nikki with soft eyes. "In your arms, it's as if I'm home, but the rest of your apartment... the rest of your life...is unfamiliar to me. I don't want to make any mistakes. Does that make sense?"

"I guess. But we're probably both going to make mistakes, Kate. It's how we deal with them that will determine if the relationship will work."

Kate nodded and selected a CD to place in the portable stereo, one of the few classic discs Nikki owned, soft rock from the seventies. As it started to play, she returned to the bed and slipped between the sheets, snuggling up to her new lover.

"Cold?" Nikki enfolded her in her arms.

"A little." Kate rested her head on Nikki's shoulder and closed her eyes. "Warm me up?"

"I thought you'd never ask," Nikki said, kissing her gently. Settling happily against the pillows, she rested her cheek on the auburn hair, feeling such overwhelming joy spread through her that it brought tears to her eyes. Every second, she had to remind herself this was real, that Kate was actually in her arms, in her bed, and whatever she had done to deserve this paradise, she would keep doing it.

"I'm glad it's Sunday," Kate murmured. "I'd have hated to leave you this morning in order to open the store."

"I wouldn't have liked it much either. But I wouldn't want to deprive the book buyers in town just because I'm in love with the bookstore owner."

Kate nuzzled her neck. "Do you mean that? I know you said it last night, but last night was—"

"I know it's easier to say it in the heat of the moment. In the cold light of morning, it can be a different thing. But in the cold light of morning, I still love you, Kate Shannon. I feel like I've been in love with you forever."

Kate rested her chin on Nikki's shoulder. "I know. I've been making you a part of my life since you first walked into my store a year ago, whether I knew it or not." Kate turned her head to drop a soft kiss on Nikki's collarbone. "It drove me crazy when you started coming in only once a week. I was afraid I had offended you or something. I would tell you how a specific book was coming in on Friday, or how another was coming in on Monday, in hopes you would take the hint, but you wouldn't show up until Wednesday. It became so bad that I would wake up incredibly happy on those mornings, and I wouldn't understand why until I realized that was the day you'd be stopping by. Then, on Thursday morning, I'd be incredibly cranky because I knew I'd have to suffer through another week before I'd be able to see you again."

Nikki didn't respond right away, astounded.

Kate obviously took her silence for something other than it was, because she blushed. "I guess I shouldn't have told you that."

"No," Nikki managed. "I...damn it, Kate, I forced myself to come in only once a week because I was afraid that any more than that would let you know how much I was attracted to you. I didn't want to scare you, or make you uncomfortable. Honestly, you don't know how much I cherished my weekly visit and our talks. Sometimes they were the only reason to get out of bed."

"God, we're a fine pair, aren't we?" Kate rested her hand on Nikki's chest, her fingers spread over her breastbone. "You've lived around Truro all your life, haven't you?"

"Yeah…except for a few years in the city a while back."

"So why didn't I meet you until this past year?"

"Different circles, I guess. We always did our shopping at the mall when I was growing up. It wasn't until I moved back to town, and one of my friends told me that Novel Companions had started carrying a large gay and lesbian section, that I thought I should check it out." She looked down at Kate. "I guess if you hadn't started selling lesbian mysteries, we wouldn't be here now."

Kate laughed. "I'm glad I decided to expand my clientele." She snuggled closer. "Do you believe in love at first sight?"

Nikki drew her fingertips lightly down Kate's forearm. "I believe in instant chemistry," she said. "It's rare, and I've never felt it as much as I felt it for you, but that isn't love. Love, if it happens, doesn't develop until later, I think. For me, it was when I realized I was willing to never see you again if that's what it took to make you happy." She swallowed, feeling the lump in her throat. "No matter how hard it would have been for me."

Kate hugged her, kissing her neck. "I really didn't understand what I was feeling for you at first," she said. "It didn't make sense, and I tried to turn it into something else. I started reading every book I could find on the subject. Everything I had in the store, everything in the library. I even special-ordered a few, trying to apply what I read to myself, trying to see why I was suddenly so attracted to a woman. Finally, I realized it probably wasn't the first time. It was just the first time I was prepared to acknowledge my feelings consciously." She took a shaky breath. "You came into my life at exactly the right time, darling. I've become so tired of pretending not to be who I am."

Feeling her heart catch, Nikki hugged her lover. "I'm glad." She ran her fingertips idly up Kate's spine, memorizing each bump. "Is that why you started carrying gay and lesbian books in your store? Did you start to suspect a little earlier, maybe?"

Kate tilted her head. "I don't know. Maybe. I was so confused, and I didn't think I could tell anyone what I was going through."

Nikki kissed the top of Kate's head affectionately, feeling very close to her. "I'm sorry it was so difficult."

"I should never have married. So many years of chasing something that I could never achieve. I was never physically attracted to men, but I never had the courage to recognize what that meant."

Running her knuckles lightly along Kate's jaw, Nikki tilted her head. "Did you love your husband?" she asked, though unsure she had the right to do so.

"Oh, yes. David is a dear man, but I was never *in* love with him, and only now am I realizing what that means and what I cost both of us. He didn't deserve to marry someone who couldn't love him the way he needs to be loved...the way Ellen loves him."

"Ellen?"

"His wife. He married her a year after we divorced. They have two little boys."

"Was it difficult? Being married, I mean?"

"Not really. It was, as far as those things go, a fairly decent marriage because David and I have been friends since junior high. It was more a constant sense of...missing something. Not necessarily grand passion, because I know that comes and goes, but the feeling of being...I don't know, of belonging somehow." She kissed Nikki on the side of her mouth. "It's what I feel now, lying here with you. I *belong* here."

"Why did you marry him? If you weren't in love with him, I mean, and not attracted to men in general." Nikki wasn't sure why this question was so important to her, but it was, and she was glad that Kate seemed willing to talk about it.

Kate shook her head. "Looking back, it seems ludicrous, but at the time it made perfect sense. Everything just fell into place—high school, university, marriage. It was like being on a train that never stops, Nikki. Furthermore, I wasn't supposed to want it to stop. I was doing everything expected of me, receiving everything I was supposed to want from life."

Kate seemed distant and serious. "I know it sounds strange, but I wasn't just living the life society expected me to live. I was also living a life that most women actually aspire to, believing I could gain true happiness exactly that way. I had a fulfilling social life, was active in countless projects and charities, and had a loving, hardworking, and generous husband in a beautiful home in the suburbs." She quivered a little, as if what she was saying surprised her in some way. "All that was missing was children, and they were expected to show up eventually, at what would be the proper time. I would have been considered insane to suddenly stop and say, 'This isn't me, this isn't what I should be doing.'"

"You never knew you were gay?" Nikki lifted a fingertip to trace lightly over Kate's brow, trying to smooth out the furrow that marred it.

Kate frowned. "I never knew what 'being gay' meant. As much as I've never been physically attracted to men, I've never been particularly attracted to women, either...not until I met you. I was astonished to discover I was thinking of you all the time and wanting to spend all my time with you. Now, just lying here in your arms, touching you...I can't get enough of it." Suddenly, she pressed her body against Nikki's, kissing along her jaw and making Nikki shiver. "I want to wrap myself completely around you and stay here forever," she said. "I feel as though if you leave, you'll take my skin with you, and I'll be left completely exposed to all the elements."

"Flayed alive," Nikki said in a small voice. "I know how it feels. It makes you very vulnerable."

"Yes, it does. It's frightening...and so incredibly exhilarating."

"It can hurt you so much," Nikki whispered, suddenly afraid.

"I can see where it would." Kate rose to her elbow, looking down at Nikki with dark eyes. "You speak as if you've experienced it. Who hurt you like that, my darling?"

Nikki was taken aback, not only by the question, but also by the endearment that was a bit old-fashioned, but that sounded extremely charming in Kate's throaty tones. As she tasted it in her mind, she decided how to respond to the question that prodded old wounds.

"Her name was Anne," she said finally. "I met her five years ago at the tennis club. We were friends while she lived in town, even though she worked in the city, and then suddenly I fell in love with her. It was impossible, of course, because she was straight...or at least more hetero than homo."

"I think I understand."

"Anyway, one thing led to another, and we started sleeping together." Nikki faltered briefly, suddenly realizing that it no longer hurt as much to talk about that time in her life. She wondered when that had happened. Unconsciously, she entwined her fingers with Kate's where they rested on her stomach. "When she moved back to the city, I moved too, just so I could be closer to her. I up and left my family and friends, found a job, and took the apartment next to hers, though we were practically living together..." Her hand tightened convulsively on

Kate's. "I worked so hard to be like she was, like someone she admired, but it wasn't enough for her to love me back."

She tried to say the words lightly, able to understand how foolish she had been, but remembering how devastated she had felt at the time, she trailed off uncertainly. "Eventually, Anne decided that she 'wasn't gay,' whatever that means, and would rather be with men. After that, she didn't want to even let on she knew me. That's when I quit my job and moved back home, though my parents weren't pleased with the whole situation."

"I'm sorry." Kate leaned down and kissed her gently. "You deserve better than that."

Nikki shrugged. "At least they let me stay at the farm until I got myself together financially and went back to school," she said quietly, feeling a lump form in her chest. "All I had to do was not talk about why I had moved to the city in the first place."

"It must have been difficult to live with such restriction. To not be able to talk about how hurt you were or why."

"I still had my friends," Nikki said, trying to put a more positive spin on the whole situation. "They helped me a lot, listened to all my sob stories, kept me from...well, giving up on the whole thing."

Kate's dark eyes searched Nikki's face. "I wish I had known you then."

Nikki reached up and kissed her on the nose. "I wish you had, too," she said, smiling crookedly, still trying to lighten the mood. "Because it certainly would have let me know that much better times awaited me."

"Flatterer," Kate said after a few seconds, apparently accepting Nikki's desire not to talk about things she couldn't change. Kate kissed her, which led to one more kiss, then to several more, before she finally sighed, drawing back to stretch lightly. "I'm sorry. I really do have to go home sometime today." She gazed at Nikki, obviously trying to convey the honest regret behind her words. "It's not because I want to, darling, but I didn't plan to spend the night away. I'm not even sure if I turned down the heat."

"I understand." Nikki was disappointed but aware Kate had responsibilities. That was part of why she was so attracted to her—her maturity and composure. The other women she had known seemed flighty now rather than exciting. "In the meantime, let me make you some breakfast, and we can read the Sunday paper in bed."

Kate smiled, her eyes shading to blue at the invitation. "That sounds delightful. I don't suppose you have any coffee."

Nikki abruptly realized she could read Kate's mood just from that telltale shift in pigmentation of her irises. The bluer they were, the happier she was, and Nikki laughed. "I'm afraid not. I could pop over to the convenience store across the street. They have a coffee machine."

Kate tightened her hold. "No. I'm not sure that I'm going to let you leave this bed yet, let alone the apartment."

"I can live with that."

They cuddled, and after a while, Kate finally broke the comfortable silence. "What did you mean last night when you said it wasn't the same?"

Nikki frowned, confused. "What do you mean?"

"Last night, just before we went to sleep. You mumbled something. You said 'it wasn't the same.'"

"What wasn't the same?"

"I don't know, you said it." Kate propped her chin on her palm and regarded Nikki, seeming curious.

Nikki tried to remember what had been going through her mind last night...other than the woman in her arms.

"The gun," she said, the thought coming to her suddenly, a jagged edge of memory that knifed into her mind. "It wasn't the same gun in the drawer the second time. The gun we found originally had a shorter barrel and a brown grip, not a black one."

"Are you sure?"

Nikki hesitated, an agony of indecision. "No," she admitted finally. "Not enough to swear to it in court, but I honestly think it was a different gun."

"Rushton must have exchanged them. It was risky, because if either of us was familiar with weapons, we'd be able to tell immediately that she'd switched them, but we couldn't." She frowned. "I'll wager she also took certain papers from the file folder. Remember how I said the business wasn't exactly on the up-and-up? Some of those papers indicated shady practices on their part. Even if she had nothing to do with the murder, she should have been afraid to be implicated in illegal behavior."

"Yet she didn't seem too worried when Rick took the file into evidence. She must have removed any incriminating information and left the rest for him to seize." Nikki shook her head, feeling sick. "I think Rushton used our showing up at Edwards House to do an end run around the local police."

"I think so as well," Kate said. "Obviously, she's a very clever woman. But how do we prove it?"

"Investigate further?"

Kate's eyes grew darker, more concerned. "If we do, then we're going to have to be more careful, as well as a little more organized. We need to dig a little deeper into what was going on with Rushton and Sam, and what exactly Mosaic Estates was doing."

"It couldn't be too successful, or Rushton wouldn't have had to start selling everything. Which, in itself, sort of provides a motive for murder. What if Sam...I don't know, cheated her in some way?"

Kate held up a finger. "Right now, we're just guessing. We need to find more tangible information."

Nikki leaned forward and kissed the elegant finger. "Do you really want to?" She was pleased to discover this adventurous streak in Kate.

"Of course. Even if she hadn't made a fool of us...which really aggravates me by the way...I certainly wouldn't let you investigate this situation without being there to watch out for you." Kate traced Nikki's lips idly as she thought. "Actually, this might be the time to acknowledge that this investigation could become a little dangerous. One person has already been killed, and Rushton, if she's involved, is already aware that we were snooping around. Are you sure you really want to pursue this venture?"

Nikki considered her words seriously. Fun was fun, but Kate had a valid point. She wasn't necessarily worried about herself, but she couldn't bear it if something happened to Kate. "Rick seems to be a pretty sharp guy," she said reluctantly. "Maybe we should leave it for the professionals."

"Maybe that would be best. Rick may be only letting her think she's fooling him."

Nikki drew Kate closer, shifting position and pressing her down onto the mattress as she moved over on top of her. "Besides, I think we have enough to occupy us for the foreseeable future."

Kate kissed her, slipping her arms around her neck. "I think I like the sound of that," she murmured. "What exactly did you have in mind?"

Desire sent a tiny shiver of delicious excitement through Nikki's body as she felt the soft curves beneath her. "Maybe I'd better just show you." She pushed her knee between Kate's, spreading her legs and pressing into the warm hollow between them as she felt the moist heat against her upper thigh. Kate's hips undulated slightly, and she rubbed herself against Nikki's leg as she kissed her. "God, you feel so good," Nikki murmured when their lips finally parted.

Kate made a small sound of agreement and rising demand. "So do you." She spread her hands over the small of Nikki's back, pulling her closer to increase the friction from the small movements of her hips. "I just want you so much."

"You have me." Nikki looked down into the bluish gray eyes, completely mesmerized by the passion in their depths as she moved slowly against her lover. "Is this enough?"

Kate gasped. "Not nearly," she said. "Will you—"

"Shh," Nikki murmured, shifting so that she was on her left side, freeing up her right hand. She slid it down over the soft swell of abdomen, raking through the fine patch of hair to the wetness below. "I've got you."

Nikki listened to Kate groan as she rubbed her, fingertips swirling over the firm ridge that was slippery and hot, swollen with need. Nikki watched the play of emotions over Kate's face as she fondled her, enjoying the unguarded expression of desire and pleasure in the classic features. Her lover drew up her left leg, and Nikki accepted the invitation, altering her caress to slip her fingers into the tight opening.

The slick walls closed about her, and Nikki's eyes closed involuntarily before she forced them open again so she could watch Kate. Her head was thrown back, her mouth open as she panted for breath, the pulse beating rapidly in her throat. Nikki leaned down and brushed her lips over the fluttering pulsation as she began to slowly thrust into Kate with a steady tempo, using her thumb to resume the caress of the protruding nodule, rubbing gently back and forth over it in rhythm with her strokes. She didn't seek out the g-spot this time, letting Kate find her own rhythm as her hips rolled firmly against her hand.

Kate began to moan in Nikki's ear as the sensation intensified, mewling with every exhalation. Aroused by the sight and sound of Kate and delighting in the knowledge that she was the one granting her such pleasure, Nikki felt her own respiration quicken as Kate gripped her shoulder, her other arm snaking around her back and holding her tight. When she began to tremble, Nikki knew her lover was close. She increased the depth but not the speed of her thrusts, keeping them steady and firm.

"Nikki!" With a helpless cry of liberation Kate suddenly clenched tight around Nikki's fingers. At the same moment, she slipped her hand up to the back of Nikki's neck, pulling her head down into a demanding, open-mouthed kiss.

Nikki returned the kiss hungrily, knowing Kate needed her as close as possible in that instant of release, pushing her tongue into her mouth as deeply as she plunged her fingers one final time into her body, wanting to possess all of her as she felt the pulsations draw her even deeper.

She drew Kate close as her final ripples of pleasure seemed to slow and fade, unable to imagine any better feeling than being in this moment with the woman she loved.

CHAPTER SEVENTEEN

Feeling as if her feet weren't quite touching the ground, Kate unlocked the back door to her building and climbed the stairs, her mind and body still remembering how it felt to be with Nikki. She ached as she realized how long it would be before she would see her again and found herself counting the hours until their dinner together Monday night, the date they made before she had left Nikki's apartment. As she opened the door to her own apartment and walked in, the sight of the woman standing by the dining room table, hands on her hips and an extremely aggravated expression on her face, brought her up short.

"Where the *hell* have you been all weekend?"

"What?"

"I waited up for you all last night!" Susan Carlson said, waving her hands. Short and stocky, with prematurely gray hair and green eyes sparking with Irish outrage, Susan seemed to have been honestly afraid for Kate. "I thought I'd have to call the police! I didn't know where you were, none of your other friends have heard from you in more than a week, and your cell phone was turned off. I didn't have the slightest clue where to start looking!"

"Oh," Kate said, slightly bemused as she hung her coat in the closet. "I'm sorry. I didn't know you were coming up this weekend, or I would have been here to meet you. What *are* you doing here, anyway?"

"I came up for the funeral," Susan said, still looking concerned. "What's going on, Kate? Is something wrong?"

"No. Everything's fine."

Susan stared at her. "Is that a…hickey?"

Kate clapped her hand to her neck where she remembered Nikki had become a little enthusiastic earlier that afternoon. "Don't be ridiculous."

"If I'm being ridiculous, how did you know exactly where the hickey was?"

Fearing she had turned an unflattering shade of red, Kate shut the closet door and strode into the kitchen, brushing past Susan. She was pleased to discover a pot of coffee already made and promptly poured a cup. As she sipped, she watched Susan sink onto the love seat. A book lay open on the coffee table in front of her, along with a mug and a plate next to it containing the remains of a sandwich. She had obviously made herself at home in the apartment, but since it wasn't the first time, Kate didn't mind. She was just disconcerted by Susan's presence right now, particularly when she proceeded to stare at Kate as if she had never seen her before.

"I believe you actually got *laid*," Susan declared finally. "That's wonderful! Not to mention *highly* unusual."

Kate couldn't demur without lying, but this wasn't exactly how she had wanted to broach the subject with her best friend. As Kate considered what to say, Susan retrieved her mug and watched her, obviously waiting for her to spill the beans. "So who is he? What does he do? Does he live here in town?"

Kate took a long swallow of her coffee, feeling the buzz from the caffeine settle within her as she sat down in the chair opposite the love seat. Leaning back, she glanced at Susan from beneath her lashes. She could do this gently, she decided, or she could just blurt it out. She wasn't sure which would be better, but it seemed inevitable that she would have to share this news with her best friend. It never occurred to her to simply make something up and let Susan continue to believe she'd been with a man. "Her name is Nikki," she said finally. "I'm in love with her."

She supposed she should have waited until after Susan had finished swallowing. She watched as her friend choked and sputtered, spitting coffee across the room as she snatched at a napkin to cover her mouth. "What?" Susan wheezed, once she had her breath back.

Gathering her courage, Kate said, "We met a year ago. She came into the bookstore and bought a lesbian novel. We started talking, became friends, and a few days ago...well, things intensified a great deal."

She was aware that if she had been telling Susan about a man, they would have immediately celebrated and shared their joy in her newfound love. Instead, she recognized a distinct fear within herself that her dearest friend would suddenly look upon her with revulsion and reject her totally. If Nikki lived with this type of fear every day, then Kate understood why she was so reserved in certain matters, why she was so careful about opening up to others.

"Are you telling me that you're gay?" Susan's eyes were wide.

Kate firmed her jaw. "I'm saying that I've fallen in love. That person happens to be female. I didn't expect it to happen, but it did. I'm certainly not going to hide it or pretend it didn't."

Susan continued to stare at her, and Kate was aware of her own measured respiration as Susan digested the news. "Well," she said finally, shaking her head as if recovering from a blow. "I won't say this isn't a surprise, but I guess it does explain a few things."

"What things?"

"Why you never wanted to date after David," Susan said, counting off the points on her fingers. "Why you never dated anybody but David in the first place. Why your marriage broke up—"

"That's not why we divorced. He wanted children. I didn't."

"Isn't that a bit of a clue as well?" Susan held up a finger, clearly attempting to slow things down a bit. "So, you've met this woman, and you spent last night with her. Is this an ongoing thing?"

"Last night was the first time we slept together, if that's what you mean. But it wasn't a one-night stand, and I fully intend to pursue a relationship with her."

Susan shook her head. "Have you thought about what this will look like?"

Kate frowned, her brows drawing down. "I don't care what people think."

"Bullshit." Kate flinched and Susan lifted her head. "Kate, I'm not trying to be homophobic here, but you're going to shake up the town's perception of you, and we both know people in this town really don't like being shaken up. Have you thought about your business?"

Anger rose dully inside Kate, without direction or a target. It made her defensive. "I've been carrying gay and lesbian books in the store for over a year. No one protested except Abigail Jenkins, who objects to everything new that happens without her personal approval anyway. Believe it or not, Truro is being dragged into the twentieth century, even if it's already the twenty-first. I bet you didn't even know that there's a gay community in this town."

"Of course I did," Susan said. "They hold dances and potlucks over at the Lyon's Club. But I didn't know you were going to join their committee."

Kate, who hadn't a clue about the potlucks or the dances, opened her mouth and then paused. "I'm not talking about that," she said. *There's a committee?* She took a breath. "Nikki and I escalated our relationship only recently. We haven't had a chance to…explore all the repercussions of it yet."

"Okay, fine." Susan leaned back against the cushions. "So her name is Nikki. Do I know her?"

"I don't know. Her last name is Harris. She grew up in Old Barns."

Susan gaped at her. "Nicole Harris? Little Nikki Harris? Holy Mother of God, Kate, she's still in high school!"

"She most certainly is not," Kate protested, her face feeling hot. "She's twenty-six."

"You're forty—old enough to be her mother!"

"I am not. Well, all right, technically, I suppose I am, but she's very mature, Susan, and highly intelligent. The talks we've shared about books and current events have been the most stimulating and provocative I've ever experienced."

"Are you sure she's not after your money?"

"What money? The bookstore barely makes enough to cover the overhead and pay for the heat and lights."

"The bookstore doesn't make that much," Susan said, "but you personally, Kate, are worth more than most people in this town, even if the larger percentage of it is tied up in your trust funds. Between what your grandfather left you, what your parents left you, and the legacy from your Uncle Abner—"

"All right," Kate said, holding up a hand to slow her down. "Nikki doesn't know about that. To her, I'm just the owner of Novel Companions, trying to make ends meet. She probably doesn't even know I'm the granddaughter of Irene Taylor."

"Has she been up here?" Susan waved a hand to indicate the apartment. "It wouldn't take a genius to figure out you're financially solvent from the way you furnished the place or the car you drive. I know you like to live frugally, Kate, but quality shows."

"She's not after my money!" Kate barked, leaning forward in her chair. She glared at Susan and then relaxed, acknowledging that things had become a bit heated and recognizing the need to cool down a bit. She forced herself to control her annoyance as she accepted that her friend was only trying to look out for her.

"All right." Susan eased her body language. "I'm not trying to bad-mouth Nikki, Kate, honestly. If you care about her, then she's obviously someone pretty special. You certainly wouldn't waste your time on just anyone. I'm simply trying to look at it from all angles. You have to admit, this is sort of coming out of the blue."

"It was a surprise to me, too. But it feels right, Susan. For the first time in my life, it really feels right."

Susan sighed. "It must," she said, in an almost envious tone. "I've never seen you like this. You're positively glowing."

"I am?"

"You are. So last night was...all right?"

Kate hesitated but was unable to keep the smile from spreading over her face. "Last night was incredible. So were this morning and this afternoon."

Susan leaned back in her seat and sipped her coffee. "I think I'm jealous. Do women really know what other women like best?"

"You just want the lurid details." Kate eyed her friend. "I'm not about to give them to you."

"At least tell me if it was better than being with David."

"Oh, Susan, there's no comparison," Kate said before she could stop herself. She forced herself to be fair. "That's not David's fault. He was always...very gentle, very giving. And he always did his absolute best by me when it came to sex. If I wasn't able to respond in the way another woman might have, well, in hindsight, that was my doing, not his."

She crossed her legs, feeling a bit of a twinge at their juncture as she abruptly remembered what it had been like with Nikki, the surge of desire catching her by surprise. "Don't get me wrong, Susan. It wasn't *horrible* being with him. I think I even managed...well, an orgasm now and again. With Nikki..." She stared into nothing, almost able to taste her on her lips, remembering the intensity of their joining, the heights of ecstasy Nikki had inspired in her, the sheer heat that threatened to incinerate her alive—

"Kate!"

Kate jumped. "What?"

"You just zoned out on me. Nikki must really know her stuff."

Kate felt the temperature of her entire body rise. "It's not the sex, it's the love. If I'd felt about David what I feel for her, we'd still be married."

Susan laughed and shook her head. "This is unbelievable. I came up here expecting to get all the dirt on Sam and how he died, and instead I discover my best friend has made a complete change in lifestyle."

Kate felt exasperated as she glanced at Susan. "I hate that term. It makes it sound as if I changed careers or something. I haven't changed my lifestyle at all. I'll be living exactly the way I always have. I'll just be able to share it with someone for a change. I'm still the same person."

"Oh, who are you trying to kid?" Susan scoffed. "You're not the same at all. You're all lit up like a Christmas tree, you're more animated, your voice is louder, and every so often you sort of mentally wander off and develop a stupid grin on your face. The sun's a bit brighter, food tastes much better, even if you'll forget to eat half the time, and frankly, after a while, you'll be so damned insufferable that the rest of us poor people not freshly in love will just want to slap you silly!"

Kate laughed, and Susan waggled her finger at her. "See what I mean? You laugh at absolutely nothing." She took another swallow of coffee. "So when am I going to meet this wonder woman?"

"She's coming over for dinner tomorrow night." Kate hesitated, and Susan started to chuckle.

"It was supposed to be a romantic dinner, wasn't it? Are you really sure you want me around? I can stay in a hotel."

"Don't be silly," Kate said, though a certain part of her felt a pang of regret for the change in plans. "I know she'll enjoy meeting you. After all, you're my best friend, and I want her to be a part of my life." She paused deliberately. "But after dinner, maybe you could go stay with your folks?"

Susan threw a pillow at her, and Kate laughed again. She really did feel giddy and agreed she truly wasn't the same person. Susan was also right about how life tasted so much sweeter now, how the world around her seemed to glow with a luminescent appeal. On the way over from Nikki's apartment, she had been captivated more than once by the incredible view of streetlights glinting off the fresh layer of snow, the deep dark blue of the sky punctuated with bright pinpoints of stars, the sheer joy of being alive and in love.

Susan was right, she thought happily as she finished her coffee. She was insufferable.

CHAPTER EIGHTEEN

Nikki entered the Mayflower Diner on feet that almost defied gravity, not even seeing her friends as she strolled happily toward the table in the corner. She felt someone reach out and grab her by the arm as she passed their booth. As she turned, she spotted Kim and her lover, Lynn, and smiled beatifically. "Hi," she said. "How are you doing?"

They both stared at her. "Where the hell were you Saturday night?" Kim asked. "I tried calling about ten times. You don't usually forget about us like that."

Nikki belatedly remembered that Kim had invited her over for a gathering to commiserate her lack of love interest and general dissatisfaction with life. "Oh, God, I'm sorry," she said as she sat down in the booth next to Lynn. "I...uh, I unplugged my phone Saturday night. I didn't remember to plug it back in until last night."

"Why would you unplug your phone?" Lynn asked. Darker, older, and quieter than Kim, she was also quicker to spot things that were unusual and tended to get quickly to the heart of the matter. She also had a way of commenting on things that left others in stitches...once they had the chance to realize what exactly she had said.

"I was...with someone."

Both stared at her again, and she started to squirm.

"Get *out*," Kim said, a grin spreading across her face. She glanced around, then leaned closer. "You don't mean..."

Nikki felt cornered and smug at the same time. "Kate and I...spent the day together. One thing sort of led to another—"

"Oh, God, not again." Lynn groaned.

Nikki wasn't surprised that Lynn already knew all about her romantic interest in Kate. Kim would have told her almost as soon as she had found out. "It's not like that. She loves me. She's already said she does." ·

"That in itself is a little quick, don't you think?" asked Lynn. "Sometimes saying it too often and too early is as suspicious as not saying it at all."

"Well, I'm glad to know you're happy for me."

"It's not that," Kim said. "It's just that...hell, this happened fast. Only a few days ago you were telling me that she was straight. Can you blame us for getting a sense of déjà vu?"

"Sometimes it just works that way. After all, I knew Anne for two years before anything happened, and that didn't make things go any smoother in the end. Kate and I..." Her gaze became distant. "We just click, you know?"

Kim and Lynn looked at each other.

"She's got it bad," Kim said.

"It's going to be unbearable," Lynn agreed.

"We're just going to have to put up with it for the time being."

Nikki was more annoyed. "Will you guys *stop*."

Kim shook her head. "Well, it's obvious that we can't talk to you right now. You're fully into that stupid stage new lovers go through. Let's give this a month or so, then we'll be able to talk sensibly." She lifted her brows. "I suppose we can also expect you to disappear for the next little while."

"Disappear?"

"Just like you did Saturday night," Kim said, flipping her fingers in the air. "Oh, you'll probably call us now and again, but I think you'll be blowing us off for the foreseeable future while you hang out with Kate and her sort."

"What do you mean, 'her sort'?"

"You know, the upper crust in town," Lynn said. "All those mucky-mucks on the town council, all the members of the golf club, the curling club—"

"Or is she just going to keep you in the closet?" Kim tilted her head. "I know. She'll probably give you a new job. You can be her new part-time help at the store."

"All *right*," Nikki said, putting enough of an edge in her voice to let them know the teasing had crossed the line. "That's enough."

"Okay, we're sorry," Lynn said. "Is she going to visit this side?"

"Of course," Nikki said promptly, aware that Anne hadn't been interested in participating in the group's events and expecting much better of her new love. "She'll be part of our community."

Kim smirked. "I wouldn't count on that. I can just picture Mrs. Shannon at our next dance, particularly when the guys start groping each other. She'd probably call the vice squad."

Nikki frowned. "She's not like that," she said, starting to become angry.

Kim must have sensed she had gone too far, because she put her hands up immediately. "Maybe not. Fine, Nikki, bring her around, but don't be surprised if she begs off. Just because she's with a woman doesn't mean that she's prepared to embrace 'the lifestyle.'"

Nikki rolled her eyes. "We don't have a 'lifestyle.' We have dances at the fire hall, barbeques in the park, pizza and videos, exactly like straights. We're so excruciatingly middle class we'd bore the hell out of the society pages."

"Yes, but we don't want them to know that," Lynn said. "They want to think that our events require pentagrams painted on the floor and that we throw orgies in the church pews. Who are we to disappoint them?"

"Has anyone ever told you that you're nasty?"

"Frequently." Kim smiled fondly as she glanced at Lynn. "Fortunately, I love her anyway."

"Someone has to." Lynn glanced at Nikki. "So you and she did the deed?"

Nikki finally nodded. "Yes."

"And?" Kim prodded.

"It was great." Nikki hugged herself as she stared off into space. "Everything I could have imagined and then some."

"Remember when it was like that for us, Kim?" Lynn sighed wistfully.

Kim frowned. "You mean it isn't anymore?"

"Who the hell have you been sleeping with?"

Nikki shook her head in exasperation at her friends who could take the romance out of a sunset and glanced toward the counter, hoping Addy would drop by to take her order.

Addy must have been waiting for a break in the intense conversation, because as soon as Nikki looked her way, she moseyed over, bearing her pad. "You decide?"

"Soup of the day. Tuna on whole wheat. A glass of milk."

Kim nodded approvingly. "Good. Healthy. Got to keep up your strength now."

Nikki shot her a dirty look, but Lynn and Kim were busy with each other.

"You got this, Kim?"

"Sure."

Nikki moved out of the way as Lynn slid out of the booth, her lunch finished, saying that she had to get back to her office.

As Lynn left the diner, Nikki asked Kim, "Are you off today?"

"I have the evening shift." Kim dug into a large hot fudge sundae. Her friends found it a constant aggravation that Kim could eat just about anything and never gain an ounce. Of course, it undoubtedly helped that she led three classes of aerobics a day. "So what are your plans for the rest of the week?"

"Well, tonight Kate and I are having dinner at her place."

"Ah, a romantic dinner."

"Originally." Nikki made a face. "Kate called last night. Apparently, an old friend of hers came up from the city to go to Sam's funeral tomorrow and is staying with her. So I guess it's more a meet-my-best-friend sort of dinner."

"Best behavior, babe. At least it's not a meet-the-parents type dinner."

"Kate's parents are dead, so I won't have to go through that. It's too bad I couldn't take Kate home to meet Mom and Dad, though. I think they'd like her a lot...if she were my friend rather than my lover."

"They'd flip, Nik." Kim licked the whipped cream off her spoon.

"Yeah." Nikki felt a twinge again, sadness at a reality that she doubted would ever change.

"Not because she's a woman. Because she's twice your age. They'd think she's cradle robbing."

"She's not twice my age. She's only..." She did the math; twenty-six from forty left... "Okay, so she's fourteen years older than me. Big deal."

"It could be. I'm not trying to bring you down, Nik. I'm just saying that for some people, it could be a problem."

"Age doesn't matter."

As Addy deposited Nikki's soup and sandwich, Kim exchanged a glance with the waitress before she reached over and nudged Nikki. "So, anything new on the murder?"

Nikki tried her soup and found it delicious, as always. "You wouldn't believe what happened Saturday." Between bites, she filled Kim in on all the events two days earlier.

"You think Rushton did it?"

"I do. It just bothers me how cool she was, though. I think she had a chance to hide the more incriminating stuff before we went back."

"Maybe you and Kate should take another look through the house."

"Maybe we should," Nikki said, forgetting that they had agreed to let it rest. "Meanwhile, do you think Lynn could track down some things for me?"

"I'll ask her." Kim picked up her coat. "Give her a call tomorrow night. I have to go. See you later."

"Bye," Nikki said and, alone, she finished her meal, thinking over what she had learned about Katherine Rushton and Sam Madison, frequently interspersing this information with random thoughts of her new love and the memories of the night they had spent together. She had never felt so in tune with another person, so peaceful on so many levels, and the new sensations made her realize how frantic and uncertain her feelings about Anne had been. She and Kate were just so comfortable, and when they made love for the first time, it was as if they had been making love with each other forever, unafraid to tell each other what they liked and didn't, communicating openly without fear of rejection or hurt.

She realized she had finished her soup when her spoon scraped the bottom of the bowl, and she grinned at herself, knowing she had to get these mental jaunts into the ether under control. She'd have to get out there and start rattling the bushes for a job again, check out the listings at the unemployment office, and see what else was going on around town. She was determined to find something better for herself in Truro. No way was she going to move back to the city now.

Glancing up as Addy approached, bearing a piece of chocolate cream pie, she was dismayed when the waitress put it in front of her. "I didn't order this." She was embarrassed because she knew she couldn't afford it. She could barely afford the soup and sandwich.

Addy shrugged. "Kim put it on her bill, along with the rest of your meal. Since it's already paid for, you might as well eat it."

Touched beyond measure, Nikki grew warm with pleasure and picked up the fork. She didn't know why people chose to be so kind to her. Such continual surprises made her feel warm inside. She decided that she was extraordinarily fortunate in her choice of friends.

Addy sat down opposite her, the diner quiet for the moment. "I heard that Marlene Shay's heading to the city once she marries Wade next month. That means her job will be open soon, and Sandy is probably already looking for someone."

"The night dispatcher at the police station? Am I qualified?"

"I don't know. I don't know what Sandy does besides pick up donuts here every morning for the station and keep track of where the officers are in the course of a shift. Why don't you give it a try and find out? The worst that will happen is that you won't get it, and you won't be any worse off than before."

"Good idea, Addy. I'll find out what's required and start working on my résumé right away."

"Plenty of time. Enjoy your pie."

CHAPTER NINETEEN

K ate fussed over the exact placement of the flowers in the center of the table until Susan finally said, "Give it a rest, Katie. What are you trying to do, intimidate the poor kid?"

Kate glanced at her. "Don't refer to her like that."

Susan held up her hands in surrender. "Fine, but you're driving both of us crazy, and from what you tell me of this ki—young woman, she's very down-to-earth and probably wouldn't be impressed anyway."

"She is." Kate sighed. "You're right. I'm acting crazy."

"Besides, it's not as if you're trying for a seduction," Susan said as she leaned back in her chair, scanning the daily newspaper. "I'm going to be here." She grinned at Kate. "Unless you were serious about wanting me to make myself scarce afterward?"

"No. I guess I'm just a little nervous." Kate left the table for the moment, wiping her hands as she returned to the kitchen where the pasta was boiling and the tomato sauce simmered slowly. Since Nikki liked lasagna, Kate assumed pasta was a safe choice. "This is our first date, remember?"

"Is that a gay thing?" The paper rustled as Susan turned the page. "First you sleep together, then you start to date?"

"Don't you dare say anything like that to her."

Susan laughed. "God, Katie, you don't want me to say anything about the age difference, you don't want me to say anything about the gay issue, you don't want me to say anything about money. What's left? Politics and religion?"

"Don't say anything at all. How about that?"

Susan shook her head. "You're hopeless."

The doorbell chimed and Kate whipped off her apron, smoothing her hands over the navy wool skirt she had chosen to wear. "That's her," she said, feeling her heart rate make a decided jump. "Remember, be nice!"

"I'm always nice," Susan said as Kate sprinted from the apartment and down the staircase, almost tripping in her haste.

Catching her footing, Kate forced herself to calm down and take a deep breath, descending the rest of the way down the stairs to the landing below in a more dignified manner. When she opened the door, Nikki beamed at her, and Kate felt her heart ricochet about her chest. "Hi," she said, unable to manage anything more articulate.

"Hi," Nikki said in her shy, absolutely adorable way.

They locked eyes for an eternity before Kate realized that she was not only leaving Nikki standing out in the cold, she was letting all the heat from her building escape into the snowy outdoors. "God, come on in," she said, taking Nikki's arm.

She rushed in and smiled bashfully. "You look wonderful."

Kate lowered her head momentarily. "Thank you."

They gazed at each other for another long minute before Nikki unzipped her jacket and Kate slipped her arms inside. Wrapping them snugly around Nikki's waist, Kate kissed her until she feared they were both in grave danger of passing out from lack of oxygen.

"Kate, we *are* going to have dinner sometime tonight, aren't we?"

Dizzy, Kate forced herself to draw back, glancing up the stairs to discover Susan standing on the upper landing, watching them. She looked back at Nikki, dismayed to see that she'd smeared lipstick all over her mouth. "That's Susan."

"Hi, Susan."

"Hello, Nikki. I don't suppose you remember me? I taught you in Sunday school."

Nikki frowned while Kate closed her eyes, wanting to groan out loud. "Miss O'Brien?"

Susan tilted her head, a hint of amusement in her face. "Yes, though it's Carlson now. How are your parents?"

"Fine."

Kate, who still had her arms wrapped tightly around her lover's waist, realized Susan was staring at her.

"She can't make it up the stairs with you hanging onto her like that, Katie," she said, and then disappeared back into the apartment.

Nikki glanced back at Kate, who managed a weak smile. "I guess I have to let you go."

"Not by my choice." Nikki hugged her tighter. "I'm perfectly happy to stay here all night kissing you."

Kate laughed and reluctantly released her hold. Then she reached up and wiped Nikki's lips gently. "I'm afraid I covered you with lipstick."

"I'll freshen up before we start dinner." Nikki plunged her hand into her coat pocket. "I have something for you." She pulled out a small package, gift wrapped with a bow. "It isn't much."

Delighted, Kate accepted the box and opened it. Inside was a small teddy bear about four inches high.

"It's so you'll have something to cuddle when I'm not there."

"I love it," Kate said, slipping her arm around her lover's neck and kissing her again. A bashfully pleased expression on her face, Nikki offered a soulful look from beneath lowered lashes, and Kate took her hand. "Come on."

Upstairs, Kate took her coat and directed Nikki to the bathroom where she could remove the lipstick. In the meantime, she carried the small stuffed toy over to the breakfast bar and placed it prominently on the counter so that she could look at it while eating dinner.

Susan, in the kitchen stirring the pasta, eyed the bear irreverently but didn't say anything.

Kate shot her an admonishing glance before turning to greet the freshly scrubbed Nikki.

"Anything new?"

Nikki shook her head. "I may have a line on a new job. A dispatcher at the police station. I'm going to do some research on the Net to find out exactly what a dispatcher does, then emphasize those skills on my résumé before I drop it off."

"I think you'd enjoy that." She made a mental note to lean on Rick as much as possible the next time she saw him; maybe he could put in a good word for Nikki. "Plus, you'd actually be involved in solving the cases."

"At least dispatching the guys that do."

Again, Kate discovered they were staring at each other, and with an effort, she led Nikki over to the living room. "Here. You and Susan get to know each other a bit better while I finish making dinner. We're having rigatoni."

"Sounds wonderful."

Kate returned to the kitchen and took the spoon from Susan. "Be nice," she murmured again in a low voice, as Susan obediently moved into the living room.

As Kate checked the pasta, she tried to keep tabs on the conversation going on in the living room. Susan was behaving herself as far as she could tell, utilizing her not inconsiderable charm to ask Nikki what was going on in town, skillfully drawing out a great many personal details from her in the process. But now the conversation was turning to Kate and their relationship, and she wasn't sure she was entirely comfortable with that topic.

"So you met Kate when you heard she was carrying gay and lesbian books," Susan said. "Was it love at first sight?"

Nikki looked vaguely uncomfortable. "No, we became friends first. I mean…she's very attractive—"

"For a middle-aged woman," Susan agreed amiably and glanced into the kitchen where Kate favored her with a poisonous look.

Nikki straightened on the sofa, her eyes narrowing. "Do you have a problem with our relationship, Mrs. Carlson?"

Kate stopped stirring for a moment, listening closely.

Susan, apparently realizing she had gone a bit too far in the jibe aimed at her friend, lifted her hands up in a gesture of surrender. "Not at all. I adore Kate. I'm just glad someone else does, as well."

Nikki leaned back. "I think that you only have so many chances in this life to love. You can always find reasons not to pursue a relationship, but what do you gain by that?"

"Not being hurt?"

"We all get hurt in life, Mrs. Carlson."

"Will you please call me Susan?"

"Susan," Nikki repeated obediently. "I'm just saying that an opportunity might not always work out the way you hope, but at least you tried. Otherwise, at the end of your life, all that's left is regret for the things you didn't do."

Susan was silent for a moment before finally nodding. "You're probably right."

Kate was relieved when she realized the pasta was cooked. She lost track of the rest of the conversation as she became busy draining the noodles, transferring them to a large glass bowl, and filling another with sauce. She carried them out to the table and then returned to the kitchen to retrieve the bread and pitcher of water. On the counter, a bottle of Jost's finest red wines was breathing, ready to be served. "Dinner's ready," she announced, pulling out a chair for Nikki as she, followed by Susan, walked over to the dining area.

From the corner of her eye, she saw Susan flick an eyebrow as she sat on the other side of the table. She also noticed Susan smile faintly as she watched Kate fill Nikki's plate with pasta, making sure she had precisely the right amount of sauce, pouring her a glass of wine, and retrieving some garlic bread for her. Susan could serve herself as best she could, Kate decided. She wanted there to be no secret of where Nikki ranked on her list of priorities.

Returning her attention to her lover, she saw how tentatively Nikki sipped her wine. "You don't like it?"

"I, ah, don't really drink it as a rule. I'm sorry."

"I'll get you something else," Kate said immediately. "What would you like?"

"Water's fine." Nikki picked up her other glass containing the ice water. "The food is really delicious, by the way."

"Have I told you how exquisite you look?" Kate asked, captivated by her soft eyes and shining hair. She hadn't even really seen what Nikki was wearing and only belatedly looked over the blouse and trousers...probably the best outfit she owned...which at least combined into a reasonable ensemble. She could have used some jewelry to set it off, Kate noted, and wondered if she dared remedy that lack sometime in the near future.

Until now Kate hadn't been aware of her emphasis on appearance. Suddenly she realized it was probably just a by-product of the community in which she had grown up. She had acquired the same unconscious, automatic appraisal of other women that most in her social circle routinely utilized. Nikki's lack of such an emphasis had clued her in on her own attitude.

Nikki blushed at Kate's compliment. "Thank you."

Though Kate was totally engrossed in Nikki's appearance and her thoughts about her attitude toward appearance, in a tiny corner of her mind, she watched Susan roll her eyes and dig into her meal. Kate supposed she felt left out and experienced a momentary twinge of guilt. She fleetingly thought about how they had grown up in the same community, though Susan's family was a little less well off than the Taylor household had been. They had both attended the same Catholic private school, then the public junior and senior high schools in town. Applying to Acadia University, they lived as roommates in the same sorority house. Susan had been her maid of honor at her wedding to David, and she had performed the same function for Susan when she later married Ted.

She supposed Susan was shocked at what was happening with her, and perhaps even a little dismayed at this unexpected side of her old friend. But Kate knew that Susan had experienced things through her children's eyes while they grew up, which helped her to realize certain of her cherished perceptions and beliefs weren't always necessarily proper, or even enlightened. Perhaps she was really doing Susan a disservice. Perhaps at the moment, she was less interested in worrying about what the rest of their social circle might think and far more concerned that Kate might be hurt in this relationship.

Surely Susan must see the love in her eyes when she looked at Nikki. She couldn't deny that Nikki had touched something new in her. Something David hadn't. Kate could only hope that her best friend would just be happy for her and not make any further judgments on something that was obviously beyond her influence to control.

"Nikki, Kate tells me that you and she have been investigating the Madison murder," Susan said suddenly.

"I don't know if you'd call it investigating," Nikki said, lifting her brows. "We've just been poking around to see what we can find out." She explained what had happened Saturday, filling in some of the details that Kate had left out, such as how impressive she'd been, first in the harrowing drive up the lane, then, by the amazingly cool...Nikki's word...way she had dealt with Katherine Rushton.

"Katherine Rushton," Susan said thoughtfully. "Which branch of the family?"

"I don't believe any of those around Colchester County," Kate said, feeling disdainful. "She looks as if she may have had money at one time." Kate knew there were two types of wealthy people in the town: those who flaunted their money as if it somehow made them better, and those who simply existed with it because it was there. Sam Madison, with his shiny red Corvette, and this Katherine Rushton, in her black Lexus, were of the former type.

During their dinner conversation, Kate felt relieved to discover that Susan apparently liked Nikki. She had known Susan long enough to recognize what was politeness on her part and what was sincere interest. Perhaps Susan was beginning to understand some of what Kate saw in Nikki: her honesty and her protective fierceness. No matter what happened, Kate understood instinctively that Nikki would stand by her, prepared to do whatever it took to support and care for her despite her youth. Susan would respond positively to that allegiance, particularly since she had such a protective streak of her own.

After dinner, the women retired to the living room with cake and coffee—chocolate milk for Nikki, which generated an amused look from Susan directed Kate's way—where they discussed the weather, books, and current events. Susan appeared pleased to discover that Nikki was quite knowledgeable about the issues of the day, though her opinions varied greatly from those of the older women, which wasn't necessarily a bad thing. She was able to present her views concisely and intelligently, forcing them to reconsider their assumptions. Every time she did, Kate felt achingly proud of her, which made Nikki respond with a vulnerably pleased look all her own, while Susan bit her bottom lip, amusement glinting in her emerald eyes.

When it was time for Nikki to leave, Kate escorted her downstairs to say good-bye.

By the time she finally wandered back, the dishes had been washed, dried, and put away, with Susan comfortably tucked up on the sofa with her novel. She peered at Kate over the top of her book. "Sweetie?"

Kate started, as if awakening from a trance. "Yes?"

"You should really learn to button up your blouse correctly if you're going to make out in the stairwell."

Horrified, Kate glanced down to see her shirt was open to below the line of her bra, feeling her face burn as Susan let loose the laughter she'd undoubtedly been holding in all evening.

CHAPTER TWENTY

Heading toward the police station after work to drop off her résumé, Nikki took the time to enjoy the fresh layer of snow on the ground, the intense blue of the sky overhead, and the sheer joy of being alive and in love. Kate was constantly in her mind, and a quick glance at her watch told Nikki that her love, along with her best friend, would be at the funeral home now. Nikki had detected some wariness in Susan the night before, but she was undoubtedly worried about her "straight" friend becoming romantically involved with a woman. She couldn't blame Susan for that. In her shoes, she'd probably be worried as well, and all she could do was hope that Susan would eventually understand how much she truly loved Kate.

In any event, Susan would be heading back to the city later that afternoon, and Nikki began to plan for the evening. The heated kisses and caresses they had shared in the stairwell of Kate's building the night before did little to compensate for having to spend their night in their separate cold and lonely beds, deprived of each other's company. They would have to make up for it later.

Striding past Kiwanis Park where ducks crowded about the thawed outlet of an ice-covered pond, Nikki watched as the vigorous creatures waddled about the frozen reeds, searching for food. Though a large sign instructed people not to feed the ducks, well-meaning animal lovers over the years had ignored it and had ended up disrupting the normal migration patterns of the flock. Nikki considered that no duck in his right mind was going to fly thousands of miles overland, dodging buckshot and predators, when he could settle into a nice northern town pond with shelter and all the free food he could eat, plus several other ducks to keep him company.

Now the town was stuck with the animals, having to continue to feed them through the winter or have them starve to death en masse in the park, which would outrage the animal-loving taxpayers, most of whom had caused the problem in the first place. These ducks were doomed never to leave town, Nikki knew, because they had essentially become domesticated. Worst of all, the population never seemed to diminish, the permanent settlers laying eggs every spring to produce a new generation that contained a certain percentage of birds that also refused to migrate south in the winter.

She could easily imagine herself and Kate sitting on a park bench some lazy summer evening, watching those same ducks and the dance of fireflies, and she laughed at herself, already seeing herself growing old with Kate. We haven't even managed to get through this first week, she reminded herself as she crested the hill and started the incline toward the downtown core. But her niggling doubt didn't stop her from dreaming, and she scarcely noticed the cold weather as she neared the central part of town.

Nikki had almost reached the police station when a familiar car passed her, and suddenly, she focused on something other than her new relationship. Intrigued, she watched as Katherine Rushton parked her Lexus in front of another car that she easily recognized as belonging to Terry Bishop. Obviously, she hadn't been arrested, which meant that Kate had correctly assumed that the truly incriminating papers had been removed from the folder. But Rushton must have been called downtown for a reason. Deciding that this was too good an opportunity to pass up, Nikki quickened her step, pleased to have a valid excuse to be at the station.

Inside the front lobby, she strolled over to where Sandy Wright, the station's dispatch supervisor, was covering the desk. Through the window in the back, Nikki could see Rushton and Bishop in heated discussion with a constable, and she wished she could be a fly on the wall. In lieu of that, she wished she could read lips and made a mental note to learn as soon as possible.

According to rumor, Sandy, a rawboned woman in her early thirties, really ran the police station, and the rest of the constables, including the chief, actually worked for her. Chief Wallace wouldn't necessarily deny the assumption, either. "Do you know what's required of a dispatcher?" she asked, her blue eyes obviously appraising Nikki.

"I believe so." Nikki launched into what she had learned on the Net, trying to make it sound casual. "I know the position requires a lot of independent judgment, along with excellent verbal communication skills, the ability to think clearly and act promptly in emergencies, and to recall essential details quickly. I also know the surrounding geography quite well, and I'm pretty good at reading maps."

Sandy looked pleased, as if Nikki was the first one who seemed to understand the position required more than just going for donuts and keeping track of the constables during their shifts. "We're not as busy as the city, of course," she explained. "Most outside area 911 calls go to the Mounties, but we still get a lot of calls from people in trouble, and you need to be able to handle some pretty tense stuff at times."

Nikki nodded, even as she kept half an eye on the drama being played out in the other room. Rushton seemed to be yelling a lot, while Bishop seemed to be doing his best to calm his client. "I'm also willing to do shift work," she said, trying not to be too distracted. "I don't have kids or anything, so I'm available all the time, even on holidays."

"If you make it past the final culling of the résumés, you'll still have to take a written exam," Sandy told her. "The scores will count for a lot on who gets the job."

"I'm ready for that. I can type fifty-five words a minute, and I'm familiar with a lot of the current software programs. I'm comfortable with computers. I know it's a really challenging and vital position, Sandy, and not everyone is capable of handling it, but I believe I'm ready for it."

Sandy nodded. "I'll make sure this goes to Personnel."

Nikki knew that was the stock response and that her résumé could easily end up at the bottom of the pile, but she still felt a bit of optimism. Though Personnel would obviously have the final say, she suspected Sandy would have a great influence over who actually made the final cut for the examinations, and acknowledging how important the dispatcher's job was in the station hadn't hurt her chances. Passing the exam would be up to her, of course, but at this point she wasn't worried. If she couldn't do well on the exam, she didn't deserve the position.

The door to the other room suddenly flew open, and Rushton stomped out, followed by Bishop. She was clearly agitated, and when she spotted Nikki, she immediately centered her fury on her. "What is that dyke doing here?" she demanded, pointing a shaking finger at her.

"She's the one who should be locked up as a deviant instead of being allowed to run around and interfere with my business."

Nikki grimaced, while Sandy looked profoundly embarrassed. Of course, thought Nikki, everyone knew there were gays and lesbians in the town, but to point them out at the top of one's lungs displayed extremely poor taste. Even if someone privately shared Katherine Rushton's opinion of homosexuality, most people considered it rude to publicly air one's prejudices, particularly when the minority in question was just standing there minding her own business. If the average Canadian tried to avoid one thing, it was rudeness.

"Let's get out of here," Bishop said, his hand on Rushton's arm, propelling her toward the entrance.

"I want to bring charges against her for trespassing," Rushton said, not budging as she glared open hatred at Nikki. "You and that Shannon woman. I don't care what she thought she saw last week. She's not going to railroad me into prison for a murder I didn't commit."

Nikki was as uncomfortable as anyone to be the target of such vitriol, but she held her head high. An idle thought crossed her mind; she wondered what Kate would do in this situation. She asked quietly, "What are you so afraid of?"

Perhaps it was the simplicity of her question, the depth and variety of meaning that could be derived from such an implication, but where Bishop could not get his client to back down, Nikki deflated her with one well-placed needle. She was rather proud of herself.

"The same thing you should be afraid of," Rushton hissed before allowing herself to be dragged out of the station, and Nikki suddenly had a totally different perception of the situation. Rushton *was* scared, and it wasn't necessarily of what she and Kate had found in her house before she disposed of it. This was a deeper fear, and Nikki was left to ponder exactly what was going on.

"You just manage to find trouble wherever you go, don't you, Nikki?" Pete McGinnis said, his arms crossed over his chest.

The constable was a friend of Nikki's brother, and even if he didn't know Nikki well, he knew the family. He had dated her older sister, Julie, at one time, and shared Julie's antipathy toward her, though she had always found him such a pompous little prick that his opinion didn't bother her a great deal. "I'm just standing here, Pete," she replied evenly. "You're the one who made her mad."

He snorted and shook his head, not rising to the bait, then returned to the interrogation room, leaving her eaten alive with curiosity about the confrontation between him and Katherine Rushton.

She nodded briefly at Sandy, who waved, then left the station. Outside, she took several deep breaths and headed for home. *What had Rushton so scared? Where would she have hidden that first gun after she replaced it with the second? Where had she stashed the other papers from the file?* Of course, at this point, Rushton had more than enough time to return to Edwards House and hide them somewhere else, or even destroy them entirely. Perhaps if she and Kate had gone back to the estate later that night while Rushton had been at the police station, rather than going to Nikki's apartment to have dinner and...

Well, all things considered, Nikki didn't really regret missing the opportunity to search Edwards House over the weekend. Her good humor restored, she checked her watch, wondering how long the memorial service for Sam Madison would take. There would be no actual burial, of course, because the ground was frozen solid, but this event would formally end one man's existence in the world.

Strolling down the block, she stopped by the sporting goods store to check out the new spring arrivals. An avid camper and hiker since childhood, Nikki was a familiar customer, and she enjoyed chatting with the clerks about all the various luxury items designed to make the urban cowboys more comfortable while out in the wild. But as amusing as it was to make fun of the extravagant equipment, it also occurred to her that this year she might have to seriously consider items to coddle a novice camper during her first outdoors adventure. Such items were pricey, but if she was hired for the well-paying job at the police station, she could afford to outfit Kate properly. She was now doubly determined to pass the exam, if she made it that far, and decided to do more research to be as prepared as possible.

Maybe Kate absolutely wouldn't enjoy camping, but Nikki decided not to contemplate that unpleasant alternative. Why look for clouds on an otherwise bright and beautiful day?

CHAPTER TWENTY-ONE

K ate took a seat in the funeral home beside Susan, glancing around at the various townspeople attending the memorial service for Sam Madison. She picked out Margaret in the front row, attended by her mother and sister. Sam didn't have any family representing him, only friends and business associates. Kate was intrigued that Katherine Rushton wasn't one of them, and she wondered where she was. Turning her head, she noted that Rick Johnson had predictably positioned himself near the back, probably so he could watch everyone who came in and out of the small chapel.

Looking over at a group of women she knew from the golf club, Kate became aware that they were glancing at her and then putting their heads together to whisper. She felt uncomfortable as she settled back in the pew and wondered if they were talking about her.

Susan shrugged when she asked her about it. "It could be that you were the one who called in the fire. It might also have gotten out that you placed this Rushton woman at the scene."

"What if it's about my relationship with Nikki?"

"Then it may be something you'll have to get used to, Kate," Susan whispered, not unkindly. "Do you think your new status as a lesbian lover would have spread so quickly?"

Kate wondered if it were possible, considering that she and Nikki had only became truly close within the last week. Of course, in this town, all it would require was for the right person to observe Kate becoming friends with her, and the news would spread from there, growing and altering until god only knew what they were saying about her at this point. What she felt for Nikki was precious and private, and she didn't appreciate the idea that others might attempt to make something so special into something tawdry or crass.

But Kate was also aware that how she dealt with this situation would give others a cue as to how to react. If she seemed somehow embarrassed or ashamed of what she was doing, then by definition it was a shameful thing. If, however, she conducted herself with the same dignity and assurance that she did in the rest of her life, then eventually the rumors would die down, and the gossips would move on to something far more delicious.

She lifted her chin higher, determined to be as confident in her relationship with Nikki as she had ever been with David. "Lesbian lover?" she said from the corner of her mouth.

"As in the lover of a lesbian," Susan said. "Not necessarily a lesbian who is considered an extraordinary lover."

"Ah. Thank you for the distinction…I think."

"My pleasure." Susan tilted her head toward Margaret Madison in the front row. "Maggie seems rather broken up about this."

"Wouldn't you be?"

"I wouldn't have married him in the first place, let alone kept him around after the first time he strayed. I just find it hard to believe she would care so much that she was finally rid of him."

"Perhaps they understood each other, Susan. Enough to let him do what he wanted so long as he maintained the letter, if not the spirit, of the marriage."

"No, I can't see that. Maggie was always a bit of a cold fish, especially at university. Remember how she turned in Sadie for having a boy in her room?"

"It *was* against house rules."

Susan chuckled. "Maybe, but even you weren't so stringent, Kate. Maggie wasn't just determined to play by the rules. She wanted to see anyone who broke them punished immediately and to the fullest extent. I just find it hard to believe that she didn't hold Sam to the same standard."

"It's possible she didn't know about the affairs."

"She knew. But why did she put up with it?"

"Maybe because she truly loved him," Kate said. "More than any rules." She shifted a little on the hard wooden bench. "We never really know what's going on inside a person's head or heart."

"You can say that again. Still waters run deep. I suppose she could be mourning the fact that her meal ticket is gone."

Kate shook her head. "No, the money was all on her side. It had to be love, because he brought nothing else to the marriage but himself."

"Maybe she's a masochist."

Which made Kate think about what Nikki had revealed to her about Abigail Jenkins, and for a moment, she was hard-pressed not to chuckle as she spotted the mayor's wife sitting next to her husband only a few rows up. She almost leaned over and told Susan about what she had learned before remembering that she had promised Nikki she wouldn't tell anyone. Biting her tongue with an effort, she settled back in her seat. It was a new experience, not sharing everything with her best friend, but Nikki had trusted her, and promptly betraying that trust would be a sad way to start the relationship.

"What?" Susan prodded.

"Nothing. I was just thinking of Nikki."

"Big surprise. Are you ever *not* thinking of her?"

Kate didn't respond, which was an answer in itself. The minister appeared at the podium, and Kate settled back to listen to the service, studying the other people around her as the various tributes were made. Toward the end of some rather lengthy prayers, she heard a stir at the rear of the chapel and turned to look back, along with everyone else, as Katherine Rushton defiantly took a seat in the last row and stared straight ahead. "That's Rushton," Kate whispered.

Susan snuck another glance over her shoulder at the woman and then turned back to the front as the minister regained control over the service. When it was finally finished, the townspeople started to file out, some moving on to the gathering at the Madison home, others returning to work or going home.

Kate would have loved to go to the house, but since she was not really that close to Margaret, she wasn't brave or crass enough to crash the gathering. As she and Susan exited the chapel, she saw Margaret Madison and Katherine Rushton facing off in the foyer of the funeral home. Though she and Susan had previously assessed Sam's wife as distantly brittle, Kate soon realized she was also emotionally volatile.

"How dare you show up here?" Sam's wife hissed, the veins standing out in her neck as she glared absolute hatred at Rushton. Margaret's mother and sister were attempting to draw her away, while Rick Johnson observed unblinkingly from the entrance.

"I was Sam's business partner," Rushton said, her face a furious red, but standing her ground. "It was appropriate that I be here."

"You killed him. You ruined him, and then you killed him."

"You're hysterical," Rushton said, which Kate thought was pretty accurate at this point, despite her dislike for the woman.

Margaret was sliding out of control, which was completely unlike the mousy, rake-thin, morose woman. Gray strands streaked her light hair. She seemed to have aged twenty years since the death of her husband, a distinct contrast to the cold but artificially attractive Rushton. But Margaret's voice remained strong, and it was apparent that very little beyond a single remaining shred of propriety kept her from striking Rushton.

"Wow," Susan muttered. "Truro is a hell of a lot more entertaining now than I remember it."

"Shush." Kate shot her an admonishing look.

However, Margaret Madison spotted her and raised her voice. "Kate Shannon," she said loudly and strode over to them. "You saw her there that night, didn't you?"

Embarrassed and helpless, Kate glanced at Rick for instructions, who merely shrugged minutely, which she assumed meant that she could say whatever she wanted. She wondered if the information was so useless as to be irrelevant in building a case against Katherine Rushton, or if Rick was trying to use it as a lure to discover something more vital. Either way, she found it exceptionally distasteful.

"I saw a car that resembled Katherine Rushton's parked in front of the insurance office that night," she admitted woodenly. She reached out and clumsily patted Margaret on the shoulder. "You're overwrought, Maggie. Try to calm down."

Margaret didn't calm down, but she didn't continue to pursue Kate either, instead turning on the police officer. Kate breathed a sigh of relief that everyone else's attention shifted with hers.

"Why haven't you arrested that bitch?" Margaret demanded, gesturing at Rushton. The slur sounded odd coming from her pinched mouth, despite the obvious and searing hatred that motivated it.

"Miss Rushton admits that she was there," Rick said easily. "She also says that she left long before the fire began, or the estimated time of death."

"She lies," Margaret stated flatly.

"I have no evidence to support that accusation," he said. He took Margaret gently by the shoulders. "Margaret, people are waiting back at your home to share your pain. You need to go with your mother and sister."

She stared into his face; then, as if deriving some comfort there, some measure of assurance and peace, she nodded and turned away, walking over to where her family waited. All the animation had gone out of her like air from a balloon, and after she left the foyer, all eyes turned to Katherine Rushton. She raked them with a disdainful look, but didn't say anything as she strode from the room with as much dignity as possible.

Kate looked over at Rick, wondering what he was up to.

"You're sure about the time you heard the car drive away?"

"I am."

He nodded and then left in the wake of the other mourners who had vacated now that the show was over, leaving only Kate and Susan standing there.

"Goodness, Kate, but your life has certainly become exciting since I last saw you."

Kate put her fingers to her temples, rubbing them as the beginning of a headache feathered through her head. "I don't know that I can survive this much excitement," she said as they descended the outside stairs, heading toward Susan's car. As they got in, Kate exhaled, her breath a frosty cloud. "That was odd."

"What do you mean?" Susan asked, glancing over as she started the car and allowed the engine to warm up.

"I mean, it just doesn't feel right. You'd have to be pretty cold-blooded to come to the funeral of the man you shot between the eyes and left to burn up in the fire you set."

"Maybe she is." Susan lifted her brows. "Are you an authority on cold-blooded killers now?"

"No, but I'd like to think I know people," Kate said quietly as Susan pulled out of the parking place and drove slowly down the street. "If Rushton and Sam were only involved in a business relationship which was unknown to the general public, why use it as an excuse to come to his service? Maybe she felt she had to be there."

"To put on a good show?"

"No." Kate shook her head. "I think it's because she cared for him, and that's something I hadn't considered. If she did, then maybe this isn't all about money after all. Maybe it goes back to what everyone first thought it was...a crime of passion."

Susan pursed her lips. "If you say so," she said, slowing for the light at the end of Willow Street.

As she did, Kate put a hand on her arm. "Instead of taking me home, drop me off at Nikki's. I'd like to talk to her about this."

"Talk?"

"Yes." Kate's face began to feel warm.

"Who are you kidding? It's been two whole days since you had any—"

"Susan!" Kate shook her head. "You're unbelievable."

"Me?" Susan said between chuckles. "You're the one who can't go one day without seeing her."

"Just drop me off, will you?"

"What if she's not home?"

"Then I'll walk back to my place. It's only a few blocks. She's on the corner of Commercial, the big gray building."

"Convenient," Susan said dryly, which Kate dutifully ignored. Susan slowed to a stop at the corner of Commercial Street and parked next to the curb. Turning to Kate, she smirked. "Try not to sprain anything." When Kate just looked at her, Susan relented. "Seriously," she said, "take care of yourself, sweetie. You could really get hurt with all this, and I'm not talking about being too energetic in the bedroom."

"I'm willing to take the risk."

Susan stared at her, then nodded. "Okay." She reached over and hugged Kate tightly. "Keep in touch. I'll want to know every bump and curve you run into while pursuing this new interest."

"I'll call you." Kate smiled. "Drive safe. The weather's clear, but I hear there are some slippery spots between here and the city."

"I will. You watch out for your own slippery spots tonight."

"Susan!" Kate shook her head as she opened the car door. "Sometimes you're so crude."

"I know, but you love me anyway," Susan said with a crooked grin. She leaned over, looking through the open door. "Come visit me in the city. Bring Nikki with you."

Touched at the invitation, Kate nodded. "I will." She carefully picked her way across the sidewalk and around the corner where the door leading to the upstairs was located on the side of the building facing Queen Street. Doorbells lined the entrance, and she was forced to try one when the lower door proved to be locked. After a pause she heard faint footsteps descending the staircase inside, and the door opened to reveal Nikki, whose face lit up like a morning sunrise.

"Hi."

"Hi." Kate grinned foolishly at her.

Without hesitation, Nikki reached out, took her hands, and pulled her inside, kissing her deeply before leading her upstairs.

CHAPTER TWENTY-TWO

Did you learn anything at the funeral?" Nikki lay with her cheek resting on Kate's stomach, listening to the gentle gurgles within her lover, who sprawled happily across her bed.

Kate laughed, a low sensual chuckle that rumbled through her abdomen. "That's actually why I stopped by. Not necessarily for...uh, this, though it was certainly quite lovely."

Nikki suspected Kate was not being entirely honest about her reasons for dropping by, considering how quickly Kate had pounced on her once they were in the apartment. "I'm sorry. Next time, I promise we'll talk instead."

"Let's not be rash." Kate raked her fingers lavishly through Nikki's hair.

Nikki chuckled also, rubbing her cheek against the soft skin beneath her face before turning her head slightly to kiss Kate's belly button, making her squirm. "Ticklish?"

"Not at all," Kate said demurely, and Nikki filed the obvious fib away as something to pursue later. For the moment, she proceeded to kiss her way up the length of Kate's body, inhaling deeply as she passed through the warm valley between her modest breasts, loving the way she smelled, before finally settling on her side next to her lover and kissing her ear.

"I think you *are* ticklish," she murmured. "One of these days, I plan to find out exactly how much."

"Fiend," Kate said placidly.

Nikki growled and bit gently at her earlobe, wrapping her up in a warm embrace. "Back to the topic. What did you learn at the funeral?"

Kate snuggled into her arms and proceeded to tell her about the scene at the funeral home.

Nikki was alternately shocked and amused at the recounting, while adding the bit of information she already had at appropriate places.

"She must have gone straight to the funeral home after the police station," she said, before telling Kate about her recent encounter with Rushton.

Kate was quiet after she had finished. "Despite our decision to stay out of it, we keep being drawn in. I suppose, since it brought us together against all odds, to maintain the cosmic balance of the universe, it's predetermined that we solve this case."

"Okay," Nikki said, not having a clue what Kate was talking about.

Kate drew her head down, kissing her gently. "I have to go home."

"You can't stay the night?"

"No, I need to get an early start tomorrow." Kate hugged her in unspoken apology. "I already had to close this afternoon for the funeral, and I'm way behind on my paperwork. It wouldn't be wise to let my responsibilities slide while I spend all my time with you, as much as that idea appeals to me."

"You're right." Nikki sighed. "I suppose one of us needs to make a living instead of a subsistence."

Kate seemed about ready to say something, but she hesitated. Nikki waited expectantly, and Kate smiled. "You'll get the dispatcher's job. I believe in you."

"Thank you." Nikki accepted the comfort and encouragement of the statement, if not the veracity, since she knew Kate had no control over the job situation. She leaned down and gently kissed her again. "Let me make you some dinner before you leave, and then I'll walk you home."

"My heroine," Kate whispered, nuzzling her lovingly.

Nikki blushed, pleased, and rolled out of bed. "Do you want to shower first?"

To her surprise, Kate stretched lavishly, resplendent with sensual contentment. "Not really. I want to keep the way you smell on me as long as possible."

Laughing, Nikki scooped up some jeans and a sweatshirt, pulling them on without undergarments. She checked out Kate's dress, which was lying on the cedar chest, and the pumps she had worn to the funeral. "You can't walk home in those."

"Any suggestions?" Kate sat up. "It's not as if I brought a suitcase."

"Give me a minute," Nikki said, ignoring the delectable display with an effort as she turned to her dresser where she pulled out a pair of sweat pants and a T-shirt, along with a pair of thick socks. "These are too large, but they'll be all right for walking home in. Far better than that dress would be." She tilted her head, thinking for a moment, then moved over to the bedroom closet where she found a pair of slightly worn hiking boots. "I have no idea why I kept these around all this time," she explained as she offered them to Kate. "I guess it really bugged me that I'd saved so long for them as a teenager and only had the opportunity to wear them for about three months before I outgrew them. Now I see that somehow I was saving them just for you. They're size eight."

Her face vulnerable, Kate accepted the gift. "Thank you."

Nikki beamed. "Would you like an omelet?"

"Sounds wonderful."

Nikki left her lover in the bedroom to dress as she went out to the kitchen. In the living room, Powder glared balefully from his perch on top of the bookcase, obviously displeased at being continually banished from the bedroom where he was used to sleeping. She wrinkled her nose at the cat, completely unrepentant, as she washed her hands at the sink, then pulled out some ingredients from the fridge: eggs, ham, mushrooms, green peppers, and shredded cheese. By the time Kate had joined her, looking adorable in her borrowed clothing, Nikki already had the ingredients for an omelet cooking nicely. On the counter, her newest acquisition burbled quietly.

"That can't be coffee I smell?" Kate's eyes were wide.

Nikki shrugged lightly. "My friends, Kim and Lynn, had an extra coffeemaker they weren't using, so they offered it to me," she said as the dark liquid gurgled and burped in the device on the counter. "They also recommended the brand of coffee."

Kate examined the packaging of the coffee that Nikki had bought earlier that day. "This is fine. More than fine." She wrapped her arm around Nikki's neck, drawing her down for a kiss. "Thank you, love. You're very thoughtful."

Nikki shrugged again, this time to hide her embarrassment, but she was pleased. "Do you want to make the toast?" She handed Kate a loaf of bread.

Kate immediately popped two slices into the toaster. For the next few moments, they became incredibly domestic, working side by side as they prepared their supper, and Nikki basked in the simple joy of their easy companionship.

"I like this," Kate said suddenly, rising to her tiptoes to kiss Nikki on the side of her jaw. "It's so homey."

"I really like it too." Nikki hesitated, then added in a casual tone as she slipped the finished omelets onto two plates. "You know, if you'd like, you can start leaving a few things here so you don't get caught short again."

Kate glanced at her as they carried their meals over to the table, sitting in the same chair as she had Saturday night. "Like what?"

"You know, a change of clothes," Nikki explained as she retrieved the butter, salt, and pepper, trying not to sound nervous. "Fortunately, I had a new toothbrush for you Sunday morning, but you might want some other things, like your own brand of deodorant and shampoo. Not that I mind you using mine, of course. I just want you to be comfortable staying over if you need to."

Kate tasted her omelet, chewing it contemplatively. "That might be more convenient. Of course, feel free to do the same at my place."

Nikki let her breath out slowly. "Thank you," she said, managing a calm tone. Perhaps it was a bit soon in the relationship to be setting such things up, but on the other hand, they would probably spend more than a few more nights together in the near future. It only made sense to be prepared. Making love was fine, Nikki thought, but sleeping together held more intimacy, and she regretted they would miss out on it today.

"What are you doing tomorrow after work?"

"I'll probably stay in," Nikki responded absently. "I need to do some laundry and clean the apartment."

"But it's Wednesday."

Nikki paused, confused by the apparent unhappiness of her new lover, and then smiled as she realized she was being teased. "I'd never miss my weekly visit to the bookstore."

Kate grinned crookedly at her. "Why not drop by at closing time? I can cook you that romantic dinner we didn't have Monday night."

"What about my laundry?"

"Can't you do it Thursday night?"

Nikki grinned back and said with mock reluctance, "I suppose I could."

Kate made a face at her before swallowing another mouthful of omelet. "You know, you're really good around the kitchen."

Nikki laughed. "Don't be too sure. My repertoire is fairly limited, and you've probably tasted my best to date. But I *am* pretty good at cooking on a grill or over a campfire."

"You really enjoy camping, don't you?"

"I do." Nikki studied Kate from beneath her lashes. "I'd love to take you out with me some time."

Kate bit her lip, as if she'd never considered such a thing. "I don't know how well I'd do."

"Everyone has to start somewhere." Nikki took a bite of her omelet, slightly disappointed at the lack of enthusiasm in Kate's voice.

"I suppose you're right. I certainly can't judge if I would like it unless I try it."

Nikki decided that was fair and probably as much as she should expect from someone who had grown up in town. "What do you like to do in the warmer months?"

"I play a lot of golf." Kate's face took on a certain glow that rather alarmed Nikki.

For her, to whom golf was slightly less interesting than watching paint dry, this expression clearly indicated that she was in the presence of a real aficionado. She exhaled. If Kate was willing to take a chance in the woods, then she should at least muster up a certain amount of appreciation for her lover's favorite sport. "I've never played." Nikki didn't bother to add that she couldn't imagine ever wanting to. "Perhaps you could teach me."

"I'd love to." Kate's eyes were actually sparkling, and Nikki tried not to wince at the thought of plodding after a little white ball with a club.

"I'm sure that once you've tried it, you'll fall completely in love with it."

Nikki reached over, entwining her fingers with Kate's. "I'm sure I will, too."

They returned to their meal, still holding hands. Afterward, Nikki found a bag in which to put Kate's dress and pumps, and they bundled up before walking out into the cold. Above the buildings, the stars glittered, softened only slightly by the lights from the town. "Out in the country, they're like diamonds," Nikki said, glancing up at them. "That's the thing I miss most living in town. That, along with crickets in the summer and fireflies in the spring."

Kate's breath created a white cloud as they stepped gingerly on the icy sidewalks. "What made you move into town rather than find a place out in the country?"

"Finances. I could either live at my parents' and buy a car, or get a place of my own." Nikki hesitated, saddened at the memory of having to make such a choice. "It seemed more important to have my own place."

Kate glanced at her, apparently picking up on her tone. "Was living at home that unpleasant?"

Nikki shook her head. "No, just awkward. I felt like I had to hide a part of myself all the time, and that's not easy. Besides, I didn't want to be a drain on my parents any longer. I wanted to be on my own."

"That makes sense. You know, if you ever need a vehicle, you're more than welcome to borrow mine."

"Ah, now I know it must be real love." Nikki deliberately lightened her tone as she slipped her arm across Kate's shoulders. She hugged Kate and deposited a quick kiss on her temple, but as a car approached from down the street, Nikki promptly dropped her own arm and edged away from Kate while they walked. Her reaction was so automatic that she didn't even notice it.

"Why did you do that?" Kate stared at her oddly as they turned down Prince Street.

"Do what?" Nikki was baffled.

"Move away from me." Kate took her hand. "Are you ashamed of me?"

"Not at all," Nikki said, releasing Kate's hand uncomfortably as they strolled through the more populated areas of town, jamming her own into her coat pockets. Several cars were driving by, even this late, and people were very visible on the sidewalks, taking their evening constitutional. "But as far as it's come in the last little while, I don't think this town is ready for me to walk down the street holding hands with you."

"What are you afraid of?"

"Some jerk coming out of the tavern who's had one too many and taking a swing at you because he thinks he has a right to," Nikki responded readily. "One of your friends spotting us as she drives by and freezing you out of all the organizations you've worked so hard for all these years." She inhaled slowly and painfully. "Never underestimate the small minds of people when they see a chance to make someone else more miserable than they are."

"Aren't you letting the bigots win by acting this way?"

Nikki considered the idea as they turned into the alley by the bookstore. "Maybe," she said finally. "But I also know that a certain amount of tolerance in this town comes from the fact that we don't flaunt anything. It was hard to achieve that much. Why risk losing it just for the sake of holding hands?"

Kate stopped on her doorstep, turning around and gazing at Nikki. "I don't think I agree with you, but you've obviously lived with being gay for a lot longer than I have."

"We still have a lot of things to fight for," Nikki tried to explain but found it difficult when she didn't fully understand the entire situation herself. "I guess it's a matter of picking your spots. You strike a blow for holding hands when you've won all the other, larger issues."

Kate studied her, then reached out and cupped Nikki's cheek in her gloved hand, leaning forward to kiss her gently on the lips. "We'll probably need to discuss this issue again. But for now, I'll play it your way."

Nikki nodded unhappily, not feeling that she had won anything with this concession.

Kate hesitated and then kissed her again, more lingeringly. "I'll see you tomorrow."

"Good night, Kate."

Nikki waited until her lover had disappeared into the building before turning to leave. She had a lot to think about as she trudged home under stars that appeared a lot duller without Kate to share them with her.

CHAPTER TWENTY-THREE

Kate opened her eyes as the alarm went off and gazed at the ceiling above her. Inhaling deeply, she could still smell Nikki, not only because she hadn't showered since yesterday, but also because she had slept in her T-shirt. She wondered if she could convince Nikki to let her keep it. If she couldn't have Nikki in the bed with her on a regular basis, then wearing her T-shirt at least offered her a bit of comfort in the night and allowed her to sleep.

Kate had always been amazed when people chose to marry after knowing each other only a few weeks, considering such stories hyperbole or the participants drunk out of their minds. But lying in her lonely bed, wanting Nikki with every molecule of her body, she completely understood such impulsive behavior. She didn't want to spend any time away from her new lover and wished fervently that she could ask her to move in. Even as she thought it, however, she knew it was way too soon, and that Nikki would probably not agree.

But oh, how it ached to wake up without Nikki next to her, and the hours that remained before she would see her again seemed to lie before her like a gray desert, an empty space of time that she had to endure. Never had her apartment seemed so sterile and empty, never had it seemed so incredibly lonely, and she had to exert an effort to roll out of bed and pull off the T-shirt.

Kate tucked it under her pillow, managing a brief smile as she glanced at the small teddy bear on her nightstand. She felt like a teenager, finally comprehending all those inane gestures people in love were so famous for. Previously she considered herself beyond them, far too mature to indulge in such silliness, but she was realizing she had merely avoided falling in love. *Poor David. Did he love me like this? What a pitiful return he received for his emotion if he did.*

Strolling into the bathroom, Kate started the shower and then noticed her solitary toothbrush in the holder looked somewhat worn. Frowning, she opened the vanity drawer, relieved to find two more still in their packages. She selected one for herself, replacing the old one, and then placed the other carefully on the sink on the off chance a certain someone might require it the next morning. Smiling, she slipped under the shower, feeling better about her day as she washed her hair and luxuriated under the hot water for a sinfully long time.

Dressed in black trousers and a teal green blouse, she had a bagel with cream cheese and coffee before returning to the bathroom to make up her face. Kate was abruptly aware of how many bottles and jars of cosmetics she had scattered over her vanity compared to Nikki's tiny selection and wondered if her need for makeup indicated yet another difference between them. Those differences preyed on her mind as she walked downstairs and began the routine of turning on the lights, bringing up the heat, and transferring the float to the register before unlocking the front doors and starting another day at Novel Companions.

Only a few customers stopped by, and she spent the morning working on the paperwork she had been letting slide since beginning her romance with Nikki. As she studied the legal documents requiring her signature, she realized the fire had occurred only a week ago. So much had happened in such a short time.

The jangle of the bell made her glance up, and she stared in amazement as her ex-husband walked into the store, almost as if thinking of him earlier in the morning had somehow predicated this visit to her store, his first in more than a year. "David?"

"Hello, Kate." He smiled at her as he stood in front of the counter. Of average height, with light brown hair and brown eyes, he had never been particularly well built, but neither was he running to fat now that he had moved into middle age. His second marriage did seem to agree with him, softening the hollows of his face, and Kate was honestly happy to see the contented light shining in his eyes. Whatever else had occurred between them, they had been friends for a very long time. "You're looking extremely well."

"Thank you," she said, slipping off her glasses and placing them on the clipboard, which she slid beneath the counter. "What brings you by?"

He started to speak, looked vaguely uncomfortable, and then

glanced around the store, almost as if he wanted to make sure they were alone. "I'm sorry, Kate," he said finally. "I've just been...well, hearing some rumors around town, and I thought I should probably stop by to see how you are."

She leaned back against the counter. "What kind of rumors?"

He gazed at the bookmark display, his thick fingers tapping the polished wooden surface of the counter. He was obviously finding it difficult to look her in the eye, but they had always tried to be honest with each other during their marriage and even after it. "There's been some talk," he began in a very deliberate tone that she recognized as his way of delivering bad news, "that you've been spending a lot of time in the company of...well, someone who is gay. A lot of people in various circles have taken that to mean that you're probably gay, as well."

"And?"

He frowned. "Isn't that enough?"

"David, I don't really give a damn what people think of me," she said, squaring her shoulders as she slipped off her stool. So it begins, she thought. "At least, not anymore. In any event, what difference does it make if people want to talk?"

"If people are spreading lies—"

"They're not lies," she said evenly, seeing how the words jolted him, but not backing down. The sooner she laid it out there, the sooner they could all get back to their respective lives. "I have no doubt the stories have been exaggerated a great deal, but yes, I've met someone, I've fallen in love, and yes, that person happens to be female. Anything else you want to know?"

He paled, then flushed, and then paled again, the colorful progression somewhat intriguing to Kate, though she rather hoped he wouldn't have a heart attack in the middle of her bookstore. Waiting with a touch of impatience as he slowly adjusted to her news, she tapped her fingers on the counter, unconsciously mimicking him.

"I see." He inhaled deeply. "How long—"

"Not long," she said, recognizing what he was really asking. "Not back while we were married, at any rate. It just sort of happened over the past few months, but I'm not going to deny it. If people have a problem with it...well, it's their problem, David, not mine." She considered him, feeling a muscle twitch briefly in her jaw. "But I was never attracted to women before I met Nikki, though I was never really attracted to men, either. That lack was what probably ended our marriage, but honestly, David, I didn't know until recently."

He inhaled audibly. "You never loved me?" He sounded bleak.

"Not in the way that perhaps you loved me." She wanted him to understand for his own peace of mind. "I loved you dearly as a person and as my friend, David, but I was never in love with you. Unfortunately, I never understood that distinction at the time. For that, I'm truly sorry, because I realize now what you offered me, and what I couldn't return. You deserved better."

He stared at her for a moment before exhaling. "This is kind of a shock, Kate," he said finally. "Maybe it shouldn't be, since we're no longer together, but still..."

She slowly nodded, acknowledging his attempt to comprehend the situation. "I guess I can understand that," she said, not unkindly. "It would probably have shocked me if the person you became involved with after the divorce had been named Eddie rather than Ellen. But this ultimately has nothing to do with you, David. This is my life, and for the first time, I'm living it in a way that perhaps I always should have."

He bent his head to study his hands resting limply on the counter, and she noticed that his hair was thinning on top. "Maybe you're right. Until Ellen, I didn't realize what I was really missing in our marriage, either." He sighed. "What a mess."

"It's old news, David."

"The marriage is, but this isn't. If people have been coming to me to try to dig for information, it's probably all over town by now. You could be facing a bit of difficulty in the future."

She squared her shoulders as she thought of those challenges that lay ahead. "Somehow, I'm not surprised, but again, I'm not too concerned. Give it another month or so, and they'll be talking about something else."

"Michelle Greenwald is going to try to get you kicked out of the golf club."

Kate didn't flicker. "Let her try."

He snorted. "Yeah, that's what I said too. People tend to forget how much clout you really hold in this town. I don't know what the hell Michelle's worried about anyway. No woman in her right mind would want her on a bet."

"Is that what she's up in arms about?" Kate said disbelievingly. "That the next time we're in the locker room together, I'll be unable to resist her 'charms'?"

"There was some mention that she would be afraid to shower in the event that 'others' would be 'checking out her body.'" He smiled ruefully.

Kate laughed out loud. "If anyone checks out her body, it's because it's such a miracle of modern architecture with all the plastic surgery she's had."

"You're being awful, but it's true. You can always find the funny side of any situation." He sobered a little, seeming wistful. "I think that's why I married you. I thought it was a good marriage, at least until the matter of kids came up. Were you so very unhappy all that time, Kate?"

"Not at all, David." She grasped his forearm. "I was...there was just something...lacking between us, and maybe I never would have figured out exactly what it was if things hadn't worked out as they did. It's entirely possible that if I had any maternal instinct at all, we'd have gone ahead, had kids, and still be together raising them."

"Of course, you still might have met this girl and realized exactly what it was you were missing," he suggested, surprising her with his prescience, just as he always had. Behind the placid exterior lurked a keen intelligence and a kind heart. She supposed she wouldn't have married him otherwise. "Then where would we all be?"

"God, that would have been awful," she said, taking his conjecture to its inevitable conclusion. She lifted her head, thinking about the possibility. "Let's just be thankful it didn't play out like that. Fortunately, I'm single now and in a position to make my own choices without hurting anyone else."

"Except yourself." He sounded honestly concerned. "Kate, it might not be easy for you. This town is small and, like a lot of small towns, it can be cruel."

"I know, but who said life was easy? Anything that really matters always requires an effort."

"This girl is worth it?" His gentle eyes were steady on hers.

Kate lifted her chin. "Oh, yes, she's worth it."

He continued to regard her and then grinned. "Well, I certainly wouldn't want to be the one who tried to get in your way." He straightened his shoulders as if accepting Kate's new status. "I can't say I completely understand this, Kate, because I don't, but I wish you the best. You've been a good friend and a class act since the moment I met you in junior high. I hope this girl realizes what a special person she's getting."

"Thank you," she said, pleased by the compliment. "I also want to thank you for coming over and...well, warning me."

"I still care about you, Kate. Regardless of what happened between us, there's a part of me that always will. You're still the girl who kept me from being a complete loser in high school, and the one person who believed in me when no one else did. The success I achieved in my life was mostly because of you."

"You're a good man, David," she said, squeezing his forearm fondly. "You never needed me."

He patted her hand. "Yes, Kate, I did." He lowered his eyelid in a bit of a wink, a familiar tic that she had grown to know well over the years. "Take care of yourself."

"You, too," she said as she walked him out.

She stood there at the door, gazing out at the street for a long time after he left, considering what he had said and thinking back over her life, over all the steps that had led her to this moment. Wondering where they would lead her in the future.

CHAPTER TWENTY-FOUR

Home at three-thirty, too restless for sedentary pursuits such as surfing the Internet or reading, and finding it too early to go to Kate's for their five o'clock date, Nikki decided to drop by Lynn's accounting office to see if she had discovered anything. Dressed appropriately in layers and sporting a backpack to carry whatever she might require later, she locked the door behind her before she set off on her hike, cutting across the marsh leading to Bible Hill.

It was good to be out in the fresh air, even when it was faintly flavored with car exhaust in the busier parts of town, and she recognized that sometimes she allowed winter to keep her inside too much. She really had to fight against hiding from the cold weather. Every so often, she entertained the notion that she would do much better in a more southern climate, one that was warm all year round, yet the thought of leaving Canada always caused a twinge within her. Of course, now that Kate was in her life, Nikki wasn't about to move anywhere.

Her thoughts kept returning to the mystery of Sam Madison's murder. It was a change from thinking of Kate all the time, and not necessarily an improvement, but unquestionably the events of the past week had profoundly altered her life.

If Katherine Rushton had murdered her business partner, discovering the proof would provide Nikki with a sense of accomplishment, something she had lacked lately. One of the most insidious things about being in a dead-end job, particularly in winter, was the ennui that arose, the sense of each day running into the next, of feeling time pass and not knowing where it was going. If she couldn't find a better job, then at least pursuing the mystery of Sam's death, as much as she could in her amateur fashion, provided her with direction and purpose. She needed those to feel useful, to feel worthy of being with Kate, of being someone she would find attractive.

Yet for all the evidence slowly being gathered on Rushton, Nikki harbored a tiny doubt. She couldn't forget that look of fear in the woman's eyes when she'd faced her in the police station the day before, and while she did believe that Rushton had switched the guns she and Kate had discovered in Edwards House, was that because the first one had been used in a murder? Or was it because someone had planted it on her, she panicked, and then switched it so as not to be implicated?

Or am I just making things unnecessarily complicated? Nikki obviously needed more information before she could formulate any real conclusions. Hopefully, Lynn had made some subtle inquiries into Mosaic Estates and found out exactly what Sam and Katherine Rushton had been up to.

Kim and Lynn's modest home sat on the top of one of the higher hills surrounding Truro, and Nikki was puffing slightly as she finally crested it and strode along the sidewalk leading to the house. Crossing the yard that had been cleared for parking, she greeted their dog, a small brown animal of undetermined breeding, before ascending the short flight of wooden stairs. Lynn's office had once been a second bedroom they had remodeled, deciding that the cost of doing so was cheaper than continuing to pay rent downtown.

Lynn was just finishing up with a client, so Nikki slipped her backpack off and placed it on the floor before quietly taking a chair in the tiny waiting area, flipping through a magazine about computers until he left.

"Any news?" she asked, wasting no time as she hurried around the small partition which had been set up to provide a bit of privacy. This was tax season, Lynn's busiest time, and Nikki was fortunate to have caught her during a bit of a slow period. Since the phone could ring or another client could come in at any second, she was determined to take full advantage of the brief time she had.

Lynn pulled out a file. "Nothing anyone would admit to knowing," she said, equally concise. "But from what I've picked up from scuttlebutt, Sam and Katherine created Mosaic Estates to buy up Edwards House and all the land surrounding it."

"Why?"

"Apparently, they were thinking of creating some vacation resort, renovating Edwards House into a hotel, and using the rest for a recreational area."

"Who'd want to build out there?" Nikki glanced at the notes Lynn had collected. "There's nothing around."

"Ah, but there is." Lynn tapped a finger on the topographical map that she had probably retrieved from her friends at town hall. "A lake in the woods next to the Edwards House, right in the middle of the Gilles property, undoubtedly full of fly fishing and resort potential. I don't think a lot of people knew about it. It isn't accessible from the road, and certainly, old man Gilles never let on it existed."

Nikki regarded the map with interest. "So what went wrong? Sounds like a good deal so far."

"Gilles moved to Florida, did you know that?"

"Yeah." Nikki eyed her curiously. "He won the lottery, didn't he?"

Lynn spread out her hands. "That's the story that went around, but I don't think so. I think he charged an arm and a leg for his lake. That was the property that counted, after all, since it had the prize on it." She leaned closer, lowering her voice confidentially, though no one else was in the office. "I think Sam made a mistake and bought up all the other land first, which tipped off the old man, and he refused to sell out for a reasonable price. Without the lake, the whole deal wasn't worth anything. I think Mosaic Estates paid up to five times what the land was actually worth, rather than let the whole thing fall through."

"So they overextended themselves?"

Lynn nodded in apparent agreement. "It sounds like it. I don't have anything concrete, of course. I'm only repeating what the innuendo in financial circles has indicated."

"If Rushton had already used up a lot of the other money renovating the hotel," Nikki said slowly, thinking out loud, "they might have got caught short, but it isn't illegal to overextend, is it?"

Lynn lifted a dark brow. "Depends on where and how they got the money to set the deal up in the first place, or how they tried to cover the bills later." She closed the file and gave it to Nikki. "I don't know anything about that, and even if somehow I found out, I'd be ethically obligated not to pass it on. It would be privileged financial information."

Nikki propped her chin on her palm. "Okay, fair enough. Speaking hypothetically, how would one go about finding out if they started doing illegal stuff to cover this deal?"

"Paper trail," Lynn said. "Follow the paper trail, and it will usually lead you to all the messy details."

Nikki frowned. "Kate would understand that better than I would."

"Wow, ten whole minutes before her name came up. Is the honeymoon finally over?" Lynn grinned.

"No, I was trying to discipline myself."

"It didn't work."

"Is this all you have?" Nikki ignored the teasing.

Lynn spread her hands. "That's all I could get on the company. I'll keep my eyes and ears open, of course, but that's probably all that's available without potentially stirring up legal problems."

Nikki certainly didn't want Lynn to get into trouble. "This is fine." The door opened behind her, and she realized that her time between appointments had just run out. She flashed Lynn a smile and stuffed the file into her backpack. "See you later."

"Call us when you get a chance," Lynn said, already concentrating on her next client.

Nikki took a deep breath of cold air as she stepped outside, slinging the bag over her back. As she shifted her shoulders to settle it into place, she felt a few twinges in her calves, indicating that she had probably overdone it after a winter of sloughing off. She stretched a few times to loosen up and set off again, grateful that the return trip was mostly downhill, including one stretch of rarely traveled road that didn't even have a sidewalk, only a graveled shoulder that had fortunately been plowed back to the ditch.

While she walked along it, she worried the information she had received like a puppy with a bone, trying it from all angles in an effort to force it all to make sense. She wondered if Sam and Katherine had a falling-out over the way the deal had gone flat. Certainly all the money Rushton had poured into the Edwards House had probably affected their cash flow, perhaps at a particularly crucial time.

The blare of a car horn abruptly jolted her out of her thoughts. Startled, she half turned, horrified to catch a glimpse of a dark bulk bearing down on her from the otherwise empty street. She leapt for the nearest ditch, plunging into the wet snow filling it. The icy cold went down the back of her neck and up under her coat as she floundered around, thoroughly soaking herself. Unbalanced by the weight of the pack on her back, she finally struggled upright and stared breathlessly after the car that squealed around the corner and sped up Willis Avenue. It was already too far away for her to see the license plate, but she easily recognized the dark-colored Lexus.

Nikki studied the snow on the side of the street and noted that the tracks, which came so perilously close to her footprints, indicated studded tires...undoubtedly the same ones that managed to traverse a long driveway during a blizzard in order to secrete a weapon in the false bottom of a desk drawer. Taking a deep breath, she hefted her pack and started down the road again, constantly alert to her surroundings and quick to glance around whenever she heard a car approach.

CHAPTER TWENTY-FIVE

Kate felt the ripple of sensation settle into her stomach as Nikki entered the store, and she wondered if this intense reaction to the sight of her lover would ever ease. She supposed it would over time, but for the moment, she cherished the feeling, nurturing it like a fragile plant. Fully engaged at the moment, Kate could do little but offer her a brief smile in passing, which Nikki acknowledged with a nod before Kate focused her attention back on the customer making his purchase.

By the time she had finished and the man had exited, Nikki was not in the main part of the store. A glance at the security mirror revealed that she had wandered into the rear to check out the used books...just as if this was any other Wednesday. Smiling fondly, Kate made sure there were no other customers and moved over to lean in the doorway, observing Nikki as she scanned the mysteries displayed on the shelves. "Do you need any help?" she asked, purposely dropping her tone into a husky, sensual trill.

Nikki started briefly and then managed a wan grin at the invitation implicit in Kate's voice. "Maybe later."

Kate immediately sobered. "What's wrong?"

"Nothing." Nikki looked away.

"I don't believe you. Tell me."

Nikki hesitated before taking a quick breath. "A car almost hit me this afternoon."

"What?" Kate strode over to her, grasped her by the arms, and examined her intently before she quite realized what she was doing. Nikki remained still as Kate assured herself that her lover was unscathed. Kate had a sick feeling in her chest, a sense of absolute terror that anything could take Nikki away from her so quickly and easily.

"It missed me. I don't think they were really trying to hit me... probably just scare me a little bit." Her azure eyes were somber. "It looked a lot like the car belonging to Katherine Rushton."

Horrified, Kate stared at her. Then, without another word, she strode purposely out into the front part of the store and snatched up the phone, punching in numbers with cold fury.

"Sandy, give me Rick Johnson. I want to speak to him right now." She was peripherally aware that Nikki had followed her and now stood regarding her, eyes wide. As soon as Rick came on the line, she was all over him. "This has gone on long enough," she snapped. "I want Katherine Rushton arrested immediately. She just tried to run down Nikki in broad daylight. What the hell kind of department are you running there?"

After a pause Rick inhaled, his breath a rush in her ear. "Is Nikki all right?"

"She appears to be, but she's white as a ghost and shaking like a leaf. Damn it, I want this woman stopped, Rick." It was not a plea for help, it was an order, issued in a tone that few people cared to argue with. Kate didn't use it often, but when she did, people jumped. Well, she thought, most people did.

Rick merely sighed. "Is Nikki there with you now? Let me talk to her."

Still riding the wave of outrage and fear for her lover, Kate hesitated, glancing at Nikki. "He wants to speak to you. Are you all right with that?"

Nikki nodded and held out her hand.

Again Kate hesitated, wanting to protect her, but finally handed over the phone.

"Hi, Rick," Nikki said calmly, just as if he had called her up to ask about the weather.

Kate could hear only her lover's side of the conversation, but it seemed to her that everyone was taking this whole situation just a little too casually, which heightened her sense of dismay.

"I was walking down College Road after visiting my friend Lynn, and a car nearly sideswiped me."

There was a pause, during which she was obviously listening to a question.

"It's possible, but the street was dry, Rick, without any ice on it at all. In any event, whoever it was didn't bother to slow down to see if they hit me or not. By the time I crawled out of the ditch, they were burning rubber up Willis Avenue. … It looked a lot like the car belonging to Katherine Rushton, Rick. In fact, that was my first thought." She scratched her head. "No, I didn't see the driver because the windows were tinted, but I'm sure I recognized the car." She looked surprised. "Really? Isn't that interesting?"

Nikki listened a few seconds longer, then handed the phone to Kate.

"What are you going to do about this, Rick?" Kate demanded, not waiting for him to say anything.

"I'm going to have a talk with Miss Rushton. But you should know that she reported her car stolen earlier this morning, long before this occurred."

"She's covering her tracks."

"Maybe. In the meantime, I want you to take it easy and let me handle it."

"You're doing such a wonderful job so far," she snapped icily.

Kate subconsciously realized he kept a rein on his first response.

"I know this scared you, Kate," he said, not unkindly, "but you won't do anyone any good by losing your temper."

"I want this stopped, Rick," she demanded again before hanging up. She turned to look at Nikki, taking deep, measured breaths.

"Kate, are you all right?"

"No, I am *not* all right. I'm not all right at all. I can't bear the thought of anything happening to you."

Nikki shrugged. "Nothing did. To be honest, I'm not sure anything was intended to. Whoever it was blew hard on the horn before they took a run at me, giving me plenty of time to turn around and get out of the way. I think they were only trying to scare me...and let me get a good look at the car."

Kate felt her mouth tighten, anger and fright warring for supremacy within her. "What do you mean 'whoever'? It was Katherine Rushton."

"It was her car. But the sun was reflecting off the windshield so I didn't get a good look at the driver. Besides, the windows are tinted."

"Who else could it be?"

Nikki shrugged. "That's the question, isn't it? Who else would want Sam dead? Better still, who would want to frame Rushton for his murder?"

Kate was astonished. "You can't be serious."

"I'm not saying it isn't her. Just that for a smart woman, it's pretty dumb to try a half-assed hit-and-run like this on someone who honestly doesn't know anything more than the cops already do, and probably a hell of a lot less."

"Maybe," Kate said, not convinced, "or maybe she thought that reporting her car stolen would give her an alibi before the fact."

Nikki seemed to consider her point. "Maybe you're right."

Kate exhaled slowly, apparently still upset.

Moving closer, Nikki squeezed her arms gently. "I'm fine."

Kate lowered her head, swallowing hard at the lump that had abruptly appeared in her throat. "All right."

Suddenly she began to tremble. Nikki enfolded her into a warm embrace, murmuring "It's all right," as she rubbed her back soothingly.

Kate took a moment to compose herself, surrendering to the sanctuary of the strong hug, allowing it to warm and comfort her. "Don't do this again," she whispered.

Nikki held her closer. "I won't."

Finally, Kate drew back, checking the time. "It's past five. Let me close down, and then I'll make that dinner I promised you."

"Can I help?"

Recognizing Nikki's honest need to contribute, Kate retrieved the clipboard and some other files from behind the counter and handed them to her. "Could you take these upstairs for me? Put them on my desk. I'll be up in a minute."

While Nikki obeyed, Kate went over and locked the door. Shutting the blinds before she transferred the float from the register to the safe, she discovered she was glaring out at the street, as if expecting someone to try for her lover again.

Turning out the lights, she headed upstairs where she felt a twinge when she saw Nikki sitting uncertainly on a stool at the breakfast bar, not even taking the opportunity to explore the apartment. Obviously, her near miss with the vehicle had sobered her considerably. Not that Kate blamed her in any way. She still felt a little sick when she thought about it. "Darling?" she asked, putting her arms around Nikki's waist and hugging her tightly.

Nikki managed a wan smile. "Maybe I *am* a little shaken by what happened. I'm sorry. I know you planned a big evening for us, but would you mind if we did it some other night? I'm not feeling particularly... romantic at the moment."

"We can have our romantic dinner any time," Kate told her gently, "but I certainly don't want you to go...unless you really want to?"

"No," Nikki said in a small voice, resting her head on Kate's shoulder. "I don't want to leave."

"Then don't," Kate whispered, holding her protectively. "Let's just have a quiet evening in. I'll make something light, and we can relax, maybe watch a little TV, talk a bit." She tenderly kissed Nikki on the temple. "Then we can go to bed and fall asleep in each other's arms."

"Hmm, that sounds perfect." Nikki nuzzled into the hollow of Kate's neck and shoulder.

Kate closed her eyes and hung on, feeling the tremors finally subside. It was clear to her from her reaction to Nikki's close call, this was no passing infatuation. The thought of anything happening to Nikki absolutely devastated her, and the need to protect her, to keep her safe, not only from freak instances such as this, but from all the hatred in the world, was so strong it was difficult for her to breathe freely.

Nikki seemed to sense Kate's disturbance, and she hugged her again. "Everything's all right."

"I know." She smiled suddenly. "Have you noticed that we keep taking turns reassuring each other?"

Nikki chuckled lightly and drew back, her blue eyes warm as she regarded Kate. "Isn't that what partners are supposed to do? Lean on each other when the going gets tough?"

Kate felt her heart give an extra thump. "Yes, it is. That's exactly what partners do." She gazed at her lover for another moment and then reluctantly released her to maneuver around the breakfast bar into the kitchen. Looking in her fridge, she tried to figure out what would be quick and easy to make. "I have some leftover turkey. Would you like a sandwich?"

"Do you have any rice chips? Or potato chips?"

"Uh, let me check." Kate searched her cupboards and the pantry, finally finding an unopened bag near the back left over from Christmas. The expiration date had passed, but since it hadn't been opened, she didn't think they had gone stale. "Here we go." She glanced over at Nikki. "I wouldn't have pegged you for junk food."

"I have my moments," she admitted. "In this case, it's the sandwiches. If we're not having soup with them, then I have to have chips. It's a quirk left over from when I was a kid."

Kate laughed. "I get it," she said, tossing the bag on the counter. "I need to have milk whenever I have donuts."

When Kate returned to the fridge, fortunately she found some lettuce left in the crisper, not too limp, and some mayonnaise, along with some green pepper and onion. Rather than bread, she chose some steak sandwich buns, preferring them for this sort of meal.

"Can I do anything?" Nikki peered over the breakfast bar.

"Would you slice up a pepper for me?" Kate asked, wanting her to feel at home.

Nikki obligingly came around the breakfast bar, washing her hands before joining Kate at her cutting board. For the next little while, they shared the same sense of domestic comfort they had at Nikki's place the night before. In some ways, this was a more important sensation to Kate than the searing flash of desire and attraction she felt every time she saw Nikki. The sheer intensity would fade, she knew, but the sense of companionship, the natural ease she felt in her presence, was what made up the substance of their relationship.

After they had made the sandwiches, Kate filled a bowl with potato chips and, with Nikki's assistance, carried them out to the table. Nikki poured herself a glass of milk without having to ask where things were and then looked inquiringly at Kate.

"Juice," she said, smiling as she saw Nikki retrieve another glass from the cupboard and pull the bottle of grape juice from the fridge. There might have been a twinge of territoriality within Kate, a small sense of having her space invaded by an intruder, but overpowering that was a stronger sense of things being absolutely right with Nikki moving so comfortably in the kitchen.

It occurred to Kate that her apartment no longer seemed sterile or cold. Instead, it felt like home, and that was a sensation that she didn't intend to give up any time in the near future, regardless of who tried to take it away from her, be it ignorant townsfolk or a killer who was trying to avoid being brought to justice.

CHAPTER TWENTY-SIX

Snuggled up on the sofa with music playing softly in the background, Nikki felt her lingering sense of uncertainty finally dissipate. Kate was leaning back in her arms, her head resting on her shoulder, her body a warm comfort against her. The sheer bliss of physical contact overrode her fear and shock over the earlier incident. Nikki brushed her lips over the curve of the delicate ear next to her mouth. "This is nice."

"It is," Kate agreed lazily. "You and I haven't had much chance just to sit back and contemplate everything that's been going on." She turned her head slightly, rubbing her temple against Nikki's chin. "Not with Sam's death, I mean. About us, and where we're going from here."

Nikki drew her closer, kissing her ear again. "Where *do* you see us going from here?"

"Much as we are, growing closer the more we get to know each other." Kate hesitated. "Eventually living together."

Nikki laughed before she could stop herself.

"What?" Kate's voice held a touch of pique.

"What does a lesbian take on a second date?"

Kate turned her head, a baffled expression on her face. "I don't know."

"A U-Haul." Then, as Kate still looked baffled, Nikki leaned forward and kissed her on the jaw. "It's a joke. Everyone feels that temptation to move in with each other immediately. It's really strong in the beginning. Maybe it's because women are nesters by nature and expect it from each other as well."

"So you feel it, too," Kate said, a little relief in her voice.

"Oh yes. I want to go to bed with you every night, wake up in your arms every morning, and spend every spare second in between with you."

"But it's not practical." Kate sighed slightly.

"No, it's not." Nikki hugged her. "That's not to say that some relationships don't work out when the women move in together quickly, but they're few and far between. Living together is a huge step, and it can make or break a relationship. I'd like to take time to make sure ours is strong before we start thinking about living together." She kissed the side of Kate's head. "With us, it might take a while because we're such different people."

Kate entwined her fingers with Nikki's where their hands rested on her stomach. "What's the biggest difference between us?" she asked, almost as if she were afraid of the response.

Nikki suddenly sensed that this was an interesting moment for them. She could gloss over it, indulge in inconsequential talk that would leave it unacknowledged, or she could take the opportunity to be completely honest and reveal her deepest fear right away. It might be too soon, possibly even scare Kate away, but on the other hand, it was an issue they would have to address sooner or later.

"The whole straight/gay thing," Nikki said finally. "I knew when I was young that this was who I was and just sort of accepted it, even if I didn't do much about it while my parents held the reins. But you've been straight most of your life, Kate. It's not easy being different. You might eventually decide that it's not worth it, no matter how much you care for me."

Kate was silent, obviously recognizing that Nikki was prepared to reveal things about herself this night that perhaps she hadn't expected. But when she finally responded, Nikki was astonished at how she had ferreted out the real truth of the statement.

"I think you're less afraid I'll reject the 'lifestyle,'" Kate said gently, "than you are that I'll decide somewhere down the road that it's men I really want...that I'll hurt you exactly the same way that Anne did."

Nikki felt her heart catch and whispered, "Yes."

"I'm not Anne." Kate turned so that she could look at Nikki. "But I also know it's not easy for you to accept that fact so soon in our relationship. Even if you know it in your head, a part of your heart will hang back and wait to be proved wrong. It might take a long time to convince that part of you."

Ashamed, Nikki bowed her head. "I'm sorry."

"Don't be, Nikki. I'm not going to change my mind, nor am I about to stop loving you. Of course you're wary. But when it becomes really bad for you, when you're feeling especially vulnerable, please tell me so that we can try to figure out a way past it together."

"I promise." Kate's understanding touched Nikki profoundly. "What about you? Does anything frighten you about this?" She raised her head. "You'll probably come across some cruel and harsh things in the future. It's not going to be easy to love me in this town...not openly."

"I'm aware of that. My ex-husband dropped by today to let me know people are already talking about me and making value judgments on my life that are absolutely none of their concern."

Nikki felt sick, knowing that this type of reaction was inevitable, but disappointed that it was happening so soon. "I'm sorry," she repeated, blinking against the tears stinging her eyes. "Was he very unpleasant to you?"

Kate shook her head. "Not at all. He was just worried about me." She sat up so that she could turn to regard Nikki face to face, her intense bluish gray eyes studying her carefully. "Why would you think he'd be unpleasant to me?"

Nikki felt off balance. "I've heard a lot of men don't like it when they find out that the women they've been involved with actually prefer women. I figured he'd be the same."

"David's a very kind and compassionate man. Honestly, Nikki, would I have married anyone who wasn't decent and honorable? More importantly, if I had, what would that say about me? How could I trust my judgment about you if my judgment about him was so flawed?"

"I hadn't thought about it like that," Nikki said. "I guess I'm just so used to hearing horror stories from other lesbians about the men they married in their effort to be straight that I just assumed that...well, that you had the same experience."

"I suppose I can understand that, but it's not what happened. I married David because I loved him, and he was the best man I had ever met. In a lot of ways, he still is."

Nikki didn't like to hear this assessment but accepted it as Kate's view of the situation.

"Would you prefer if he were an obnoxious Neanderthal who came by to spout religious text about why I was now on a one-way trip to hell for my choice in lovers?"

Nikki squirmed. "I think...it bothers me that you're so complimentary about him," she said, deciding that since they were being perfectly honest, she would reveal exactly what was on her mind.

"Ah," Kate said in that already familiar way of hers, a sort of verbal pause to gather her thoughts. Her expression gentled. "You're worrying that I'll change my mind about loving a woman...that if I care for David so much, it might mean that I can't care for you."

Nikki nodded, close to tears, and Kate leaned forward and kissed her.

"I am who I am, Nikki. I don't know how to be anything else. I wasn't always comfortable in my skin when I was married to David, and that's probably why we divorced, regardless of the issue of children. I do feel comfortable in my skin with you, but I'm not always going to feel at ease with all the things about 'being gay' that you probably take for granted. It may seem like I'm disagreeing with 'the lifestyle' at times, but it has nothing to do with how I feel for you."

"All right," Nikki said, wanting to believe Kate more than anything else in her life. "It's still not going to be easy for us."

Kate lifted her expressive brows. "Probably not, but nothing worth having ever comes easy, darling. Loving someone, maybe. But staying with them, getting past the obstacles? That's the true test. Have you forgotten what you told me? That how we deal with the problems we face will determine what our relationship will be?"

"No. I haven't forgotten."

"As long as we talk things out, then you and I will be able to find a way through all the landmines other people want to plant in front of us."

"You've been thinking a lot about this."

"A little. Definitely since speaking with David this morning." Kate tilted her head, her features altering slightly as her smile dimmed a little. "You know, being considered 'gay' isn't really what worries me."

Nikki stroked Kate's cheek with her fingertips. "What does?"

"The fact that you're twenty-six. I'm forty. How long before you want someone your own age, someone who can share the things with you that I can't?"

Astonished, Nikki stared at her. "The age difference doesn't matter," she said in complete honesty. She took a breath, knowing she had to be as calm and as rational in diminishing Kate's fears as her lover had been in helping her. "Kate, you're probably the most beautiful woman I've ever met. I'm not looking for a mother figure. I have a mother, and we get along fine for the most part. And I'm not looking for someone to think for me. Otherwise, I doubt I would be very attractive to you in the first place. I kept coming into your store not necessarily because I wanted you physically, but because our talks stimulated and intrigued me. That need to be with you knows no age boundaries." She hesitated. "Do you think I'm too young to hold your interest once the passion wears off?"

"God, no," Kate said, faltering as she was forced to look at the other side. "I just...I don't want to ever hold you back."

"You won't," Nikki said with conviction. "But I guess you'll worry about it, just like I'll worry that your loving me will hurt everything you've worked so hard to accomplish." She took a breath. "We'll just have to deal with all these things when and if they happen. We can spend all night thinking up potential problems. In the end, it comes down to whether the end result is worth the effort. I believe it is."

"I believe it is, too." Kate smiled, her eyes shading to blue, a clear light color that Nikki now associated with happiness. "You know, for a kid, you're pretty smart."

"For a straight chick, you are, too," she countered. It was as if, by being able to joke about their fears, they shrank and became more manageable.

Kate leaned closer and kissed Nikki, gently at first, then with more demand. "I'm sorry," she said, drawing back. "I know you aren't in the mood."

"I'm quickly changing my mind," Nikki murmured, pulling her closer and kissing her insistently, feeling her own desire rise quickly. She ran her hands under Kate's silken teal blouse, feeling her lover tremble as she touched the warm skin of her abdomen and sides. "You're so beautiful."

"In your eyes," Kate whispered. "That's all that matters."

Carefully, Nikki unbuttoned the blouse as Kate leaned back, straddling her hips. Their eyes locked as Nikki slipped the blouse off the smooth shoulders, letting it fall to the sofa, then slipped her fingers underneath the bra straps and pulled them down. She loved the convenience of the front fastener, and she broke off her gaze with Kate to look as she opened the bra slowly, her mouth going dry at the sight of the small breasts.

"Beautiful," she said again, drawing her fingers lightly over them.

Kate shivered. "If you only knew what that does to me. No one's ever made me feel this way, Nikki."

Reassured, Nikki used her mouth on the swells, enjoying the soft sounds of delight that issued from Kate, inflamed by the way the velvet tips hardened beneath her lips, how Kate wrapped her arms around her head and held her to her chest. It was slightly difficult to breathe, being hugged so tightly, but it was exciting as well, knowing how much pleasure she was providing her lover.

"Let's go in the bedroom," Kate urged, drawing away.

Requiring little convincing, Nikki rose from the sofa, pausing briefly as Kate switched off the stereo, and then followed her into the bedroom. She had never been in this room, and like the rest it was decorated with antiques and feminine touches. The tiny teddy bear sitting on the nightstand didn't look at all out of place, and Nikki smiled as she saw it. She was even more amused as Kate drew back the covers to reveal a familiar garment tucked beneath the pillow. "You slept in it?" She nodded at the T-shirt.

"You realize, of course, that you're never getting it back," Kate said as she turned around.

Nikki rested her hands lightly on her lover's waist and gazed at her. "I'm glad I didn't give you my favorite shirt, then."

"Which one is your favorite?" Kate asked, slipping Nikki's sweatshirt off, along with her bra, her hands warm and gentle as they stroked Nikki's body.

"The black one." Nikki unbuttoned Kate's trousers and pushed them, along with her underwear, over her hips and down her legs.

"Ah, the one that's too small and shows everything you have?" Kate asked, stepping lightly out of the clothing crumpled around her feet. She tugged at Nikki's jeans, having a little more difficulty removing them than Nikki had found with her garments, but persisting nonetheless.

"You noticed?" Nikki said, pleased, as both of them finally crawled into the large bed where they settled into the center, side by side, hands exploring avidly, immediately seeking out the places on each other they had learned provided the most pleasure.

"You were wearing it the first day you walked into the store," Kate said huskily. "How could I not? It might just be my favorite of all your shirts as well."

"I'll remember that. I'll wear it for you on our next date."

"When might that be?" Kate laughed, a little shakily, Nikki noticed, as she stroked Kate lightly between her legs.

"Soon," Nikki promised, leaning close to capture her lover's mouth in a searing kiss. "Very, very soon." She kissed her again and then nibbled a line along her jaw. "Lie back."

She urged Kate down onto the mattress. Kate didn't resist, taking a shuddering breath and offering no objection as Nikki kissed down her throat and over her chest.

Nikki smiled briefly as she bent over her lover, brushing her lips over the soft texture of Kate's right nipple. Licking it gently, she was rewarded by a quiet gasp and an even deeper moan when she closed her lips around it and sucked lightly. Kate tangled her fingers in Nikki's short, blond hair, holding her lover's head to her as Nikki paid worshipful attention to her breasts, alternating back and forth between them in an effort to make sure neither felt neglected.

After several lovely moments, as Kate expressed her appreciation with a series of throaty whimpers and moans, Nikki resumed her meandering trail down the compact body, brushing her lips over the slight swell of stomach and nuzzling gently in the thin thatch of auburn hair. Kate shifted and groaned, spreading her legs in open invitation that Nikki wasn't slow in accepting. Settling comfortably on her belly between the smooth thighs, Nikki glanced at the treasure offered, grateful that they had not turned off the bedside lamp and prevented her from seeing the delicate shades of pink, glistening with the moisture her attentions had inspired.

Kate's scent was ripe and womanly, heady in its richness, and Nikki inhaled deeply before lowering her head and extending the tip of her tongue, drawing lightly along the tiny erection of flesh, tracing its outline with careful precision.

"Nikki…" The name was a whispered benediction, utter adoration wrapped up in a single word of aching desire.

Nikki smiled again and leaned closer, sinking her mouth happily into the moist folds as Kate's thighs closed about her ears and her fingers raked through Nikki's hair, urging and loving at the same time. She loved how Kate tasted; the warm, musky flavor of her was better than the finest of wines, and she drank deeply. Her tongue never ceased laving the sensitive ridge, and before long, Kate was shuddering beneath her, a soft rush of additional moisture and a single, incoherent cry giving evidence of the deep pleasure she felt as she peaked.

Nikki offered a few final kisses to the over-stimulated flesh, making Kate twitch helplessly, before kissing her way back up the sated body, to be welcomed into loving arms and a woman thoroughly intent on paying back tenfold every bit of pleasure she'd been granted.

CHAPTER TWENTY-SEVEN

S upremely content, Kate turned off the light. As she settled back onto the pillows, she felt Nikki wrap around her from behind and thought it was impossible to feel any more satisfied and fulfilled than she did. She sighed contentedly as she snuggled back against the warm embrace. "Happy?"

"Ecstatic. This is a *really* nice bed."

Kate laughed. "With no one to share it, comfort was the only thing I had in mind when I bought it."

"Well, I like it a lot, but I don't think I could ever buy one."

Kate felt a tiny uncertainty, aware of the difference in their financial situation, wondering if Nikki felt it too. They hadn't discussed it earlier, and she wondered if they should have. "It wasn't that expensive," she said, though she realized it probably would be for Nikki,

"I wasn't referring to the cost. Just that I could never find another one that came with what I like most about it."

"What's that?"

"A sheet warmer that also knows how to make a killer turkey sandwich."

Caught, Kate nudged Nikki's ribs with her elbow as she laughed. "Fiend."

"I am, aren't I? But you love me anyway."

"Totally." Kate yawned, the day and the exertion of their lovemaking catching up to her. "I also love having you spend the night."

"Hmm, I love being here," Nikki said, pressing against her. "There's something special about being able to wake up in your arms." The quiet of darkness surrounded them like a warm shroud. A passing car hummed softly on the street outside. Suddenly Nikki asked, "What time did you go to bed last Wednesday night?"

Kate forced herself awake. "Around nine-thirty. I read for about an hour, until I couldn't stay awake any longer."

"So you were asleep by ten-thirty or eleven?"

"Hmm, I'm not sure." Kate wondered at Nikki's interest. She sounded as if she had a specific purpose in mind. "Probably. Why?"

"You don't really notice the sound of cars, do you? I mean, cars go by all night on Prince Street. After awhile, you'd have to tune them out to get any sleep at all."

"I suppose so."

Nikki hugged her lover closer. "Is it possible that Rushton did drive away around eleven-thirty, and another car parked there afterward? That a second car is what you heard when it drove away?"

"Ah," Kate said, realizing where this was going now. "It's possible."

"Then maybe Rushton *is* telling the truth."

Kate felt a touch of annoyance. "Maybe. Or maybe she's lying through her teeth. Who else would want to kill Sam?"

"His wife?"

That statement woke Kate fully and she sat up, turning to Nikki in the darkness. Unable to make out anything, she reached over and switched on the light, blinking painfully as her eyes adjusted. When she could see again, she noticed that Nikki looked absolutely delightful tangled in the bed linens, blinking as well in the sudden illumination. "Margaret?" She considered it. "I don't think so."

"Why not?"

"Because...well, what possible reason would she have?"

"Sam lost all their money on a bad deal," Nikki suggested. "Or maybe it's a little closer to home than that."

"Such as?"

"Maybe Sam's affair with Rushton wasn't just an affair. Maybe this time, it was for real, and he wasn't going to come back to her."

"Where on earth are you getting all this?"

"The card," Nikki said, rising up on her elbow and staring seriously at her lover. "The one that started all this."

"Rushton said the weekend at the Keltic Lodge didn't mean anything to either of them."

"So?" Nikki made a face. "She didn't even admit it happened until she was pinned down. I just can't help but remember that Sam signed it with all his love."

Kate snorted. "That doesn't indicate anything significant."

"Maybe not, or maybe it means everything."

Kate stared at her and then shook her head. "I don't know. It's pretty flimsy. Margaret might have loved her husband enough to do anything to keep him, but she's always been such a cold fish that it just doesn't fit."

"Really?" Nikki regarded her speculatively. "How well do you know Margaret?"

"Not that well," Kate said, horrified by the implication in Nikki's voice. "Certainly not well enough to grill her about her marriage."

Nikki sighed. "Too bad. We'll have to tackle it another way."

Kate crossed her arms over her chest. "We don't have to tackle it at all. Or have you forgotten what almost happened to you today?"

"We're already in this, Kate. If someone's going to take a run at me, I'd rather be doing something about it than stay out of it and be a target anyway."

Kate wanted to refute Nikki's logic but couldn't. She thought she should be able to see a way around her argument, but perhaps it was too late in the evening, or perhaps it was too difficult to disagree with Nikki when she was lying there all soft and mussed from their lovemaking, with golden hair and the brilliant eyes that regarded her with the innocent sensuality of a goddess. "Damn," she said, frustrated. It was beginning to occur to her that she could refuse Nikki very little.

Nikki, unsure what had prompted the curse, smiled slightly anyway. She reached out, coaxing Kate down beside her. "Let's sleep on it. Things always look better in the morning."

"I doubt that," Kate said, but she allowed her lover to embrace her, freeing a hand briefly to switch off the light again. Ensconced in comfortable darkness once more, Kate settled into Nikki's arms, surrendering to the sheer pleasure of silky skin and a strong heart beating against hers.

"I know you were scared today," Nikki told her fondly, tucking her under her chin. "I was, too, but sometimes you just have to do what has to be done, no matter the risk."

"I couldn't bear it if anything happened to you," Kate said, but it was hard to muster much debate when she was being held in an embrace so intoxicating.

"So we stop this before anything does. We find out who killed Sam and discover enough evidence so that Rick can arrest them."

"Piece of cake," Kate said sarcastically, not at all reassured by Nikki's quiet laugh or gentle kiss. But despite her disquiet, she was able to fall asleep in her arms, not stirring the entire night.

Waking up was a joy, surrounded by the familiar confines of her bedroom, her lover molded warmly around her. She lay there, basking in the blissful reality of their new life together. She knew Nikki was right about their needing time to know each other better, to be more assured of their relationship, but if she dared, she'd ask her to move in that day, just so she could be sure that she would be able to wake the next morning in the exact same manner.

Nikki woke with a simple intake of breath, snuggling closer. "Good morning."

"Good morning, love. Sleep well?"

"Oh, yes." Nikki kissed her neck. "You?"

"Like a baby."

"I've always wondered about that saying. Babies don't sleep well. They wake up every two hours or so."

Kate chuckled. "Good point. Okay, then, I slept like a log."

"Inaccurate, but more descriptive than the baby analogy."

"Ugh, are you always so precise first thing in the morning?"

"I'm a morning person. You're not?"

"Until I get my first cup of coffee," Kate said, "I'm unbearable."

"Hmm, maybe." Nikki slipped her hands longingly over Kate's body, pressing her back against the mattress. "But you're certainly not untouchable."

"Obviously not."

Nikki moved over her lightly, stroking Kate's hips and thighs as she whispered hotly in her ear. "Now you know why I'm a morning person."

"Does this ever end?" Kate murmured between the sweet kisses that seemed to make every molecule in her body hum with sensation.

"What?" Nikki asked, slipping between her legs where her fingertips did the most amazing things to Kate.

"This incredible desire," Kate whispered. "This need to be with you."

"If we're lucky, never."

"But it can't possibly be this intense forever," Kate said, gasping as she felt Nikki's fingers press against her tenderly, then into her with firm assurance.

"You could be right," Nikki agreed, flexing intimately within her, "so let's enjoy it while it lasts."

"Oh," Kate said, and that was approximately all the coherent conversation she was capable of for the next little while. Later, they showered together and somehow managed to wash between the caresses and kisses that took up far more time than had they showered separately. "Did you bring the stuff you needed?" Kate asked as she toweled her hair dry in the bedroom.

Nikki finished pulling her shirt on over her head. "In my backpack. A few changes of underwear and other things."

Kate opened a drawer in her dresser, scooping out the few clothes she had in it and shoving them in another drawer. "Is this enough room?"

"Plenty." Nikki pulled out some panties from her bag, a few pairs of socks, a pair of sweat pants, and a couple of T-shirts, placing them neatly in the drawer. "Those are mine," she said in a warning tone. "Don't wear them to bed."

Kate laughed and hugged her from behind. "Stay over enough nights and I won't have to."

Nikki turned in the embrace, sobering as she looked down at her. "You really don't mind my leaving some stuff here? I don't want to impose."

"You're not. I want you to feel comfortable here."

Nikki kissed her lightly. "I want you to feel comfortable at my place, too. Is there anything you want me to take back when I leave?"

"Good idea," she said. "I'll give you some things." Kate found some of her lesser-worn casual clothes, some underwear, and a spare pair of jeans. Nikki packed them into her bag before they went to prepare breakfast.

"Can I ask you a question?" Nikki said as they sliced some grapefruit. In the background, the radio, tuned to the local station, played country music interrupted occasionally by the incessantly cheerful morning DJ.

"Of course," Kate said, removing some bagels from the toaster oven.

"Did you...enjoy sex with men?"

"Whew," Kate said, a little breathless. "That's not a breakfast question, love. That's a question asked after several glasses of wine over dinner."

"Do you want me to take it back?"

"No, it's okay," Kate said, sucking her thumb lightly where she had singed it on the hot bagels, then carrying the plate over to the breakfast bar. "I, uh, guess I did." She thought about it. "David, my husband, is the only one I've ever been with," she admitted after a minute. "He really worked at making love, and I mean that in a good way. We started out so awkwardly, as most young people do, but he honestly tried to please me, and as time went by it got to a point where I...ah, found it reasonably...acceptable. I even managed to...well, climax a time or two." She laughed. "I'm sure Ellen was just thrilled by the time she got him, however." She shot Nikki a look. "Can you tell me why you asked?"

Nikki flushed faintly and said in a small voice, "I guess...I wanted to know it isn't just the sex between us."

Kate tried to decide if that comment should insult her. "So how was the sex between you and Anne?"

Nikki started, then flushed even harder. "It was a really bad question, wasn't it? I'm sorry."

"I can't change the past, Nikki," Kate said quietly. "I can't predict the future. I can only be who I am right now."

Nikki stared at her, then nodded. "Anne and I were...it was good," she said finally, obviously trying to be as candid as she could in exchange for Kate's honesty. Kate wasn't sure if she really wanted to know the answer to her question, but she wanted to make the point that this was information that had to be volunteered, not finagled.

"As good as I could imagine...the first few times. But the longer we were together, the less she seemed to want it...want me, and it didn't take long before I realized she was losing interest, even if I didn't want to admit it to myself. I became more and more frantic to be with her, but that only pushed her away sooner." She took a deep breath, her expression an aching mix of pain and humiliation as she remembered Anne's rejection. "It wasn't ever like it is between us, Kate. I'm not just saying that to make you or me feel better. After we make love, I feel like I could spend the rest of my existence just holding you, even if we never made love again."

Kate reached over, cupping her cheek in her palm. "I feel the same. I love making love with you, but I also love just being with you. With David, sex was always an effort, always a goal to be reached, and when we did, we actually thought we had accomplished something. With you, it's just what we're supposed to be doing at that particular moment, and it's absolutely incredible." She wished she could explain the unexplainable, but she saw the look in Nikki's eyes and knew that, somehow, she had managed.

"I'm sorry, Kate," Nikki said, hugging her around the neck. "I'm afraid my insecurities pop up at the worst times."

"Well, that's why they're insecurities. At least you know they are. It's when you refuse to recognize them that they can really trip you up."

"I suppose." Nikki kissed her. "Thanks for putting up with me."

"I love you. I'll always put up with you."

They kissed again, longer this time, and only after they finally parted for breath did they manage to pay attention to the morning news. Edwards House had burned to the ground sometime the previous night.

CHAPTER TWENTY-EIGHT

Well, if there was any evidence hidden up there, it's gone now," Kim said, studying a French fry warily before finally popping it into her mouth.

"I can't believe it just burned down." Nikki was monumentally annoyed because she'd wanted one more chance to search the place. Now that option was gone forever, and the missed opportunity rankled.

"At least they didn't drag a body out of these ashes," Addy said, putting a cheeseburger platter in front of Nikki, who flashed a look of gratitude and proceeded to dig in. "I suppose the first question should be, was it arson?"

"How could it not be?" Kim interjected. "What are the odds of Katherine Rushton's house burning down right now with everything else that's been going on in town? I bet she was insured up to her neck."

"She'd have to be crazy to burn it down now," Addy said. "Everyone would assume she did it deliberately."

"Exactly," said Nikki. "What if she's being framed?"

The other two women stared at her and Kim asked, "Is that your newest theory, Nik?"

"It's a possibility. Otherwise, Katherine Rushton is as stupid as they come, and she just doesn't seem like it. Obnoxious, rude, and stuck-up, but not stupid."

"Criminals aren't necessarily the brightest bulbs in the garden," Addy pointed out. "If they were, they wouldn't get caught."

"Addy's right," said Kim. "People do things without thinking of the consequences, then are completely surprised when things go wrong."

"People do stupid things with and about money all the time, but this is arson we're talking about, and murder," said Nikki. "She'd have to know that she'd be the prime suspect in anything like this."

"She hasn't been arrested yet," Addy reminded them. "Maybe she thinks she's invincible." Looking at them significantly, she left to wait on some other customers.

Nikki chewed a mouthful of cheeseburger slowly. "The worst part is that Kate and I never had the chance to check Edwards House out a second time. Now, we never will."

"You could sift through the ashes."

"Even if we found the remains of a gun, there wouldn't be much left."

"So what are you up to the rest of the afternoon?" Kim was obviously bored with the mystery of Sam's murder.

Nikki tried to ignore the flutters in her stomach. "I have an appointment at the police station. We're writing the exam for police dispatcher this afternoon. If I do well, I'll be hired."

"Is that what you really want to do? You never struck me as the law enforcement type, even though you do tend to stick your nose in places it doesn't belong."

"Funny," Nikki said. "It's fascinating work. The more I research it, the more interesting it sounds."

"If you say so. Does it pay well?"

"It starts at $12.50 an hour. The shift is three twelve-hour days from six p.m. to six a.m., Tuesday to Thursday night. That gives me a lot of time off."

"You might find the late nights too much."

Nikki shrugged. "Maybe, but it would be exciting, which appeals to me."

"Like you don't have enough excitement in your life now." Kim snorted. "Or are you bored with Kate already?"

"Not a chance." Nikki thought about how crucial a part of her life Kate had become in such a short time. "She's so incredible, Kim. I can talk to her, and she always knows what I mean, even when it's not what I'm saying."

"Oh, boy," Kim said, thumping her forehead with her palm. "I have only myself to blame. I'm the one who brought her up."

Nikki ignored her, lost in the thoughts of her new love. "We talked about all the things worrying us about the relationship. She doesn't hide anything from me, Kim. She says exactly what she's thinking and explains it in a way that I understand. She doesn't try to play with my head."

"She sounds perfect."

"She is." Nikki, who had responded dreamily, slowly realized Kim was being facetious and fixed her with a dark look. "You're not funny."

Kim laughed. "You're so cute when you're like this."

"Like what?"

"All soft and gooey, with big blue eyes and the look that says, 'I'm gone.'"

"I'm not laughing. Do you see me laughing here?"

Kim finally subsided. "So, are you going to see her later?"

"She's working tonight. Normally, someone comes in evenings and Saturdays, but the kid's going to some high school dance. I promised I'd call her around suppertime and let her know how the exam went. We're having dinner at her place tomorrow night." Nikki sighed, keenly aware that she hadn't had a chance to see her the previous night either, since Kate was occupied with her monthly book club meeting while Nikki had been home doing laundry. To know she wouldn't be able to spend any quality time with Kate until Saturday evening was like a nagging injury, an ache in her midsection she couldn't quite pinpoint but that left her uncomfortable.

"She asked you to move in with her yet?"

Nikki hesitated, and Kim laughed again.

"She did, didn't she? God, straight chicks are worse than lesbians when it comes to that. The joke should be, what do straight chicks who want to be lesbians take on the second date?"

"She didn't ask me to live with her," Nikki said. "But we did discuss it a little for the future. We both want to wait until we're sure about our relationship."

"You know there's a pool."

"What?"

"On when you two will move in together."

Nikki stared at her, not especially pleased. "What's the consensus?"

"No later than March 20th."

"What's March 20th?"

"The first day of spring. Everyone thinks you'll be in her place by spring, except for Audrey, of course. She says that you two have to go camping first. She believes you won't move in together unless you know for sure that Kate can and will spend the night in the woods with you."

Nikki was disgusted. "Don't you people have anything better to do?"

"Are you kidding? This is the most entertaining winter we've ever spent. Between you and the straight chick—"

"Her name is Kate."

"And Sam's murder," Kim didn't miss a beat, "there's something going on every day. Who says February is the most boring month of the year?" Kim tilted her head. "Speaking of which, what are you doing for Valentine's Day? You actually have an excuse to celebrate it this year."

Nikki felt uneasy. "I don't know. I'd like to get Kate something special, but I don't know what yet."

"It doesn't really matter, you know. This first year, you could give her weeds you yanked out of a ditch, and she'd call them wildflowers and find it romantic. It's only after you've been together for a while that you actually have to work at it."

"Meaning you're out of ideas for Lynn."

Kim sighed. "She's so hard to buy for. If she wants something, she just goes ahead and gets it without even telling me she wanted it. If she can't afford it, then I can't either, and if I did buy it, she'd only get mad because I spent so much."

"Life's a bitch, isn't it?" Nikki said in a tone devoid of sympathy, enjoying the chance to tease her friend for a change instead of being the target.

"Don't gloat." Kim raised a warning finger. "Your time's coming. You have only this initial grace period. Next year, you'll be in the same boat as the rest of us."

"You're just upset because you aren't romantic enough to think of something for Lynn. Whereas I have the imagination required to come up with something really spectacular for Kate."

Later, Nikki wished she could live up to such hyperbole as she trudged through the snow toward the police station. Truthfully, she didn't have the slightest idea what to get Kate, mostly because she hadn't been with her long enough to really figure out her tastes and desires...at least outside the bedroom. She didn't even know if Kate liked chocolate.

Sandy smiled when Nikki pushed her way through the solid doors. "Go down the hall to your right. That's where they'll be giving the exams. Take a seat anywhere."

Nikki nodded her thanks and hung her coat on the rack before following instructions. She appeared to be the last one there, other than the proctor, and as she took her seat she surreptitiously appraised the others in the room. The three men and one woman returned the glance, checking her out in a polite, subtle way. Without recognizing any of them, Nikki couldn't tell what kind of competition she would be up against.

All she could do was her best, she decided philosophically. If that was good enough, she would get the job. Otherwise, someone else with more qualifications would. She didn't believe her sexual orientation would be held against her, and besides, it was against the law in Nova Scotia to discriminate on the basis of that...assuming she could prove any such discrimination. She took a deep breath and focused on the task at hand.

A few hours later, she had finished all the tests and was walking out of the room with a sense of accomplishment. She couldn't really tell how she had done...the proctor had been inscrutable...but she was secure in her competence with the computer section of the exam, as well as her ability to type basic facts quickly while someone shouted contradictory instructions at her. That had to count for something.

She felt her heart sink as she saw Katherine Rushton talking to a constable in the outer area of the station. Not really in the mood for another confrontation, she wondered if there was another way out. But to her surprise, Rushton was slumped in one of the chairs, her face haggard and fear still evident in her eyes.

She didn't even look up as Nikki walked past, and the air of total defeat surrounding her was a marked departure from her usual haughty demeanor. Sidling over to where Sandy was covering the desk, Nikki pretended an interest in the donation box for the SPCA before she finally caught the dispatcher's eye. "Can I ask what she's doing here?"

"She had her car stolen," Sandy said. "She's here to do the follow-up report. Apparently it showed up in her driveway last night without a scratch on it, the keys still in the ignition."

Nikki knew that was as much as she dared coax from Sandy, and with a farewell nod, she shot a final glance at Rushton before leaving. As she walked outside, Nikki wondered if Rushton had finally run out of ways to hide her crimes...or had someone maneuvered her into exactly where they wanted her to be?

CHAPTER TWENTY-NINE

Kate stood behind the counter, pleased by the inordinate number of customers in the store. Even for a Friday, this crowd proved that, whatever rumors were spreading around town, they weren't affecting her business. Then it occurred to her that perhaps a few of them had come to look at her, as if she were an odd exhibit in the zoo. They were members of the golf club, or the Historical Society, who picked up one of the lesbian or gay novels with deliberate casualness, read the back, and then offered her a baffled look, as if they expected something in the blurb to explain her sudden change of status. Kate was torn between laughing at the sheer absurdity and being annoyed by the pettiness of people whom she had once considered friendly acquaintances.

Shaking her head, she accepted the money from one of her regular customers, a gentleman who preferred cold-war thrillers, though how the genre managed to survive the dismantling of the Berlin Wall so many years ago was beyond her. As soon as he left, another joined the line. Of all the evenings for Sheila to take off, this was turning out to be the worst.

At least the day's profit margin would be spectacular, she thought, trying to consider the bright side. Though she had access to funds beyond the average Truro citizen, she tried to live within the means of what the store made and the payment she received once a month from her major trust. That way she didn't have to touch her other accounts except in unusual circumstances and couldn't be unnecessarily extravagant, something her parents had frowned upon. They had taught her that having money was not merely a privilege but a responsibility.

Responding to a customer request, she looked up the availability of a book on the store computer, filled out a special order for it, and then dealt with the next customer, a parent looking for some children's books. After that, business lulled as traffic picked up outside with people leaving work to go home for supper, and Kate took a moment to gather her bearings. Making a quick tour of the store, picking up a few books that had been knocked to the floor, and straightening others on the shelves, she felt some of the tension leave her shoulders. She doubted this interest in her and her store would continue for very long, and in the meantime, she would simply have to work through it.

The treble of the phone made her hurry to the counter, and she picked up the receiver, somehow knowing who it was before she answered, her heart thumping pleasantly in anticipation.

"Hi, Kate," Nikki said, the rich voice making a shiver ripple down her spine. "Are you busy?"

"I have a moment to talk," she said, suddenly hearing her own voice lower instinctively to a sensual inflection. "Especially to you." Nikki chuckled, and again Kate felt her heart give a jubilant little twinge. "How did the exam go?"

"I think I did all right. I won't know until next week, of course, but it felt pretty good."

"I know things will work out the way they're supposed to," Kate said, then laughed. "I almost wish you could pop by tonight to help out in the store. It's been crazy here."

"It would probably take more time to teach me how things work than any help I could provide. But if you really want me there—"

"No, I was just joking." Kate laughed again. "If you were here, I wouldn't get any work done at all." She paused. "I miss you, darling."

"I miss you, too. We'll see each other tomorrow night."

"I'm counting the minutes," Kate said, wishing Nikki would say that she would stop by once the store was closed, even though it would be late. Kate wouldn't presume to ask her to come over at such an inconvenient time. The tinkle of the bell above the door made her sigh. "I have a customer. I have to go."

"Okay. I love you. I'll talk to you tomorrow."

"Until tomorrow," Kate said and hung up, wondering too late if she should have told Nikki she loved her as well. She made a vow to do something extra-special for her, not only to make up for the overlooked endearment, but because it would soon be Valentine's Day. It had been so long since she had celebrated it that she usually ignored it altogether, but this year she'd once more mark the date as a special occasion.

Kate turned around to discover her customer was none other than Margaret Madison. She couldn't remember her coming to her store very often, if at all, and she wondered what had brought her out. It couldn't have been her new notoriety as a lesbian, she thought. Margaret would have far more occupying her mind than that little tidbit making the rounds.

"Hello, Kate," Margaret said, barely smiling as she stood in front of the counter, resting her gloved hand on top of the polished surface.

Compassionately, Kate immediately covered it with her own, not knowing why, only aware that she seemed in a great deal of pain. "Margaret, how are you?"

"I'm getting by." Margaret hesitated and then lifted her chin, as if gathering her courage. "I'm not sure if you're aware of this, but Sam's death left me...in somewhat difficult circumstances. You're one of the few women I know who owns her own business, and I was wondering... if perhaps you could provide me a letter of recommendation."

"I'd be glad to." Kate tilted her head as she regarded the other woman, noting the haunted look in the eyes, the hollows of her cheeks. "I didn't get a chance at the service to tell you how sorry I am for your loss."

"Yes, the service," Margaret said, her voice a thin thread of hatred. "I still can't believe that...*woman*...dared show her face."

Kate was grateful no one else was in the store. She envisioned another scene and was already preparing herself mentally for the onslaught. "Apparently, she was his business partner."

"Business? Is that what you thought when you saw her car parked there that night, when you saw the light in the upstairs apartment?"

"Well, it's in the past, Margaret." Kate desperately tried to come up with something to defuse the moment.

Margaret stared at her and then seemed to shiver before regaining her composure.

Kate felt disturbed, aware of an indecipherable look in the widow's eyes, a sort of darkness that she didn't want to probe too deeply.

"You're right," Margaret said in a calmer tone, "it *is* over. I've finishing cleaning out his stuff from the house. Now I suppose it's time to start cleaning out his belongings at the cabin." She grimaced. "Perhaps it's fortunate that I didn't have to clean out the office. That Rushton woman saved me that task, at least."

"I'm sure Rick Johnson has the case well in hand. If she's behind this, Margaret, then he'll bring her to justice."

The door opened as more customers entered the store, and Kate felt relieved, despite her earlier wish not to involve other people in a possible scene. "I'll get that letter for you as soon as I can."

"I appreciate that, Kate." Margaret turned, hesitated, and then looked back. "Ah, I don't mean to pry, but is it true that you've...met someone?"

Kate resisted the urge to sigh. "That's the rumor." Firming her jaw, she inhaled deeply to prepare herself to utter the truth. "I've never been happier."

Margaret regarded her for a few seconds. "Then I'm glad for you, Kate," she said in an oddly flat tone. "It's rare that one can find such happiness. Don't be afraid to take it wherever you can find it, no matter what anyone else says. And never let anyone take it away from you."

"Thank you." Bemused, Kate watched Margaret leave before she glanced back at her other customers, two teenagers browsing the young adult section. Idly, she wondered why Margaret had come to her. Somehow, she didn't quite buy the excuse that she was the only business owner she knew. What about all her husband's associates? Which led back to Katherine Rushton, and Kate decided that perhaps it wasn't so strange after all.

More customers filtered into the store, and she was forced to put the conversation aside, along with the questions it raised, as she waited on them. She noticed a run on her lesbian and gay books and realized that if some of the townspeople were coming by out of sheer inquisitiveness, others were there to silently support her. She didn't know how many of the new customers were gay...though sometimes it was obvious when she was waiting on two women or two men who had that certain comfort level with each other...but unquestionably she was suddenly part of a community.

She did notice that certain people who normally came in Friday night didn't, for whatever reason. She didn't know if their absence was significant or coincidental, but in the end, she supposed it all evened out.

By nine o'clock, she was exhausted and glad to lock up. Upstairs, she found an apple in the crisper and took it along with a mug of tea into the living room, where she turned on her small television, something she rarely did. Switching it to the local news station, she caught up on the events of the day, finding little that was new. Restlessly, she flipped through the rest of the channels, searching for something to quiet her mind to the point where she could go to bed, finally finding an animal documentary.

Around eleven-thirty she shut off the television and stood up, stretching to ease the kinks from her shoulders. She went into the bathroom and prepared for bed, smiling as she saw the second toothbrush, now used, sitting in the holder. In the bedroom, she found the T-shirt tucked beneath the pillow, pulling it on before she slipped between the sheets and turned off the light. She had barely settled down before the phone rang, and she bit off a curse as she picked up the receiver, remembering that she had neglected to set the answering machine. Her annoyance immediately dissipated when she heard the voice on the other end.

"I'm sorry to call so late," Nikki said. "Did I wake you?"

"No." Kate relaxed against the pillows, a soft smile on her face. "I just went to bed. Now I'm lying here missing you more than I can say."

"Me, too. I crawled into bed a half an hour ago, but I can't go to sleep without saying good night."

"Well, I'm glad you did." Kate's voice dropped to the husky trill that Nikki evoked in her. Lying in the darkness, her lover's voice in her ears, she was abruptly aware of an ache in the lower part of her abdomen, and she turned onto her side, drawing up her legs. "Oh, dear."

"What?"

"Nothing," Kate said, embarrassed. "I'm...aroused, just hearing your voice."

"Really?" Nikki's tone rose significantly. Kate could almost see the leer on her face.

"Fiend," she murmured affectionately. "How dare you call me, set my senses aflame, then leave me here alone to suffer the consequences?"

Nikki's chuckle was low and sensual. "They say deprivation is good for the soul."

"Who says?"

"Those who are deprived, I suppose. That means us, at the moment."

"Only until tomorrow night," Kate said. "I'm counting the minutes."

"The seconds."

"You should have come over tonight."

"I would have." There was a touch of surprise in Nikki's voice. "Why didn't you ask me?"

"I...I didn't think you'd want to that late."

"You're kidding, right?"

Kate didn't have a response. For a few seconds, she listened to Nikki's respiration on the other end of the line and then laughed, unable to help herself. "I'm a fool."

"No, I should have asked if I could. I'm not...I don't always know where the line is, you know?"

"I know," Kate said softly. "It's hard to figure it out when all we can think about is being with each other."

"It's as if by deliberately staying away from you, I can tell if it's really love. That's stupid, isn't it, Kate?"

"No, it's being in love. It makes us so vulnerable, and a part of us tries to hold back so that we're not hurt."

"Yes, that's exactly it."

Kate cradled the phone closer to her ear. "I'd never hurt you, my darling," she whispered. "Not deliberately, at any rate."

"I know," Nikki said in a barely audible tone. After a long silence, she finally sighed. "I'd better let you go."

"Until tomorrow night."

"Tomorrow."

"I love you."

"I love you, too."

After gently hanging up, Kate lay awake for a long time, the ache inside gradually subsiding until finally she fell asleep, wrapped around a pillow that still bore Nikki's scent, dreaming of warm skin and an even warmer heart.

CHAPTER THIRTY

The Tidal Watch Inn on the outskirts of town, located on the shore of the Salmon River, always required a reservation. Not because people were fighting to get in, Nikki suspected, but simply because they wanted to project that sort of image. In any event, it was supposedly the best place in town to eat, not to mention the most expensive, and she wanted to do something very special for Kate on Valentine's Day. Running over from Keebler's Building Supplies during her lunch hour, Nikki made a reservation for what would certainly be a busy day.

After she spoke to the maître d' in the foyer, she glanced through the arches leading into the dining room and noted what kind of patrons regularly dined there. She was not surprised to see Terry Bishop, along with his partners from his law firm, nor to recognize Art Ryan, the owner of the largest grocery superstore in the area. But she was truly astounded to see Katherine Rushton having lunch with a woman Nikki couldn't identify from the back. They were seated next to the partition separating the foyer from the dining area, a half wall topped with a lattice that ran to the ceiling, vines growing decoratively over it to further shield the dining room from prying eyes. Not from equally inquisitive ears, however.

Nikki paused by the rack containing brochures for various tourist attractions in the area. She picked out one about a walking tour of historical sights in town and pretended to read it as she cocked her head and listened intently, trying to pick out their conversation from all the others. Fortunately, it wasn't difficult, the partition offering little soundproofing.

"I didn't try to run that girl down, Diane," Rushton said, desperation coloring her otherwise cool and haughty tones. "I came out of my condo Wednesday morning, and my car was gone. I reported it immediately."

"Well, it didn't help that it showed up in the parking lot later that evening with the keys in the ignition."

Nikki realized she was hearing Diane Miller, a junior partner in Bishop's law firm. Apparently, she had been assigned to keep their client occupied. Or perhaps Diane was a friend, and it was highly unlikely Rushton had many at this point, the two commiserating over Katherine's problems. Nikki wondered why women always desired to confide in each other, even as she was grateful for the characteristic as she listened closely.

"Maybe the girl lied," Katherine said, sounding dissatisfied. "She's of questionable character. All those types are. So is that woman she's with—"

"I wouldn't pursue that line if I were you." Diane's tone cooled. "You're not from around here, so maybe you don't know this, but Kate Shannon is one of the few truly influential people in Truro. She's not obvious about it, and people tend to forget who her maternal grandparents are, but she can pull strings that the rest of us only dream of having access to. She is *not* someone to trifle with."

"But...she runs a *bookstore*." Rushton sounded shocked.

"She *owns* the bookstore and the building it's in, among other things," Diane said. "Her grandmother is Irene Taylor, and apparently the Taylors believe that one should always be gainfully occupied. Kate continues that tradition, but she could probably buy and sell you ten times over and still have enough spare change to support a hundred girlfriends."

Nikki discovered she was leaning weakly against the rack, one hand on the side to keep from toppling. She had always understood that Kate was well off financially...she owned her own business, after all, and was older, having been in the workforce much longer...but Nikki had never connected her with being *rich*. The Taylors owned half of Truro. She was so shaken, she missed the next few words of the conversation and had to catch up.

"...set me up," Katherine was saying.

"No one had to set you up with Mosaic Estates," Diane said. "It was Sam's and your decision to try to cover your losses with money embezzled from the stockholders. Once that gets out, you'll be charged. Murder is actually the least of your problems."

"I didn't kill Sam. I loved him. We were going to be together."

"Did he tell you that? You're hardly the first woman he's indulged himself with."

"He was going to divorce his wife. I saw the papers Wednesday evening. That's why I was there. We were celebrating, but he was alive when I left. Someone else came by afterward and killed him."

"If you say so." Diane didn't sound convinced. "In any event, the most pressing problem is the fraud charges that you and Terry will face if any of this comes out. Thankfully Sam's business insurance can cover some of the losses."

Terry? Nikki thought excitedly. *Terry Bishop was involved with this, too?*

"Your firm isn't clear," Rushton hissed, a streak of vindictive hatred in her voice. "Terry had this all figured out...right up until old man Gilles stopped him in his tracks. The firm might survive without Terry, but the publicity won't do any of you much good."

"That sort of talk won't do you any good either," Diane said, active dislike coloring her tone. "Besides, with the evidence burned—"

"It wasn't at Edwards House." Rushton undoubtedly surprised the lawyer as much as Nikki. "I moved it last Saturday night, after the police finished questioning me. I didn't want those two prying dykes to come find it again."

"Is that why you burned down the house?" Diane asked, an edge of demand in her voice. Holding her breath, Nikki waited, needing to know if Katherine would reveal all.

"I didn't burn it down." Rushton's outrage sounded genuine. "Why would I do that? It was insured for its initial value, not for all our renovations. I'll be lucky if insurance covers half of what I spent."

"You'll be lucky if insurance pays at all. It was arson. In any event, you'd better hope no one finds that other file."

"It's in a safe place. Someplace only Sam and I knew about, a little cabin on the lake." Rushton hesitated. "It was where we'd go to be together." Her voice became somewhat dreamy in a way that Nikki recognized only too well. Her mood didn't last long, however, for her voice hardened perceptibly with her next words. "So you people will continue to represent me in whatever happens, and it won't come out that Terry was also a partner in Mosaic Estates."

Nikki had heard all she needed. She had to get her hands on that evidence and find out exactly what Rushton and her associates were up to. Leaving the restaurant, she crossed the parking lot and strode briskly toward the sidewalk, heading back into town. She did stop by Keebler's to feign illness, and since she rarely missed a day, her supervisor didn't question her. She thought briefly about telling Rick, but without evidence, there would be no point. But with the file in hand, he could probably do something about the situation. Nikki suspected no one knew about Terry Bishop's involvement, and something of this nature involving one of the biggest lawyers in town would have lasting repercussions.

She very carefully forced aside her first impulse, which was to run to Kate with this new information. She especially tried not to think about what she had learned about her financial status, and how it would affect them. Whenever she came close to thinking about it, a sense of betrayal and hurt started to radiate from her chest, and she had to think about something else quickly to make it ease. She wasn't ready to deal with it or examine why she was so angry that Kate hadn't told her she belonged to one of the richer families in town. Perhaps Nikki should have known Kate was descended from the Taylors, but that didn't mean Kate should have pretended she was merely another working stiff just getting by. Or in Nikki's case, barely getting by at all.

Entering the Sportsplex, she made her way to the floor containing the classes for aerobics and dance. She found Kim leading a group of puffing women, encouraging them to greater exertions by telling them class was nearly over and then they could have the hot fudge sundaes they all really wanted. Kim knew how to truly motivate people. Nikki waited until the music slowed and the class cooled down and then stood aside as the women, chatting and laughing, left.

Kim, wiping her face with a towel, picked up her bag from the floor. "Hey, bud," she said as she spotted her. "What's up?"

"I need to borrow your car."

With a look of concern, Kim dug the keys out of her bag. "What's going on?"

Nikki accepted the keys gratefully. "I came across some new information. Sam was supposed to have a cabin that no one knew about other than he and Rushton."

"Then how do you know about it?"

"A matter of being in the right place at the right time."

"Do you know where it is?"

"I'm not entirely sure, but I'm guessing it's on the lake on the Gilles property. I want to go check it out before anything else happens. I need a car to get there, though. It's too far to walk."

"Okay," Kim said, looking at her with concern. "Are you sure you should be doing this? You're nosing around a murder, after all. You should probably leave it for the police."

"If I find the cabin, I'll tell Rick. If not, then I won't look like a fool for sticking my nose in. Thanks for the keys. I'll put some gas in it before I bring it back."

"No problem," Kim said, and then called after her as she left the room. "Be careful!"

In the parking lot, Nikki tracked down Kim's little blue Honda, thankful that she knew at least one person who would lend her their car and that it was an automatic. She didn't have anything to go on but instinct, but she had an unmistakable sense of where the cabin had to be located, particularly if only Sam and Katherine knew about it. Of course, she could be completely wrong, but in a worst-case scenario, she would have a chance to go for a drive on a sunny day and enjoy the scenery. Though she enjoyed certain things about living in town, a large part of her greatly missed living in the country.

Nikki decided to start her search at Edwards House and was pleased that someone had freshly plowed the driveway. But when she saw the blackened remains of the house on the hill, she was reminded that the fire trucks would have needed it. As it was, the curving nature of the driveway and her relative unfamiliarity with driving in winter conditions made the trip a little more nerve-wracking than she would have liked, though certainly not as exciting as that first visit with Kate.

Taking a pair of binoculars Kim kept in her glove compartment, Nikki got out of the car and stood in the courtyard looking over the snow-covered fields and forest, thankful that it was high enough to give her a good vantage point. The Gilles property was located to the west, and she scrutinized the farm, the buildings starting to weather badly now that no one lived there. Yet the driveway to that property, as well as what appeared to be some sort of logging road leading into the trees on the rise behind the farm, had been plowed, the banks humped high on either side.

That had to be the access to the lake, she thought. Otherwise why plow it, though she wasn't sure whom Rushton would trust to do it. Then something else caught her attention, and she trained her binoculars on the barn, noticing that the door was half open. Inside stood a tractor with a plow blade, explaining how the road could be cleared without outside help, though Nikki couldn't quite picture Rushton operating such a piece of equipment.

Deciding she wasn't solving anything just standing there, Nikki returned to the Honda and drove gingerly back down the lane. She didn't look back at the house, now nothing more than the charred remains of an unfulfilled dream; she was too intent on discovering what lay beyond her vision.

CHAPTER THIRTY-ONE

L eaving the store in Sheila's capable hands for the time being, Kate crossed Inglish Place at the corner and strode briskly up the sidewalk toward Judith's Jewelry. Inside the small but exclusive shop, the proprietress greeted her immediately. A stocky woman with ginger hair, Judith Bishop had owned this store for as long as Kate could remember. As a fellow member of the Downtown Business Committee, Kate had a great deal of respect for her, though they didn't have much in common other than the fact that Kate had gone to high school at the same time as Judith's younger brother, Terry.

Kate suspected they had even less in common after the events of the past week or so.

"Kathryn." Judith greeted her with cool civility. "What brings you here?"

Few people insisted on using Kate's full name. She tried not to be annoyed, though she suspected Judith did it only because she knew it aggravated her. Judith was like that.

"I'm stopping by to pick up a gift," Kate said, seeing no reason to dance around the issue. "Something for Valentine's Day."

The blunt declaration made Judith seem unable to respond beyond blinking uncertainly. "I...see," she said slowly. "What did you have in mind?"

"Earrings," Kate said, inspecting the selection kept carefully under glass. "Or perhaps a necklace." She tapped the glass over a section of simple yet elegant chains with pendants. "Let me see the heart-shaped one."

Judith hesitated and then opened the rear panel to retrieve the necklace. She presented it to Kate, who examined it carefully for flaws, judging how the light fell upon the stones. Easily imagining how it would look around Nikki's neck, the pendant cradled in the soft hollow of her throat, and not one for vacillating, Kate made up her mind on the spot. "I'll take it," she said, handing it back to be boxed. "Gift wrap it, please."

"Of course," Judith said, staring at her oddly, as if she couldn't quite believe this was happening.

As Judith wrapped the necklace, Kate entertained the idea of buying some matching earrings, scrutinizing them carefully, but ultimately held back, suspecting that both would be too much for a first present. Seeming to be in a daze, Judith accepted the credit card Kate handed her, ringing up the purchase that undoubtedly increased her profit margin by a considerable amount for the day.

After she tucked the small box in the pocket of her coat, Kate formally nodded to Judith, who still looked slightly stunned, and left the store. Outside, the sunshine reflected sharply off car windows and snow, making her blink as she continued to the grocery store farther up the street, intent on picking up a few things for dinner. In the produce aisle, she ran into Lillian Salter, the member of the Historical Society in charge of the annual fund-raising dinner. It was one of the more significant social events of the town and, with plates going for well over a hundred dollars, unquestionably elite. Kate had, by virtue of her membership and the support of the Taylor Foundation over the years, a somewhat permanent position seated next to the president.

Kate was amused to see Lillian hesitate when she saw her, her face altering as if she wanted to flee in the other direction. However, she pushed her cart in Kate's direction, looking both resolute and artificially cheerful. "Kate," she said. "I'm so glad to run into you. I was wondering about your seat at the head table this year. Will you still be attending?"

"Of course," Kate said, discovering she was enjoying this encounter far more than she probably should. "I wouldn't miss it. I'll drop off my check this week."

"Ah, that's wonderful," Lillian said, her smile as false as her eyelashes. "I'll put you down for your customary place."

"Actually, this year I'll be bringing a guest. Put me down for two."

Lillian's expression froze, and a certain desperation abruptly appeared in her watery eyes. But despite her obvious dismay, she was apparently determined not to put a foot wrong. She knew as well as anyone whose signature was on the checks donated to the treasury that kept many of the Historical Society's projects moving forward. Kate knew Lillian was not prepared to insult one of their biggest contributors, even if she had a deep-seated desire to do so on some perceived moral ground.

"Both at the head table?" Lillian's voice cracked ever so slightly.

"Where else?" Kate said, staring at her blandly as she stuck in the needle. "Side by side. I want my guest seated next to me." She smiled, twisting it a bit. "Within arm's length."

Lillian gasped. "I...see."

It occurred to Kate that she was making a lot of people "see" this particular Saturday morning. That it was rather entertaining was probably just a bonus. She stared politely at the woman. "Is there anything else?"

"No," Lillian said stiffly. "I'll make sure you and...your guest...are seated together."

"Thank you," Kate responded, and continued shopping, placidly picking up some green peppers and a red one. She was aware of Lillian's eyes following her as she moved on to pick up what else she required, and she had to suppress a tiny chortle.

Kate paid for her purchases at the checkout, surprised when the same young woman who had waited on her countless times, but had rarely looked up from her register, now smiled shyly. Kate didn't know quite what to make of it, but she couldn't deny that the attitude of the people around her was definitely altering in some not-so-subtle ways. Obviously, this lesbian thing was more complex than she realized when she made her first unconscious decision to pursue Nikki.

Kate had a lot to think about as she walked home. She entered the back door, taking the bags upstairs to put everything away. The present she laid on the counter to deal with later that night. She and Nikki had agreed to meet at seven, and since the store closed at five, that would give her a couple of hours to prepare for their special evening. Smiling faintly in anticipation, she went downstairs to where Sheila was taking care of the store.

The customers weren't as numerous as they had been the previous day, but it was still busier than the average Saturday, and both Sheila and Kate stayed occupied. At three, business finally died off, and Kate had an opportunity to ask Sheila how her date the night before had gone.

"It was great," Sheila said, as they straightened the rack of bestsellers. "Billy's really nice. We danced to all the songs, even the slow ones."

"I'm glad," Kate said, genuinely pleased for the girl. "You should only date nice guys. Save the 'bad boys' for those who don't know any better."

Sheila blushed and glanced sideways at her. "Mrs. Shannon?"

"Yes, Sheila?" Kate moved over to the general fiction where she knelt to pick up a few novels that had been put back in the wrong spot.

"Some kids were...saying some things last night."

Kate felt a bit of tension ripple across her shoulders, a sort of foreboding. "Yes?" she said, not turning around, keeping her voice pleasant and even.

"They say you...well, that you like girls."

Kate inhaled deeply, summoning a calm demeanor, then rose and turned. Sheila was regarding her with a mixture of curiosity and trepidation. Kate wasn't entirely sure how to respond to this reaction, but she didn't consider diverging from the truth any more than she had with Judith or Lillian earlier in the day. She simply intended to be a little gentler in her approach until she determined Sheila's comfort level.

"I like one woman specifically," she said. "Her name is Nikki Harris."

Sheila seemed to absorb this piece of information without much change in expression. "So, what they were saying was true. You're a lesbian."

Kate opened her mouth to say she wasn't sure, that so far in her life only one person had ever made her feel as she did and that she wasn't entirely certain that deserved such a label, but decided it was too complicated.

"I guess so," she said instead, in a gentle tone.

Sheila nodded. "I guess that's kind of...cool."

Kate's smile tightened when Sheila bent her head, seeming uneasy as she fussed with one of the novels. "What is it?"

"I don't think my mom and dad agree, though."

"No?"

Sheila kept her eyes fixed on the shelf in front of her, as if she apparently found it hard to look directly at Kate. "This morning, before I left for work, Dad said that it would be a good idea to give my notice."

That statement struck with the force of a blow, completely unexpected. Kate barely knew the Fishers, and they hardly knew her. Apparently, that didn't stop them from suddenly making value judgments on her. "I see," she said with difficulty. "What do you think about that?"

"I think they're being backward, as usual. But they're my parents, you know?"

"I know." Kate strove for some kind of evenness in her tone. "You should probably go along with their wishes." She searched for something to say. "Do you think it would help if I spoke with them?"

Sheila shot a look of alarm at Kate. "I don't think that would be a good idea. Dad said some...kind of nasty things this morning. He said that I had to go to work today, because it wasn't fair to just not show up, but that this should be my last day to work for you."

Kate didn't have to use too much imagination to read between the lines of how the conversation had actually gone. "All right." She felt a lump in her throat, an acid taste of sorrow and anger, though she knew it wouldn't help to display it. "I'm sorry to lose you, Sheila. You've been a good worker, and I think this job has been good for you."

"It has." Sheila's eyes shimmered with tears of frustration. "It's not fair!"

Kate reached out to comfort her, to put her hand on her shoulder, but stopped as Sheila subtly flinched away. It wasn't obvious, and perhaps the girl wasn't even aware of her movement, but it was detectable, and Kate drew back, feeling sick inside. Was this what Nikki had experienced since coming out? Suddenly, she better understood why Nikki had refused to hold hands while walking down the street, or had difficulty showing how she felt while in public. Kate's confident assurance about her place in this town had made the morning encounters with the women of her social circle entertaining. The fondness she had for the teenager made her hurt with a profound pain.

"I'm afraid life isn't fair, Sheila," she said quietly. "Hopefully, one day, a person won't be judged on where they come from or what they look like...or who they fall in love with. But we have to live in the now, and unfortunately a lot of misconceptions and prejudices remain. I'm sorry that you're caught in the middle."

"I guess." Sheila finally managed to glance at Kate. "I never would have guessed you'd fall in love with:..a woman. You were married and all."

"I didn't know it when I was married."

Sheila stared at her, eyes widening. "You didn't know? I mean, aren't you always supposed to know, only just be hiding it?"

Kate shrugged. "I have no idea." She searched for a way to explain the whole situation, to put it into words that Sheila would understand. She glanced at the girl, wondering if she had been a little more like her, more of an outsider while growing up…if she had not been perceived as so "normal"…would she have been quicker to realize her true nature? What was her true nature?

Defeated by the complexity of things that she was only starting to consider, Kate forced a smile. "I'll give you a letter of recommendation. As well as two weeks' severance pay. That way, your employment record will show your dismissal as due to lack of work rather than... well, quitting without just cause."

Sheila flushed. "Thank you, Mrs. Shannon. You don't have to do that."

"I know. But none of this is your doing, Sheila. I've found that in unpleasant situations, a person can choose to make it worse, or they can make it better. When possible, I try to do the latter."

Unfortunately, she didn't want to make it better. She wanted to scream out her hurt and anger at the small-minded people in this town and their insidious influence on yet another generation. She wanted to call up Sheila's parents and tear strips off them, making them accountable for their prejudices, for forcing their daughter to do their dirty work. Mostly, she wanted to fall into Nikki's arms and weep, not only for the hurt she had discovered this day, but for all the hurt that her lover undoubtedly had experienced in her own life and that she was only now beginning to taste.

CHAPTER THIRTY-TWO

Nikki's fingers were tight on the steering wheel as she navigated the logging road behind the Gilles farm, and she gave thanks for studded tires every slippery inch of the way. She noticed that the forest had been extensively cut in the last few years. The old man had responsibly harvested the softwoods and replanted them, the new growth of firs and spruces only about eight feet high, while he had left the hardwoods standing. Birch trees poked from the deep snow on either side of the road, reaching starkly for the azure sky overhead, while the darker trunks of maples and poplar swayed slightly in the light wind.

As the car crested the ridge, Nikki felt her stomach lurch and had to keep herself from slamming on the brakes. Instead, she dropped into low and pressed her foot down carefully, gradually stopping the vehicle. Before her, the road seemed to drop straight down to a white expanse, obviously the frozen surface of the lake. It was beautiful, but no way did she dare drive down the sharp incline. Even if she managed to get down in one piece, it was highly unlikely she could drive back up again.

Fortunately, she noticed a cleared area, the snow plowed some distance back to the tree line as if others had also found it wise to park on the crest of the hill, and she took a few moments to laboriously turn the Honda around, grateful that it was a compact. Edging close to the snow bank, she jammed the car into park before turning off the ignition.

After Nikki got out, she stood for a moment as she searched the lakeshore laid out beneath her, able to see most of it from the rise. Only the sound of the tree branches creaking quietly in the breeze and the minor clicks and ticks of the Honda's engine cooling down broke the eerie silence of the woods in midwinter. Draping the binoculars around her neck, she fastened a small fanny pack around her waist. She had retrieved it from her apartment before leaving town because it contained the basic survival equipment that no experienced person would go into the woods without.

She hadn't been able to see a cabin from her vantage point on the hill, but she suspected it wouldn't be too far away from the road that appeared to run along the lakeshore. Her glasses shaded to dark to protect her eyes from the glare reflecting off the snow as she tramped along the icy dirt lane, impressed as always by the incredible peacefulness that pervaded the forest...no cars, no planes, no constant hum from power lines, no incessant buzz of civilization.

Nikki was grateful that such nature was so accessible, only a twenty-minute drive from her apartment, and she found it ironic that this area had been earmarked for a resort, destroying the very thing that had attracted the developers to it in the first place. She could see several excellent places to camp along the lake and knew that its waters probably contained trout and possibly even fresh-water bass or salmon.

She knew this was really why she was reluctant to return to the city. She might have had to move to Truro from the farm for purely logistical reasons, but her heart would always remain in the country. Even in the dead of winter.

As she turned the corner near a small inlet, she noticed a bridge crossing a stream that led into the lake. Beyond it, a small log cabin resided in a picturesque clearing, looking as if it had been taken from a greeting card or a painting.

Sam Madison certainly did have an eye for beauty, Nikki thought. However, he never seemed to be able to look beyond it. She noticed the way the land sloped and immediately realized that the stream would undoubtedly overflow its banks during the spring melt of the more snowy winters, as this had been, and inundate the low-lying area, including the meadow where the cabin sat.

Shaking her head at the shortsightedness of the cabin's construction, she approached the front porch, wondering if she could find a way in. Despite her desire to discover all its secrets, Nikki wasn't about to break in, and she was dismayed to discover a heavy padlock on the door. The windows looked tight, sealed against the outside, and, cupping her face with her hands, she peered through the frosted glass, unable to see much. Stymied, she left the porch and trudged around it, struggling briefly through the thigh-deep snow before it occurred to her that she didn't even know if there was a back door.

Returning to the front porch, she eyed the door again, the thought of the desk in Edwards House and how available its key had been abruptly surfacing in her mind. She removed her mittens and ran her fingertips along the top of the frame where she discovered a metal object. People were creatures of habit, and Katherine Rushton obviously had a problem forgetting her keys, developing this quirk so she could always have access to where she wanted to go.

Nikki fit the key into the padlock and turned it, needing to exert some effort to pull it open because of the ice around the edges. She understood that technically this was still trespassing, but it seemed a far lesser crime than if she had deliberately broken a window or door. It was probably only a matter of semantics, but where she would fudge a little on one, she refused to on the other. Taking a deep breath, she wrapped her fingers around the handle and pushed the door open.

Golden woodwork accented the interior, which featured a combination of expensive antiques and cottage country pieces. A fieldstone fireplace dominated one end of the living area, and if she dared, she would have lit a fire, the inside of the cabin seeming much colder than outside in the sunshine. But she discarded the idea as unwise and began to systematically search the little hideaway.

She discovered some rather interesting devices in the chest in the bedroom, forming several theories on just what kind of sex life Sam and Katherine had shared. Her find did make her pause briefly to wonder if Kate had any interest in "toys," forgetting that she was upset with her lover, and she made a mental note to take her to the Venus Envy women's shop the next time they were in the city. Inspired by this thought, she returned to the living room where she yanked out a drawer in one of the end tables with unnecessary vigor.

She froze when she saw the file she was looking for. Hands shaking from cold and excitement, she pulled it out and began to leaf through the papers that implicated Sam and Katherine, along with Terry Bishop, in a scheme that involved using stockholders' money to cover up the losses they incurred with the Gilles property and the renovation of Edwards House. She was so involved in what she was reading she didn't hear the footsteps until a board on the porch creaked.

She froze as the door swung open, the figure outlined in the bright light from outside, impossible to identify from within the dim interior of the cabin. Nikki's chest grew tight, and she could scarcely hear for the pounding in her ears.

"What the hell do you think you're doing?"

Although she knew that Katherine Rushton was a fraud and embezzler, that she might also be an arsonist and murderer, Nikki felt guilty. Straightening with an effort, Nikki faced her and attempted to look cool. "Uh," she said brilliantly.

Rushton spotted the file in Nikki's hand and, eyes widening, rushed toward her and tried to snatch it. Nikki, not really thinking about what she was doing, immediately clutched it to her chest and backed up. For a few seconds, they shuffled around the living room in a ludicrous sort of tag, and then Rushton lunged, landing on the sofa as Nikki neatly avoided her.

"How dare you?" Katherine panted, scrambling to her feet. "That's mine."

"I'll say it is," Nikki said, deciding that a good defense came by presenting a good offense. "Evidence showing your criminal activity. Embezzlement, arson, murder...is there anything you won't do?" She couldn't actually justify her accusations from what she had read, not business-minded enough to understand all the various papers, but she knew what she had heard in the restaurant.

The accusation, stated so plainly, froze Rushton. A wealth of emotion played over her face, and then she took a shuddering breath, staring at Nikki in horror. "I didn't kill him," she said in a small voice. "I didn't try to run you over. I didn't burn down anything."

Suddenly drained, she sagged to the sofa, and Nikki, still clutching the file to her chest, hesitantly stepped a little closer. "Who did?"

"I don't know," Katherine whispered, then buried her face in her hands and burst into tears.

Things didn't happen like this in the books Nikki read or on the dramas she watched. The villain didn't suddenly fall to pieces and start blubbering like a baby when her nefarious deeds were uncovered. Sometimes there was a fight, sometimes gunplay, and once in a while, even an explosion or two. This reaction was very anticlimactic.

"What's going on?" Nikki asked, slightly disgruntled though she tried to hide her dismay, actually reaching out and patting the woman clumsily on the shoulder.

"It was just a deal, you know." Katherine sniffed. Nikki glanced around, found a box of tissues, and presented one to her. "I met Sam when I was evaluating Edwards House. It was..." She shook her head, dabbing at her eyes. "It was too large for me, but it would have made a great hotel. The problem was, there was nothing around until Sam discovered the lake."

"Whose idea was it to turn the area into a resort?" Nikki wanted to keep her talking as long as she could, needing to understand what had gone on.

"Sam's," Rushton said, in a fond sort of tone. "He thought we could make this one big deal that would set us up for life. We brought Terry in to handle the legal stuff, and he was the one who suggested how we could come up with all the extra funds we needed to get started..." She paused, her face hardening. "It just went wrong so quickly. It was Gilles's fault. He demanded so much, and then we had to cover other costs..."

Nikki supposed that old man Gilles had been wise to take off for Florida as soon as he had, particularly with the amount of arson and mayhem going on, not to mention the look presently in Rushton's eyes. Or were people only assuming the man had made it to Florida? Unobtrusively, Nikki edged back a few feet. "What happened the night Sam died?"

"He called me to come over," Rushton said, her voice becoming unnaturally calm.

Her tone made Nikki shiver.

"He showed me the divorce papers. I know everyone says that it was just a deception, a game he played with women, but I know he meant it when he said he loved me."

"I'm sure he did."

"He told me about the other women," Rushton said dreamily. "He admitted that he played around and that he always went back to his wife...until me. I was different."

Nikki felt another shiver. Similar words. Had Sam meant them as much as Kate did? That finally he had found someone that filled that piece he hadn't even known was missing until it appeared? Or were both he and she blowing smoke? Of course, Nikki knew she shouldn't compare Kate to Sam, not even privately. Kate deserved far better than that. Taking a breath, Nikki refocused on Rushton. "Then what happened?"

"We celebrated, had a little champagne, and then I left at eleven-thirty. I swear he was still alive when I drove away. There was no fire, no sign of a spark anywhere."

"What was Sam intending to do? After you left, I mean."

Katherine blinked, obviously not expecting the question. "Go home, I guess," she said slowly, as if she had never thought about it before. "Tell his wife about us, and that he was leaving her. Get her to sign the papers."

"That would have gone over well," Nikki said, remembering what Kate had said about the scene at the funeral home. "He never went home."

"No." Katherine's voice broke.

"He told you first that he was going to divorce his wife?"

"Yes."

"Yet she knew all about you," Nikki said slowly. "No one else in town even knew you and Sam were partners, but Margaret knew about the affair. That's why she was so infuriated at the memorial service."

Katherine stared at her. "No," she said, shaking her head. "She only knew about the deals, the money. That's why she was mad at me."

"You think?"

Gradually Rushton seemed to realize what Nikki was saying. Finally she said, "Sam had a set of my car keys."

"Your car really was stolen?"

She nodded solemnly, as if the two were the closest of friends sharing confidences at a slumber party.

Nikki settled into the chair opposite her, propping her chin on her palm. "Okay, let's say that someone else went to the insurance office that night," she said, thinking out loud. "He or she meets with Sam, there's an argument...Wait a minute. The gun. You swapped the gun?"

Katherine started and then looked uncomfortable. "When I saw it in the desk at Edwards House, I panicked. It was Sam's, and when I found it I knew someone was trying to frame me, so I switched it with the gun in my purse."

Obviously no one had heard of the stringent gun control laws in the country, Nikki noted with annoyance. "Where is it now? Was it in Edwards House?"

"No, I brought it here with the file," she said, and reached for the drawer beneath the one where Nikki had found the file.

Nikki had a very bad moment, thinking that she had been incredibly stupid to leave a weapon within arm's reach of Rushton, chastising herself that she ought to be conducting this investigation in a more intelligent manner. She almost sighed with relief when Rushton came up empty-handed, before the paleness of her face made her realize that maybe the lack of a weapon hadn't been a good thing.

"It's gone."

"What do you mean, it's gone?"

A shadow fell over both women, and abruptly everything seemed to move in slow motion. Nikki realized someone stood in the doorway, blocking the light from outside, and she saw Rushton's eyes widen as she stared over Nikki's shoulder. Her mouth opened as if she were about to call out.

Then Nikki heard a small bang, a little crack of sound, and she stared dumbly at the hole that suddenly formed in the center of Rushton's forehead, a shocked expression appearing in her eyes before the light in them faded and went out. Nikki started to cringe away, uncertain as to what exactly was going on but very much afraid of where the next hole would appear. Something struck her on the back of her head before she had gone very far. Pain seared through her skull, and she surrendered to deep darkness, the blow sending her spinning into oblivion.

CHAPTER THIRTY-THREE

Kate smiled in satisfaction as she scanned the table, set with fine china, crystal, and unlit candles. A small gift-wrapped box containing the diamond necklace sat carefully by Nikki's plate. They were finally going to have their romantic dinner that had been preempted so many times, surprising Nikki, who was supposed to drop by after work. Dressed in a silken sapphire blouse, to set off her eyes, and a tailored skirt that reached to her knees, Kate was feeling particularly good about her appearance. Her skirt may have been a little formal for a private dinner, but she knew she looked good in it. The fact that Nikki appreciated running her hand up a nyloned thigh to the delights hidden beneath such a skirt was purely incidental.

Kate shivered in delight as she remembered the passionate kisses and caresses stolen in the stairwell at the end of their last abortive romantic evening. The tingle radiated through her limbs to settle pleasantly in her lower abdomen and succeeded in easing the tension she still felt over the day's events.

The only problem was that it was going on half past seven, and she was still waiting. It wasn't like Nikki to be late...at least not in Kate's admittedly limited experience with her...and she was starting to worry. Calls to her apartment received no answer, and it suddenly occurred to Kate that she didn't know any of Nikki's friends, or her family's phone number. The thought shamed her, regardless of the fact that she and Nikki had only been together for little more than a week. Agitated, she paced about the apartment, growing more concerned with every passing minute, along with becoming slightly angry in case Nikki had a previously unrevealed quirk, the habit of taking off without letting anyone know where she was.

The ringing of the phone nearly jolted Kate off her feet, and she stumbled as she hurried for the kitchen. Snatching up the receiver, she pressed it anxiously to her ear. "Hello?"

"Uh, Mrs. Shannon?"

"Yes," Kate said, unable to identify the voice. "Who is this?"

"This is Kim, Nikki's friend. I was wondering...is Nikki there?"

Kate felt a chill that stabbed her chest like a dagger. "No." She controlled her voice with an effort. "I was expecting her for dinner at seven, but she hasn't arrived."

"Oh, boy, I don't like the sound of that. This isn't like Nikki at all."

Kate felt her heart pounding unpleasantly. "What made you call?"

"Nikki stopped by the 'Plex this afternoon and borrowed my car so she could go investigate some cabin out on the Gilles property... something to do with this Madison murder. I didn't think too much about it at first and had my partner, Lynn, come pick me up, but now I'm starting to worry. Nikki left at one-thirty, and it's only twenty minutes out there. There's no answer at her place, so I guess I was hoping she was with you and...well, sort of forgot about things."

"No," Kate said, fear rising fast and thick as Kim talked. "You're right, this doesn't sound good. You said she went out to where? The Gilles property?"

"Yes. Nikki seemed to think that she could find some secret cabin there or something. It's next to Edwards House, to the west."

"Thanks very much for calling," Kate said. "I'll take care of it."

Kim didn't argue but simply said good-bye and hung up.

Kate picked up her address book, checked the number, and then phoned Rick Johnson at home. "Rick? I need your help."

"Kate?" Rick sounded a bit apprehensive. "What's going on?"

Quickly, she filled him in on what Kim had told her, and he muttered a curse.

"We don't have time for that, Rick. I want you to go out with me to the area to search for her."

"Kate, she's an adult, and there's a forty-eight hour rule with missing persons—"

"I know. That's why I called you at home. I'm not asking you as a police officer, I'm asking you as my friend. Help me find her."

After a pause he asked, "Where are you?" in a resigned tone.

"At home. I'm going to change clothes. I'll be ready in ten minutes."

"It'll take me that long to get over there," Rick grumbled. "Damn it, Kate, if this turns out to be some kind of stunt—"

"Just get over here."

She hung up and hurried into the bedroom to change into some warmer clothes: a sweater, some ski pants, and the thick socks Nikki had given her the previous week. She pulled on her heaviest winter boots before retrieving her jacket, making sure she also had good gloves, a scarf, and her warmest hat. Grabbing a flashlight from a drawer in the kitchen, she flicked it on to check the batteries and shoved her keys and wallet into her pocket.

By the time she exited the back door into the alley, Rick had pulled up in the police force's SUV. As she climbed in, Kate noticed a rifle holstered beneath the dash. Despite her general distaste for guns, she was a bit relieved to see it, though she wasn't entirely sure why.

As he pulled out onto Prince and sped down the street, Rick asked, "So Nikki thought this cabin was out on the Gilles property?"

"According to what I've been hearing, Mosaic Estates owns everything, including the lake behind the farm," Kate said, staring through the windshield.

Rick shook his head. "This is all I need."

As they quickly headed out of town, Kate barely noticed that the moon was full, its glory becoming more apparent as they drove through the less populated area of Lower Truro. Hills rose on one side of the road while the other flattened out to the marsh leading to the river. The smooth whiteness was unblemished, providing a perfect reflection to the moonlight brightening the night.

"What possessed Nikki to go out to the lake?"

"I don't know. I haven't seen her since Thursday morning. We talked on the phone a few times but haven't had a chance to get together."

Kate noticed Rick glance at her from the corner of his eye. "You and this girl, Kate...you're really together?"

"You have a problem with that?" At the moment Kate had little patience and less amusement for such things.

"Hell, no," Rick said. "You know me better than that, Kate.

Robbie's gay, after all. I just didn't know you were. You have to admit, this is something out of left field for you."

"I wish people would stop trying to put me in a box," she said crankily, "just so they can feel justified in whatever course of action they think that little label entitles them to."

"Bad day, Kate?"

"Bastard."

He laughed. "How come you only show how foul-mouthed you really can be in my presence?"

"You're one of the few people I truly call a friend," she said honestly. "You always have been."

"Well, I guess now is when you find out who your friends truly are," he said after a moment, his eyes distant, obviously thinking of his little brother who now lived in the city with a construction worker named Mark. He paused, as if making a startling discovery. "Is this why you never went out with me after your divorce from David?"

"I never went out with you because it would unnecessarily complicate a perfectly good friendship. Besides, you didn't really want to. Your mother pushed you into it, convinced you it would make me feel better." She smiled. "It was a mercy date."

"That's not true. I've always liked you, Kate." He glanced at her again. "Even if you are awfully puny and out of your depth when it comes to the finer things in life."

Kate agreed, thinking of the buxom, brash, and predominately Junoesque type of women Rick generally dated, who usually shared his passion for powerboating, dirt biking, and skydiving. "Nikki likes camping," Kate said suddenly, the worry for her lover once more descending upon her like a shroud.

"All the Harris kids do. Has she asked you to go camping with her?"

Kate managed a weak smile. "I'll probably have to, won't I? At least once."

"Well, before you do anything, let me outfit you. You won't do yourself or her any good by getting out in the middle of the woods and bitching about how cold you are."

"You're never going to let me forget that, are you?" Kate shot him a stony look as she was reminded of the weekend excursion she and her husband had taken to the shore with Rick and his then girlfriend.

"Kate, that wasn't even close to camping. We were in a national park with electrical outlets. You and Dave rented an RV, for God's sake. It had a satellite dish on the roof!"

"You seemed to enjoy it," she said, remembering how Rick and David had watched six hours of football on Sunday while she and Rick's girlfriend had eyed each other warily and made stilted conversation as they picked up shells on the beach. The wind had been wicked as it came off the water and had chilled her so thoroughly she didn't feel warm for a week. "Whatever happened to Jennifer?"

"Married some guy from Upper Rawdon." Rick shrugged.

Kate wondered if she was making small talk in order to ignore the tension radiating pain through her temples and the sense of things sliding rapidly out of her control. "Rick, did Katherine Rushton kill Sam Madison? No politically correct answer, please."

He didn't answer right away, his jaw moving slightly. "I don't know," he admitted finally. "But I don't think so. There's not enough evidence that says she did, and what little there is seems...manufactured somehow. It takes time to build a solid case, Kate. You know that."

"I did see her car there that night." She paused, remembering the conversation with Nikki...it seemed so long ago now. "But it's possible she left and someone else visited the office. It might have been an entirely different car that I heard drive away."

"I know. On the other hand, it *was* Rushton's car that tried to run down Nikki."

Kate tensed as he passed the driveway leading to the charred ruins of Edwards House and slowed, turning onto the next driveway a half-mile down the road at what had to be the Gilles farm. He turned left, shifting as the truck crunched over ice. There were no vehicles in the yard, but Kate and Rick spotted the cleared logging road at the same time.

"Up there." She pointed.

"I expect so." Rick guided his SUV to the narrow lane snaking into the woods and up the hill behind the farm. The road turned and twisted, going through terrain that undulated with hills and gullies, making the driving tricky. But nothing was too formidable until a few miles into the forest, where the headlights picked up the reflective glass from two vehicles.

Kate's tongue stuck to the roof of her mouth as she identified Rushton's car parked behind the small blue Honda. "Oh, Rick."

"Take it easy, Kate," he advised, parking the truck and getting out to examine the vehicles, leaving his running.

Kate sat frozen in the SUV, terrified of what he would find, watching as he shone his light into both cars and then aimed it down the road that seemed to suddenly disappear into darkness.

When he came back to the truck, his face was serious but not grim. "I don't think they dared take their vehicles down the hill in case they couldn't get them back up again. They must have walked wherever they were going. I think my truck can handle it, though."

"All right." Kate clutched the brace on the door as Rick navigated carefully down the steep incline that had a sharp left turn at the bottom, sighing in relief when they made it without incident. He accelerated slightly once they were driving beside the lake, and then Kate spotted something through the trees that made her heart pound and fear rise thick and strong in her chest once more. She clutched Rick's arm. "Oh, my God," she said, in utter horror as she saw the yellow flames and smoke through the trees. "There's a fire."

CHAPTER THIRTY-FOUR

A roaring hurt her ears, and she could barely breathe. Coughing, Nikki opened her eyes, horrified to see flames flickering through the thick smoke surrounding her. Fortunately, she had been lying on the floor where there was still some oxygen. Trying to breathe shallowly, she felt the pain in her temples pound with a rhythm that echoed the beating of her heart. As she lifted her head, she looked around blearily, starting abruptly as she met the empty eyes of Katherine Rushton. There was a neat hole in the woman's forehead, only a trickle of blood having oozed from it to pool on the polished surface of the hardwood floor.

Suddenly nauseous, Nikki tried to rise, then discovered that her hands were bound behind her back and her feet tied together with her bootlaces. In a daze, she understood that she had been left to die, and she forced back the panic rising within her. Flinching away from falling debris that showered her with sparks, she detected the strong smell of burning hair and knew she didn't have much time. The blow to her head and the ache in her lungs made it hard to think clearly, but, twisting on the floor, she struggled to devise a plan of escape.

A bulge at her belly reminded her of her survival pack, and she scrabbled beneath her coat. Clumsily, she yanked at the band running around her waist, pulling it around until the pack was positioned in the small of her back and she was able to put her fingertips on the zipper tab. She managed to yank it open and find the hard lump she recognized as her jackknife. Despite the cramping in her fingers, she pried it open and sawed at the sticky, heavy tape securing her wrists.

She hissed in pain as the edge of the blade sliced across flesh. Biting her lip, her breath a sob in her chest, she continued to hack at the bindings until they finally weakened enough for her to pull her arms apart. Her glasses were hanging off one ear, and she fumbled to replace them on her nose, though she still couldn't see much through the smoke and shadows. Not wanting to waste any more time by attempting to untie her laces, she sliced them apart and began to crawl in the general direction of the door. The constant roar and loud crackles made her feel as if she had fallen into one of the seven rings of Hell, and the crazy shadows thrown by the flames and smoke made it difficult to gain her bearings. Cringing, she shied away as more flaming debris cascaded to the floor. She discovered she was muttering a prayer of deliverance, an undirected plea for escape.

She bumped into the wall and felt along it until she found the door. Sparks fell steadily, and wood snapped alarmingly above her as she desperately twisted the handle. It took a few seconds for her to realize it wasn't budging, that someone had locked it from the outside, undoubtedly with the same padlock.

The skin on her face was scorching, and it was even more difficult to draw in oxygen. She pulled herself up unsteadily, squinting at the window nearby. Picking up a small end table, she smashed at the glass, relieved and gratified when it shattered, leaving a hole to the outside. With rapidly ebbing strength, she pulled herself through the window, yanking desperately when she felt her jacket snag on the splinters of glass around the frame.

Heat blasted at her back, and she scrabbled for the colder air that greeted her. The creaking sound of an imminent collapse hastened her efforts, and she fell weakly to the porch, rolling across it and down the stairs onto the icy path. Struggling along it, slipping and sliding, she stumbled for the trees across the road away from the inferno, falling on her face in the blessed chill of the snow as she heard the roof of the cabin crash into the interior behind her and glanced over her shoulder to see it throw sparks and burning debris for meters.

Exhausted, her head aching with a sickening pain, her lungs straining to suck air into them, Nikki was only dimly aware of the embers hissing as they dropped into the snow around her. Ash drifted lightly through the air as more collapses within the structure threw up sparks, one of which landed on her hand. She felt a burning pain and rolled over the snow bank to extinguish the spark before crawling farther beneath the shelter of the bushes, deeper into the protective white. The melting ice and snow around the cabin sizzled behind her, and the strong smell of burning wood was permeated by something even stronger, that reminded her sharply that Katherine Rushton's body was still inside.

Shaking, she vomited, losing what little remained in her stomach, and then scrambled away when she finished, trying to put more distance between her and the destruction. Gradually becoming aware that it was dark, Nikki wondered how long she had been in the cabin. The sun had been slanting low through the windows while she was searching the place, she decided disjointedly, giving her the impression of late afternoon. She looked at her watch in the light of the fire, astonished to discover it was still working and that it was 8:10. Was it the same evening?

Abruptly, she remembered she was supposed to meet Kate at seven, appalled to be late. She could think only of how disappointed Kate would be with her. Struggling to her feet, she found the going hard through the deep snow. As she staggered toward the road, she saw lights approaching through the trees and tried to identify them.

Baffled, she stared as an SUV with police markings slid to a halt in front of the cabin and both doors flew open. Kate leapt from the passenger's seat and lunged for the burning building, screaming something that Nikki couldn't quite make out through the roar of the flames. Rick scrambled from the driver's side and managed to intercept Kate before she reached it, wrapping his big arms around her to drag her back, kicking and thrashing mightily.

Nikki wondered what had upset her lover so, before she gradually realized Kate thought she was in that cabin. Feeling absurdly flattered by the depth of Kate's reaction, she raised her hand and called out to them but could make only a croaking sound. Bemused, she tried again, doing her best to move toward them, only to collapse into the snow. She tried to get up, unable to get any purchase on the crusty surface that gave way beneath her hands, swallowing her arms up to the shoulder every time she tried to use them for leverage. Floundering helplessly, she cried out, an inarticulate growl of anger and frustration.

Nikki barely lifted her head in time as Kate leapt on her, hugging and kissing her like a crazy woman, forcing her deeper into the snow. Startled, Nikki wrapped her lover up in her arms, holding onto her tightly.

"Oh, god, Nikki," Kate whispered, cupping her face in her hands, her eyes wide pools of terrified darkness. "Are you all right?"

"I think so."

"Nikki, is anyone else in there?" Rick demanded, using his considerable strength to yank both women from the deep snow and back onto the road.

Nikki stood uncertainly on the icy surface, supported by Kate's arm firmly wrapped around her waist.

"Katherine Rushton." Then, as Rick took a step toward the cabin, horror twisting his features, she added in a louder voice, "She's dead. Someone shot her."

He whirled to look at her. "You found her body?"

"No." Nikki shook her head as she tried to organize her thoughts. "I came out here to...find the file, but she interrupted me." She swallowed against a throat raw from the smoke and coughing. "We were talking. She told me she didn't kill Sam or try to run me over. Then..."

"It's all right, Nikki." Kate's strong voice soothed her, supported her. "You're safe now."

Nikki inhaled with a shudder, gathering her composure. "Someone else showed up," she said slowly, trying to remember, finding it hard to cut through the cottony fog clouding her mind. "I heard a...gunshot. Katherine had a...a hole in her forehead, and she...she fell, and I started... I was turning around to see what...who it was, but...something hit me." She shuddered again. "When I woke up, my hands and feet were tied, and the cabin was on fire."

Rick's face became stone, and Kate made a small sound of dismay. "You didn't see who it was?"

"No," Nikki said, shaking her head. She felt dizzy and ill again. "Katherine said no one knew where this place was. I just figured it out because of what she said to Diane at lunch."

"Margaret knew."

Startled, Nikki looked at Kate, seeing the drawn expression in her face.

"What do you mean?" Rick asked, looking as if he wanted to shake the information from her.

"Margaret Madison was in the store yesterday afternoon. She wanted to know if I'd give her a letter of recommendation. During the conversation, she said something about cleaning Sam's things out of a cabin."

"Could she have meant this one?"

Kate looked annoyed and frustrated. "I don't know, Rick," she snapped. "For all I know, Sam had cabins all over the goddamned county."

Nikki glanced at her with surprise, but Rick snorted, relaxing as if Kate's uncharacteristic display of temper indicated something that was currently escaping her.

"I have to call this in," he said, heading back to the truck. "Take care of her."

Nikki stumbled as Kate led her to the other side of the vehicle, urging her up into the rear seat. There, she used a flashlight to examine Nikki more closely, exclaiming as she found the cut on her arm and the burns she had incurred during her escape from the flames. Kate used a medical kit from the glove compartment to treat them and then flashed her light in Nikki's eyes as she flinched away.

"Rick, she may have a concussion from that blow to her head." Kate's words didn't quite make sense to Nikki. "I don't think her pupils are dilating properly, though it's hard to tell in this light."

"If she was unconscious, you might be right," he agreed. "I called the paramedics along with the fire department. They should be here shortly." Rick looked uncertain. "Hell, maybe I should rethink this. The fire will burn itself out, and I don't think they can get the trucks down that incline safely. We should go back and meet them on the hill where the other cars are parked."

Nikki, huddled in the backseat, found it difficult to concentrate on what was happening. She heard the words, understood on some level what they meant, but was not connecting them with herself. All she could think of was the look on Katherine's face when she saw the person standing behind Nikki. She had recognized the person, Nikki thought distantly. Who had it been?

She swayed as the vehicle moved beneath her and realized that they were driving away from the fire. Kate was on the seat beside her, her arm about her shoulders, holding her as the SUV slipped through the woods, the engine a low growl. Nikki looked forward over the front seat, watching as some parked cars abruptly appeared in the headlights of the truck.

"I shouldn't have borrowed Kim's Honda," she said weakly. "I lost her binoculars." Then she began to cry, unable to stop. She wasn't sure why she was crying or what was making her feel so sick and unhappy.

She was only aware of Kate beside her, squeezing her tighter, muttering words that didn't really penetrate her misery but sounded comforting nonetheless.

A block of time disappeared like a splice from a film Nikki had been watching, and the next thing she knew the truck had stopped, strangers were peering in her eyes, and Kate and Rick were across the road, talking intently as they stood next to Rick's SUV. Nikki couldn't quite figure out how she could be sitting in the truck at the same time the truck was several feet away and then realized vaguely that she couldn't be in the truck at all. Proud of this line of deduction, she finally figured out that she was actually in the back of a brightly lit vehicle with someone she didn't recognize who kept trying to get her to lie down on a stretcher. She kept refusing, struggling weakly because she really wanted to know what Rick and Kate were saying. No doubt they were up to something, but she couldn't seem to rise from the stretcher.

Suddenly Kate was hovering over her. "Darling?"

Frowning, Nikki tried to focus on the beautiful face that had an alarming tendency to swim out of view. "What?"

"They're going to take you to the hospital now. I'm going with Rick to talk to Margaret Madison, but I promise I'll be by to see you as soon as possible."

"What about the car?" Part of Nikki thought she should be concentrating on what Kate was actually saying, but she had seized on the Honda that she could see from the corner of her eye. She was extremely embarrassed that she had not gone back to pick Kim up at work, that she had lost her binoculars and was now apparently expected to just leave the little blue car there in the middle of the woods.

"Someone will take care of the vehicles."

Nikki pawed through her pockets, managing to find the keys. "Will you take it back to Kim?" She anxiously pushed them at Kate.

Kate hesitated and then accepted the keys. "Of course," she said, and Nikki was content, because she knew her love wouldn't promise something that she didn't intend to carry out.

"Nikki, did you understand what I said about going with Rick?"

Nikki nodded. "Yes. You're coming by to visit me in the hospital later." She paused. "Am I going to the hospital?"

Kate seemed half amused and half worried. "These people in

the ambulance are going to take you there," she said. "You have a concussion."

"All right." Nikki inhaled, smelling the medical scents of the compartment she was in. "Are you coming with me?"

"I'll be along shortly. I have to take care of something."

That's right. Kate had to take care of Kim's car. I borrowed it and never took it back. That was really unacceptable. Then she blinked and Kate was gone, and it seemed to Nikki that she was being driven through the woods again, making her wonder where the hell she was going.

CHAPTER THIRTY-FIVE

K ate watched as the ambulance carefully drove away on the logging road before she turned her attention to the police officer speaking with the local fire chief. Scarlet, blue, and gold lights from the multitude of official vehicles washed the area, and the churned ground appeared brown in their illumination. The firefighters, forced to leave their trucks on the hill, had dispatched a few men on foot with extinguishers to make sure the fire didn't spread to the surrounding trees, though that was unlikely from the amount of snow around the cabin. She wondered if these volunteers were going to start asking the town council to be put on a salary. Considering how many fires they had been forced to fight in the last week, she wasn't sure she would blame them. The situation was quickly developing a surreal quality, and at this point, she was infinitely weary of the whole thing.

Moving over to join Rick, she nodded at Tom Anderson, who looked unhappy beneath his red helmet. "A hell of a thing," he said as she approached.

"Agreed." She looked at Rick. "It's time to end this." She felt calm and cold, completely resolved.

"You're right." Rick nodded at one of the other officers standing nearby. "You two get these cars back to town. The Lexus can go to the Impound. The Honda..."

Kate held out the keys Nikki had given her. "It belongs to a girl named Kim." Suddenly she realized she didn't have a last name or an address.

The officer took the keys. "All the necessary information will be on the registration," he explained, "though I suspect I know whom it belongs to." He glanced at Rick. "I hope Nikki's all right," he added awkwardly, as if unsure he had the right to say it.

"She'll be fine, Pete."

Kate followed Rick over to his vehicle and crawled into the passenger's side. There was no question about her accompanying him. Rick certainly knew not to argue with her, and she fully intended to make sure this whole mess was taken care of before she saw Nikki again. She owed it to her, since Nikki had risked her life to uncover the truth behind these crimes.

The drive out the logging road seemed to take forever, and Kate discovered she was gripping the brace on the door until her hand ached, not because of the road conditions, but because she was furious. The abrasions on Nikki's wrists, clear indication of her being bound, the burns, cuts, and bruises on her head where she had been struck so violently were sharp in Kate's memory. She didn't want to waste time on small talk. She set her jaw so hard, her back teeth felt as if they were about to splinter.

"Kate, take it easy," Rick said quietly, obviously picking up on her tension.

"I wish you'd stop saying that." She felt like slapping him.

"I'm not entirely sure what you think you'll accomplish by coming with me."

"Margaret might be able to lie to you," Kate said, absolutely assured that what she was saying was true. "She won't be able to look me in the eye and do it."

Rick didn't look so sure. "If you say so."

They were silent for the rest of the drive to the Madison house, a large country-style home in one of the more expensive residential areas. After turning into the paved driveway, Rick and Kate got out of the SUV, and as she studied the house, she assessed the probable mortgage, knowing that Margaret hadn't exaggerated her financial straits. But was that enough to kill for? Or was some darker motive at work? At any rate, Kate was not about to stand for it any longer.

The sight of the cabin in flames and the knowledge that Nikki had been left to die in it had destroyed whatever sympathy she may have felt for Margaret. As Rick rang the doorbell, Kate inhaled deeply, realizing it was rather late. Glancing at her watch, she noticed it was almost 11:40, but she was sure she had seen lights in the upper part of the house.

"Let me do the talking, Kate," Rick warned her in a low voice as they waited.

She frowned, but nodded shortly.

Finally, the door swung open and Margaret peered at them sleepily, frowning as if uncertain why they were there. "Yes?"

Kate felt a qualm. Perhaps she was wrong. Perhaps they were all wrong. Perhaps Margaret had nothing at all to do with this, and someone else altogether was the culprit.

"I'm sorry if we woke you," Rick said. "We're looking for someone."

In a perplexed tone, Margaret asked, "You think they're here?"

"We think you might know where they are," Rick said. "May we come in?"

Margaret hesitated and then motioned them inside. She was dressed in a terry cloth robe that she clutched at her neck, while her graying hair was damp at the ends. Leading them into the living room, she nodded at the sofa and took a seat in the chair. She regarded them steadily, her face devoid of expression. "How can I help?"

"Nikki Harris has been investigating certain matters on her own," Rick said. "This afternoon, she borrowed a car to find a cabin she believed belonged to Sam. She hasn't been seen since. Do you happen to know anything about this cabin or where it might be located?"

Margaret glanced at Kate, nothing more than a brief shift of her eyes in her direction, before focusing on Rick. Kate wondered if she was remembering the conversation in the bookstore earlier and how she had revealed that she knew about the cabin.

"I don't see what...Nikki...would be investigating. But the only cabin I know about is the one he built last year on a lake out by Edwards House."

With a glint in his eye, Rick said, "Yes, Katherine Rushton told us about that one, but we visited it before we came here, and we couldn't find anyone around."

As if ignited by Rick's expression, a flash appeared in Margaret's eyes, one of disbelief and astonishment. It obviously took an effort for her not to react beyond that minute slip, and if they hadn't been on guard for a guilty look, it was marginally possible that they might have missed it.

Kate held her breath, aware that this was a very delicate moment and that Rick, after having dropped in the line, was reeling it in lightly, waiting for Margaret to take the bait.

"No one around?"

"No," Rick said. "We couldn't get inside, nor could we see through the windows. They were too frosted up, and besides, it was dark. There was a padlock on the door."

"I have the key for it somewhere," Margaret said in a distant tone. "Would that help?"

"Yes," Rick said with apparent gratitude.

Again, Kate questioned her assumptions as she saw Margaret rise from her chair and walk over to the desk. But as Margaret opened the drawer and reached inside, Kate lunged to her feet. She wasn't sure why but only knew that if she were wrong, she would have to apologize later...profusely. Instinctively, she slammed the drawer shut on Margaret's wrist and held it there as the woman yelped in pain, cowering away from her.

Rick hastily leapt to his feet, cursing as Kate gripped Margaret's arm with her free hand and slowly pulled out the drawer with the other. Margaret's fingers were wrapped loosely around the brownish grip of a handgun.

"You can forget about that letter of recommendation," Kate said coldly.

Rick's face tightened when he saw the gun. "That didn't go quite the way I planned," he said with a touch of sheepishness, forcing Margaret to release the weapon before picking it up and sniffing the barrel. "Fired recently." He stared at Margaret as she remained quietly where she was now that she had been discovered. "Will the bullets from this gun match the one we took from Sam's skull...and will take from Katherine Rushton once we recover her body from the ashes of the cabin you torched?"

"The cabin burned," Margaret said passively. "You lied to me?"

"Yes." Kate inhaled deeply, releasing Margaret's wrist, resisting the urge to wipe her hand on her pants as if it had been covered with something unpleasant and slimy. In the drawer, she noticed a file folder and pulled it out. "This was what Nikki was looking for." She glared furiously at the woman. "She's not dead, by the way."

Margaret glanced at her. "I'm glad, Kate," she said in a detached tone that matched the expression in her dark eyes. "I didn't...she never did anything to me. It made me feel good to shoot the bitch, but the girl was just in the way."

"Why kill Rushton now?" Kate ignored Rick's wince. She knew that anything said by Margaret at this point was not admissible in court, but she needed to know, if not for herself, so she could tell Nikki later. "You've been trying to frame her for Sam's murder."

Margaret regarded her without blinking. "I needed to change plans. I followed her to the cabin where I was going to shoot her, make it look like a suicide, and then direct the police there to find her, along with the file showing all her criminal activities. I didn't expect to find the girl there." She hesitated, a faint trace of annoyance crossing her face, the first expression of emotion she had displayed. "Why couldn't she leave well enough alone?"

Kate, remembering the abrasions on Nikki's wrists from where she had been bound and left to burn along with the evidence, reacted instinctively, slapping Margaret as hard as she could.

"Jesus, Kate," Rick said, stepping between the two, pushing her back gently as he took hold of Margaret's arm to prevent her from retaliating. She was staring at Kate with complete horror. Kate was merely glad to see something get through that emotionless shell. "Damn it, I told you to take it easy."

Kate didn't reply, her chest heaving as she glared at the woman, seeing the imprint of her hand appear red on Margaret's pale face. She continued to stand there, taking deep, shuddering breaths and trying to regain her composure as Rick led Margaret out of the living room. Once she was sure she was calm, she followed the pair out of the house, shutting the door firmly behind her.

Kate was silent on the way to the hospital, refusing to look either at Rick in the driver's seat or at Margaret, handcuffed and secured in the rear. Rick dropped her off in front of the emergency room with instructions to come down to the station later the next day to give a statement. When she located her in a cubicle, curtains drawn around her, Nikki seemed a lot more alert than she had out by the lake, and the bandages on her head gave her a rakish appearance.

Nikki managed a weak grin when Kate entered. "Hi."

"Hello." Kate felt a definite sense of relief seep through her. She glanced at the doctor who was writing something on the clipboard. "How is she?" she asked, easing over to put her hand on her lover's shoulder.

He looked up at her briefly. "You a relative?"

Without hesitation, Kate said, "She's my partner."

Nikki glanced at her in obvious astonishment.

He didn't flicker. Apparently, thought Kate, an ER physician had better things to do with his time than be concerned with others' sexual preference. "Will you be taking her home with you?"

Kate hesitated, but only briefly. "Yes, if she's not going to remain in the hospital."

"Ideally, we'd like to keep her here all night for observation, but with this latest bout of influenza, we're strapped for beds, so she'd have to remain in ER. It would be better for her to go home and rest than spend the night here."

Kate frowned. "Doctor, she seemed...very confused while being put in the ambulance."

"Yes, she suffered a certain amount of shock from her ordeal, and she did sustain a mild concussion, but she's lucid now and her pupils are fully responsive. She'll have a bit of a headache for a few days, but she should be fine. If she displays any other symptoms, you can always bring her back in." He patted Nikki absently on the shoulder and left them in the cubicle.

Nikki reached for her jacket. "Did you and Rick talk to Margaret?"

Kate resisted the urge to sigh. "Rick arrested her for the murder of Sam Madison and Katherine Rushton, not to mention attempting to murder you."

"Did she confess?" Nikki's eyes were wide.

"Something like that." For a moment, it occurred to Kate to wonder what would have happened had something not tipped her off, if Margaret had been allowed to pull the weapon from the drawer. Would she have turned around and shot both Rick and herself? Suddenly, Kate felt the floor become unsteady beneath her feet, and rather than put a steadying hand on Nikki, she had to cling to her lover for support.

"Are you all right?" Nikki asked, clearly anxious.

Kate brushed at her face, feeling chilled. "Just...tired, I guess," she said weakly. "It's been a long day."

"That's for sure." Nikki exhaled heavily, as if glad it was finally over. "Where are you parked?"

Kate stared at her, then shut her eyes. "I'm not." Sighing in aggravation, she turned around and, with Nikki in tow, began to search for the nearest phone to call a taxi.

CHAPTER THIRTY-SIX

Nikki silently regarded the simple silver chain with the heart-shaped pendant set with stones that looked very much like diamonds. Before she had eavesdropped on the conversation at the Tidal Watch Inn, she would have assumed they weren't, if she had thought about it at all. Now she knew they were the real thing and probably cost a fortune, particularly since the necklace came in a box from Judith's Jewelry. She swallowed hard. "I can't accept this," she said, dropping the chain back into the container and pushing it away from her, across the table to where Kate sat.

They had been having brunch at the table still elegantly set for the night before, drinking orange juice from crystal glasses, the candles flickering fretfully in the sunshine pouring through the apartment windows. After returning from the hospital the night before, Nikki had taken a shower before they went directly to bed, falling asleep in each other's arms and not waking until late morning. Nikki felt considerably better after a good night's sleep, but this gift reminded her of the previous day and how she had felt upon hearing about Kate's standing in the town.

Kate appeared hurt and disappointed at Nikki's reaction. "Why not?"

"It's too expensive."

"I can afford it."

"I know you can," Nikki said, stung. "That's the problem."

Kate sat up a little straighter. "Why?"

"You're rich." Nikki said it as if it were some sexually transmitted disease Kate had neglected to mention.

Kate put down her fork, as if she needed both hands to deal with Nikki's reaction. "Maybe I should have mentioned I have money. I didn't think it would be that important to you."

"Of course it is." Nikki threw down her napkin and stood up. "You have money coming out your ears! I barely have two cents to rub together!"

"I'm still the same person I was before you knew I was financially solvent." Kate rose to her feet. "What's changed?"

Nikki inhaled deeply, unable to answer. "Why did you hide it from me?"

"I didn't hide it." Kate spread out her hands, indicating the tasteful yet simple apartment. "This is how I live, Nikki. What's different?"

"You should have told me," Nikki repeated stubbornly.

"You act as if having money is a crime," Kate said, frowning. "Or some form of moral defect. It's not. All money is...all it's ever been...is a tool, and how one uses the tool is up to them. I don't deny that some people use their money as a form of power, but I've never believed in living extravagantly or flaunting how much I have. I don't understand why you're so upset."

Nikki looked away, unable to define why she felt so hurt, only knowing that she did. "Because it's one more thing that I can't share with you!" She gestured angrily at the necklace on the table. "How do you think I feel when you give me something like that? I can't afford those sorts of things. I certainly can't give them to you in return."

"I don't expect you to," Kate said, obviously searching for words. "Do you think that I was any less touched by the bear that you gave me the night you met Susan than if it had been covered in diamonds?"

"You probably thought it was cheesy," Nikki said, tears stinging her eyes, finding it difficult to swallow past the lump in her throat. "Susan probably laughed at it. A cheap, stupid bear from the cheap, stupid girl her friend is playing with."

Kate looked as if Nikki had just struck her." How dare you," she said, her eyes shining, her color high. "How dare you dismiss me as some kind of superficial, petty woman who believes a person's worth is measured by their bank account. How dare you dismiss Susan, probably one of the kindest people I know, as having the same kind of shallow, uneducated beliefs? Having money doesn't make me a better person than anyone else, Nikki Harris, but not having it doesn't make you better either!"

"That's not what I meant," Nikki retorted, stung by the anger in her lover's voice and the hurt in the eyes. She wanted to say more, to express what she meant, to explain all the reasons she felt unworthy of Kate. She wanted to express all the fears and insecurities that made her scared to death that Kate would suddenly realize that she was wasting her time.

Instead, she did what she always did when she was hurt and frustrated and didn't understand what was wrong. She burst into tears, completely unable to stop the helpless sobbing. It had always been her biggest downfall. Others became magnificent in their wrath, in their pain, transformed into dignified, formidable powers to be respected. Kate was like that, but Nikki simply dissolved into a helpless puddle of sobbing and mucus. Dimly, she was aware of Kate gently grasping her wrists and drawing her hands away from her face, then leading her to the sofa.

"Shh, darling, I'm sorry," Kate said, sounding somewhat helpless herself as she drew her down onto the cushions. She gently removed Nikki's glasses and placed them on the table, reaching up with tender fingertips to wipe the tears from her cheeks. "I didn't mean to make you cry. I didn't mean to hurt you by giving you the necklace."

Nikki tried to pull away, knowing everything wasn't all right but unable to articulate her feelings. Kate tightened her embrace, and though Nikki was larger and undoubtedly stronger, she was unable to break the hold.

"Listen to me," Kate said. "I know you feel, for whatever reason, that money puts a gulf between us, but it doesn't, Nikki. Honestly, if our positions were reversed, and you were the one with money, would you think I was a lesser person because I didn't have as much as you? Worse, would you believe you would be incapable of love or that I was somehow not worth loving? Do you understand how ridiculous that is?"

Nikki sniffed, finding it hard to catch her breath as she nodded wordlessly, unable to deny the logic of the questions. She knew if she suddenly came into money, she'd be dispensing it to all her friends and family, showering them with gifts and assistance whenever she could. Furthermore, she'd feel as if she was free to love whoever she chose, unafraid of what society might do to her. "I wouldn't give you a gift that made you feel bad."

"Oh, love, is that why you think I gave you the necklace?" Kate whispered. "I gave it to you because it was beautiful, and you're beautiful, and you deserve beautiful things. It wasn't to make you feel bad, and I'm so profoundly sorry that it did. I gave it to you for the same exact reason you gave me the bear. I gave it out of love. I love you, Nikki, with all my heart. Why do you think there's some kind of price tag on that? Where do you get the idea there's some kind of contest involved?"

Unable to reply, Nikki wrapped her arms around her lover and sobbed until she couldn't breathe. She had believed that money would somehow put an inaccessible chasm between them, and it hurt to know she was the one actually afraid to bridge that gulf, a result of her irrational fear that she wasn't worthy of this elegant, beautiful woman. It wasn't an easy thing to admit to herself, and it took an effort to realize she was the one actually judging others based on their financial worth, particularly herself.

"It'll be all right," Kate said softly, stroking her hair. "We'll work through this, Nikki. I promise."

"I hate it when I get like this," Nikki muttered finally, wiping ineffectually at her face.

"Like what?"

"I fall to pieces," she said shamefully. "I can't say or do anything. I just bawl like a baby."

"There's nothing wrong with that," Kate told her, kissing her temple. "You're just experiencing what you feel and expressing it."

"It makes me look stupid."

"No, it makes you look like you're frightened and hurt," Kate said gently. "So much so that it gets the better of you. It's probably to be expected after last night and whatever else that's going on that seeing the necklace triggered." She tightened her embrace. "Why do you think it's wrong to display your pain with tears?"

Nikki sniffed. "I don't know. It makes me look weak when all I can do is cry."

"That's a male thing, you know," Kate noted conversationally. "Men came up with that one so that they could dismiss any arguments from women. If you really feel for something, then you must be lesser for it. If you show how you feel, then obviously you're too emotional to think clearly."

"Not just men," Nikki murmured, thinking of how Anne had taken advantage of her in their arguments, how she grew colder and more contemptuous as Nikki became more emotional. Kate didn't do that, she realized, hiccoughing a little. She kept trying to find a way to communicate so they could work out their problem, no matter how upset Nikki became.

"No, but the society which forms us is patriarchal, like it or not," Kate said as Nikki tried to work out her tangle of emotions, the small talk granting her a bit of distance even as Kate continued to hold her tightly. "So expressing emotion is always perceived as being a flaw somehow. The truth is when you recognize and understand your feeling, and exactly where it's coming from, rather than trying to hide or suppress it, you're better able to deal with it." She kissed Nikki's cheek gently. "Where do you think this is coming from?"

"I don't know," she said, still ashamed. "From being poor, I guess. I know money doesn't make you happy, but sometimes it's so hard not to have any at all."

Kate put a finger beneath Nikki's chin and lifted it so that she was looking at her. "Do you honestly believe that my having money makes me better than you or your parents, or your friends?"

Nikki found it hard to look in her eyes. "No."

"Do you think that your not having money somehow makes you less in my eyes?"

Nikki hesitated, then whispered, "No."

"Do you think that people shouldn't love each other because of who they are, or what gender they happen to be, or what they do for a living?"

"Of course not." Nikki inhaled deeply. "I know what you're trying to show me."

"Yes?" Kate prompted, her dark eyes gleaming with wisdom and love.

"You're trying to show me that I judge my own worth in financial terms. That by becoming angry at your present, then it's really me who thinks I don't deserve it, that I don't think I'm worth what you paid for it."

"I wasn't thinking that exactly, but all right. I don't want to make you feel uncomfortable, Nikki. Not with how I live or by what I'm able to give you because I can afford it. Yet at the same time, I have money, and it's not going away. All other things being equal, I know in purely logistical terms it's better to have money than not have it. I'm not about to give it up or turn my back on it." Kate frowned, a small line appearing between her thin brows. "I honestly don't know what to do, Nikki. I want to give you nice things, but it's because you've given me so much, not because I think you're lacking without them. Does that make sense?"

"Yes," Nikki said. "I'm sorry. The necklace is...really beautiful. I just...it hurts me that I can't give you nice things back."

Kate inclined her head toward the box that remained unopened on the table. "I'm certainly glad Kim and Lynn discovered your gift for me in the backseat of their car, and it was extremely nice of them to take the time to drop it by this morning. I can't wait to open it." She paused. "Tell me, what percentage of your total worth does the cost of the gift you gave me represent?"

Nikki winced, realizing where Kate was going with the question. "Far more than your gift probably does," she admitted bashfully, thinking of the lightweight sleeping bag and backpack that were of far better quality than anything she had ever purchased for herself.

"Am I supposed to become angry with you because you gave far more of yourself financially than I was able to give you?"

"No, I want you to be happy and pleased with the gift. I guess I have a lot to learn."

"We both do," Kate said, kissing her on the forehead. "We're going to make some mistakes in the process."

"You're right." Nikki swallowed audibly. "I'm afraid people will think I'm only with you because of your money."

Kate lifted a brow and looked skeptical. "I'm sure some people will think I'm only with you just because you're so young and gorgeous," she countered. "They'd be wrong on both counts."

Nikki hesitated. "What do you believe?"

"I don't think you seduced me for my money. It was because of my books. A reader like you? You definitely seduced me for my books."

Nikki managed to laugh. "I hadn't thought of that," she said, pulling Kate close. "You're probably right, though. There's something about having all those books downstairs..."

Kate laughed too, hugging her back. "Are we all right now?"

"Yes." Nikki sighed. "I'll try not to be so stupid about this anymore."

"I promise to think about the next gift I give you a little more carefully," Kate said. "If I want to give you something...extravagant, then I'll talk to you first. But will you consider any gift on its own merits rather than by its cost?"

"Meaning?"

"Meaning this is our first Valentine's Day together." Kate tilted her head, her eyes gentle as she looked up into Nikki's face. "I've never had anyone I could give a present like this to...one that has all the traditional implications of love. I just...I would really like you to keep it."

"Where would I wear it?" Nikki was thinking that she also didn't have anything nearly fine enough to wear that would begin to match the necklace.

"The Historical Society dinner," Kate said promptly. "I want you to attend with me...as my date."

"Oh, boy." Nikki felt as if she had been punched in her stomach. "You just want to rub it in everyone's face, don't you?"

"I want people to know I love you, Nikki. Just as I would if I had met and fallen in love with a man. I'm not ashamed of you. I'm proud to have you in my life. Is it wrong to want to show you off?"

"It's not wrong. It just might not be very smart." She exhaled loudly, as if emphasizing her point. "You have to pick your spots, Kate."

"I know. I'm picking this one...the Historical Society dinner."

"I never knew you would...want to flaunt the pink triangle."

"There are probably a lot of things you'll be discovering about me."

Nikki leaned forward and kissed her. "I think you're right. I also think I'm going to love finding them out."

EPILOGUE

I'm still not sure I understand," Susan said, her voice tinny over the phone. "Sam Madison, Terry Bishop, and Katherine Rushton were all in business together?"

"Yes," Kate said, leaning back on the stool, her back supported by the breakfast bar. "They created a company called Mosaic Estates, intending to turn Edwards House and the surrounding area into a tourist resort. They started by writing ten one-million-dollar checks, backed by a loan from the company. This made them the principal shareholders. Then Rushton began filtering off holdings of some of the biggest clients so they could buy the remaining shares and renovate Edwards House. They were doing fine until they ran into a problem with the lake property. In order to make Gilles sell, Sam had to pay five times the market value, forcing them to use all the rest of their own money, plus borrow on everything they owned. They had to do this to maintain their share percentage. They had become quite greedy as they neared the end."

Kate knew that Susan was no financial wizard, unlike her husband, but she had picked up enough to easily see where this was going. "They were screwed," she said, obviously in awe that anyone could get themselves in that much trouble. "They stole money, committed fraud, and had big loans they couldn't pay. The only way out would be to sell the land quick, and who would be in a hurry to buy land on the outskirts of Truro, even with the bloody lake? It would be a huge loss with no hope of covering the mess they created." She paused. "That isn't why Sam was murdered, though, was it?"

"No, it came down to a matter of love and hate," Kate said, sighing. "Sam was going to divorce Margaret. She had gone to his office that night to discuss the financial problems they were suddenly having and saw Rushton there. She hung back and either saw the papers or heard him tell Rushton that his marriage was really over. She waited until Rushton was gone before going in and confronting him. The gun was already there, or she had taken it with her, I'm not sure which, and he ended up shot to death. She used some gas cans from her car to start the fire and then left. Probably, if it hadn't been winter, she wouldn't have had the spare cans in her car. When she managed to get away with it and then heard that I had placed Rushton on the scene...though how she heard that, I don't know...she decided to frame her for the crime, thus getting her revenge on everyone while playing the wronged widow."

"Maybe part of it was also because she enjoyed playing head games with this Rushton woman."

Kate thought about Margaret and how she had slapped her a few weeks earlier. "I think so, too," she said, suppressing a shiver.

"How's Nikki?"

"Better," Kate said. "Her headaches went away, and Rick was so impressed with how she escaped from the fire, keeping her cool under pressure, that he really pushed to get her the dispatch job. She's working this evening, though she promised to come by after her shift."

"You two still going hot and heavy?"

"Depends on your definition."

"I gather that means yes."

"She's a wonderful woman."

"She's probably a tired woman. I'm surprised she has enough strength left to go to work after you're finished with her."

"Funny." Kate made sure Susan realized she didn't find it so at all.

"So, what's this rumor you're taking her to the Historical Society dinner?"

"Damn, how do you keep up with these things?"

"I hear things," Susan said lightly. When she spoke again, her voice was more serious. "Are you really going to do it?"

"Why wouldn't I?"

Susan didn't respond, her silence eloquent.

"You're not talking me out of this, Susan."

"Did I try? Did you hear me say a word?"

"I know what you're thinking. To me, it's the perfect opportunity to settle the rumors and gossip once and for all. I love Nikki, and I don't care who knows it or what the hell their opinion might be about it."

"Aren't you putting a lot of pressure on Nikki? How comfortable is she going to be while you're waving her around in lieu of a rainbow flag?"

"She's fine. We've talked it through, and she's ready to stand by me."

"Okay, but if they run you both out of town on a rail, you know you always have a place to stay with us."

Kate smiled. "Thanks." She lifted her head as she heard the door open below and the sound of footsteps on the stairwell. Obviously, Nikki was trying out the new key Kate had presented her. "I have to go, Nikki's home."

"Well, I don't dare keep you from that," Susan said, sounding affectionate. "I'll talk to you later."

Kate hung up just as Nikki knocked quietly. The door wasn't locked, but it was understood that the key was only for the back door downstairs. Nikki had provided a similar key to Kate for her building. The next step for them would undoubtedly be an exchange of keys for the apartments themselves.

"Come in," Kate called, smiling. She met Nikki by the dining room table and hugged her tightly. "How was work?"

"Still a little confusing," Nikki admitted after kissing her thoroughly. "Once I've finished training, though, it should be all right."

"You'll do fine." Kate tilted her head coyly. "So, are you really tired?"

Nikki grinned, her expression the slightest bit lascivious. "Did you have something in mind?"

"I just might," Kate said, smiling as she took her hands and led her to the bedroom.

Both knew that when two people experienced unexpected sparks between them, either a blaze would ignite or the feeling would eventually die out, growing cold from lack of attention.

They fully intended to keep this fire burning.

About the Author

Gina L. Dartt was born and raised in Nova Scotia. She's been a lot of places in Canada and the States, including California, Texas, Georgia and New Jersey, but still considers the Maritimes the best place in the world to live. She likes playing tennis, hiking, reading, spending time with friends and following NFL football. Her favorite authors are currently Elizabeth Peters, Douglas Preston & Lincoln Child, and Nevada Barr. She lives in Truro, with a massive amount of books and two cats, and works in the office of a hardware store that has existed in the town since 1886. From the original wooden counter on the main floor, where a customer can still buy a single nail if they'd like, to the beams on the top floor that are still blackened and seared from a fire that occurred nearly sixty years earlier, she is surrounded by the history of her home town, which she appreciates and cherishes. Her upcoming works include *Unexpected Ties*, the next book featuring Kate Shannon and Nikki Harris (Fall 2006).

Books Available From Bold Strokes Books

The Traitor and the Chalice by Jane Fletcher. Without allies to help them, Tevi and Jemeryl will have to risk all in the race to uncover the traitor and retrieve the chalice. The Lyremouth Chronicles Book Two. (1-933110-43-0)

Promising Hearts by Radclyffe. Dr. Vance Phelps lost everything in the War Between the States and arrives in New Hope, Montana with no hope of happiness and no desire for anything except forgetting—until she meets Mae, a frontier madam. (1-933110-44-9)

Carly's Sound by Ali Vali. Poppy Valente and Julia Johnson form a bond of friendship that lays the foundation for something more, until Poppy's past comes back to haunt her—literally. A poignant romance about love and renewal. (1-933110-45-7)

Unexpected Sparks by Gina L. Dartt. Falling in love is complicated enough without adding murder to the mix. Kate Shannon's growing feelings for much younger Nikki Harris are challenging enough without the mystery of a fatal fire that Kate can't ignore. (1-933110-46-5)

Whitewater Rendezvous by Kim Baldwin. Two women on a wilderness kayak adventure—Chaz Herrick, a laid-back outdoorswoman, and Megan Maxwell, a workaholic news executive—discover that true love may be nothing at all like they imagined. (1-933110-38-4)

Erotic Interludes 3: Lessons in Love ed. by Radclyffe and Stacia Seaman. Sign on for a class in love…the best lesbian erotica writers take us to "school." (1-933110-39-2)

Punk Like Me by JD Glass. Twenty-one year old Nina writes lyrics and plays guitar in the rock band, Adam's Rib, and she doesn't always play by the rules. And, oh yeah—she has a way with the girls. (1-933110-40-6)

Coffee Sonata by Gun Brooke. Four women whose lives unexpectedly intersect in a small town by the sea share one thing in common—they all have secrets. (1-933110-41-4)

The Clinic: Tristaine Book One by Cate Culpepper. Brenna, a prison medic, finds herself deeply conflicted by her growing feelings for her patient, Jesstin, a wild and rebellious warrior reputed to be descended from ancient Amazons. (1-933110-42-2)

Forever Found by JLee Meyer. Can time, tragedy, and shattered trust destroy a love that seemed destined? When chance reunites two childhood friends separated by tragedy, the past resurfaces to determine the shape of their future. (1-933110-37-6)

Sword of the Guardian by Merry Shannon. Princess Shasta's bold new bodyguard has a secret that could change both of their lives. He is actually a *she*. A passionate romance filled with courtly intrigue, chivalry, and devotion. (1-933110-36-8)

Wild Abandon by Ronica Black. From their first tumultuous meeting, Dr. Chandler Brogan and Officer Sarah Monroe are drawn together by their common obsessions—sex, speed, and danger. (1-933110-35-X)

Turn Back Time by Radclyffe. Pearce Rifkin and Wynter Thompson have nothing in common but a shared passion for surgery. They clash at every opportunity, especially when matters of the heart are suddenly at stake. (1-933110-34-1)

Chance by Grace Lennox. At twenty-six, Chance Delaney decides her life isn't working so she swaps it for a different one. What follows is the sexy, funny, touching story of two women who, in finding themselves, also find one another. (1-933110-31-7)

The Exile and the Sorcerer by Jane Fletcher. First in the Lyremouth Chronicles. Tevi, wounded and adrift, arrives in the courtyard of a shy young sorcerer. Together they face monsters, magic, and the challenge of loving despite their differences. (1-933110-32-5)

A Matter of Trust by Radclyffe. JT Sloan is a cybersleuth who doesn't like attachments. Michael Lassiter is leaving her husband, and she needs Sloan's expertise to safeguard her company. It should just be business—but it turns into much more. (1-933110-33-3)

Sweet Creek by Lee Lynch. A celebration of the enduring nature of love, friendship, and community in the quirky, heart-warming lesbian community of Waterfall Falls. (1-933110-29-5)

The Devil Inside by Ali Vali. Derby Cain Casey, head of a New Orleans crime organization, runs the family business with guts and grit, and no one crosses her. No one, that is, until Emma Verde claims her heart and turns her world upside down. (1-933110-30-9)

Grave Silence by Rose Beecham. Detective Jude Devine's investigation of a series of ritual murders is complicated by her torrid affair with the golden girl of Southwestern forensic pathology, Dr. Mercy Westmoreland. (1-933110-25-2)

Honor Reclaimed by Radclyffe. In the aftermath of 9/11, Secret Service Agent Cameron Roberts and Blair Powell close ranks with a trusted few to find the would-be assassins who nearly claimed Blair's life. (1-933110-18-X)

Honor Bound by Radclyffe. Secret Service Agent Cameron Roberts and Blair Powell face political intrigue, a clandestine threat to Blair's safety, and the seemingly irreconcilable personal differences that force them ever farther apart. (1-933110-20-1)

Protector of the Realm: Supreme Constellations Book One by Gun Brooke. A space adventure filled with suspense and a daring intergalactic romance featuring Commodore Rae Jacelon and a stunning, but decidedly lethal, Kellen O'Dal. (1-933110-26-0)